BLISSFUL DISASTER

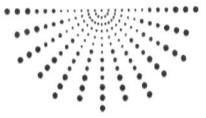

AMY L. GALE

5 PRINCE PUBLISHING
5PRINCEBOOKS.COM

Published by 5 Prince Publishing

PO Box 865, Arvada, CO 80001

www.5PrinceBooks.com

Digital ISBN: 978-1-63112-190-6

Print ISBN 978-1-63112-418-1

BLISSFUL DISASTER. Amy L. Gale

Cover Credit: Viola Estrella

First Edition 2017 Third Edition 2025

For my husband, Chris, who rocks my world every day.
For my mom, who supports me every second
and truly believes I can do anything.

ACKNOWLEDGMENTS

I am enormously indebted to many wonderful people who have believed in me and assisted in my journey to publication.

Chris Gale, my husband, biggest fan and supporter, vermin slayer, tornado warrior, and only person I'd want by my side in the zombie apocalypse. You make every day a love story. Spending forever with you isn't long enough.

Carol Riccetti, my mother, "PR manager", cheerleader, and best friend. You truly believe I can do anything and always support me. I'm the luckiest girl in the world to have you as my mom.

Bernadette Soehner, my content editor and owner of 5 Prince Publishing, who not only made Blissful Disaster shine like a diamond, but also made my dream of becoming a published author a reality. Thank you so much for welcoming me into the 5 Prince family and giving me so much artistic freedom.

Cate Byers, my line editor, with the superhuman ability to find inconsistencies and typos. Thank you so much for working with me on Blissful Disaster. You smoothed out all the rough edges and it reads so much better because of your hard work. I appreciate all you have done for me.

Olivia Howe, my PA, owner of Beautiful Promotions and Beautifully Broken Book Blog, web designer, formatter, social media wizard, and street team manager who constantly promotes me and my work. I truly believe you are my long lost little sister and I'm so lucky to have such a great friend, fan, fellow author, and promotional wizard with excellent taste in music.

Viola Estrella from Estrella Cover Art who created my beautiful cover. Thank you so much for working with me on my book covers. You always work your magic and make my vision a reality.

My 'Girls Book Club' (Sharon, Rachel, and Kelly) who started it all. Thanks for your constant support and encouragement.

Thank you all so much!

ALSO BY AMY L. GALE

BLISSFUL DISASTER

1

AFTERMATH

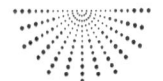

THROBBING PAIN PULSATES THROUGH MY HEAD, SENDING ECHOES OF agony through every crevice of my skull. I lift my head and grimace. Bad idea. My heartbeat pounds a fierce rhythm in my ears. If it's possible for a human brain to explode, mine wants to unleash the wrath of an atomic bomb. It's like I'm reliving the morning after my twenty-first birthday, three years later. Well, the hair of the dog theory never seemed to work for me. Maybe a little fresh air will help. I rub my eyes and spring into a sitting position. Bright rays of sunlight burst through the window, temporarily blinding me. I'm never drinking again. Sure, I've told myself that after almost every hangover. Why don't I listen? Within seconds everything becomes clearer. A ripple of soft satin flows across the length of my queen-sized bed, moving toward me like a snake slithering through the grass. A silhouette enrobed in the white sheets lies asleep on the opposite side of me. I cover my mouth holding in the scream that's dying to escape. No, I couldn't have. I mean, I came to L.A. to pursue a professional writing career and now I'm a one-night floozy. Oh my God, what the hell happened last night?

I cover myself with the rest of the sheet, and slowly slide off the edge of the bed until my feet hit the hardwood. My toes slide along a silky fabric. Great, there's my Gucci dress from last night. Never thought I'd be stepping on a dress that cost two weeks' salary. I swallow hard trying to suppress the sour tang of stale alcohol. I grab my underwear from the floor and tiptoe to the bathroom, snagging the Ralph Lauren T-shirt I left on the triple dresser on the way. Okay, it's not the end of the world. I'm sure most women have been in this sort of situation one time or another, right? Yeah, drunken sorority girls and porn stars. A bass drum pounds in my head, beating harder every time I move. I slowly close the door as quietly as humanly possible and hunch over the cool granite countertop. Memories of last night rush through my mind like a raging river. Flashes of dancing at Club X, drinking blueberry martinis, and visions of doing way too many shots with the hot guy next to me shoot through my tattered brain. Oh God, I don't even remember his name.

I turn on the sink and splash cool water over my face. Ugh, this is so bad. *I know nothing about this guy; please tell me we used protection.* Oh no, what if he's a co-worker, or someone who lives in the apartment complex. I've got a fresh start in a big city and this is how I act? I turn off the water, lift my head, and stare into the mirror. Wow, so I end my night of celebrating my promotion to field reporter by getting drunk and taking home some guy I hardly know. Way to act professional. I made it through four years of college without any one night hookups. It's like I regressed five years overnight.

A screaming guitar resonates through the air, hammering through my head. The tune plays again. I grip the countertop. Ah, must be his ring tone. Crap, now he's definitely awake. I grab the hand towel and blot my face, red veins scatter through puffy eyes. I look like death twice over. Doesn't matter, all the make-up in the world can't cover up last night. The floor boards creak as heavy footsteps slowly move along the wooden planks. I nibble at my nails and stare at the white wooden door. Oh God, he's walking around my bedroom. What am I supposed to say? It's not like there's a book of etiquette for one-night stands. I take a deep breath and slowly exhale. Ok, maybe he does this all the time and once I come out he'll just go say goodbye and go home. Yeah, that's really comforting; I'm just another notch on his bedpost. How in the world did I let this happen? He probably thinks I'm some slut who does this every night. There's no way this can be anything but a disaster. *Dammit*, I can't hide in here forever. There's no window in here so escaping isn't an option. I slug a gulp of mouthwash and swish it around my mouth. Okay, time to put on my big girl panties. I'll handle this situation the best I can. Maybe it'll help prepare me for unpleasant situations in the field. Yeah right, if I end up in this type of situation at work I'll either be fired or highly promoted. I run a brush through my tangled, blonde strands. Guess it's now or never. I spit out the mouthwash in the sink and trudge toward the door.

Please let me think of something to say to... whoever he is. I gaze down at the tan tiles and slowly turn the knob. Last time I procrastinated walking into a room was when I backed Mom's car into the tree in the yard while using the rear view mirror to apply lipstick. I'd rather relive that day than face what's on the other side of the door. My best bet is to get it over with quick, like ripping off a Band-Aid. I take a deep breath and open the door. I grip the hem of my T-shirt, trying to pull it down over my underwear. There's just no way to maintain my dignity in this situation. It's long gone.

He holds his cell phone to his ear. "Hey Lexie, is Van around?"

I swallow hard and focus. Perfectly fitted light blue jeans slightly frayed at the knee, an incredibly chiseled torso, and a multitude of tattoos gracing muscular biceps. My heart pounds, causing more distress to my already debilitated head. So guys who look like him do exist in real life. I gaze over a black leather strand fastened to his neck holding a shark tooth, and continue to his dirty blond hair hanging right past his shoulders. Women would kill for that hair. Holy hell, maybe I should get trashed more often if I could bring home guys like that. What a thing to think of at a time like this. Especially since these are the kind of guys I need to stay far away from. Maybe my brain needs to find something positive to lift my spirits.

"Hey man, it's Tyler. Running a little late. Be there soon." He presses the screen on his phone and slides it in his pocket.

Ok, so his name is Tyler. One mystery solved.

He runs a hand through his hair and turns toward me, flashing a small smile. "I know this great place for breakfast."

My stomach flutters. Not so sure food is my friend today. I loosen the death grip on my T-shirt hem and side step to my triple dresser. "Breakfast sounds great." What? Breakfast is a terrible idea. My brain seems to be operating on auto pilot.

He bends down and grabs his white T-shirt from the floor. I follow the path of the thin fabric, across his pecs, and over his six-pack abs. It's like I can't peel my eyes away from him. Guess that's how last night happened.

"Nice place, Ali."

At least he remembers my name. More than I can say for myself. Clearly he didn't succumb to the effects of alcohol quite like me. I turn around quickly and pull a pair of jean shorts out of the top drawer.

"Thanks." I wobble, trying to slide on my shorts in warp speed. "So, whose car do you want to take?"

He narrows his eyes. "You have no clue what went down last night." He presses his lips together holding in a smile.

Great, busted. Good thing I didn't come here to pursue acting. My body freezes. Come on Ali, think. There's no way anyone would have let me drive last night. Ah, my car must still be at the club. "Oh, that's right. We took your car." I bite at my lip.

He walks toward me and raises an eyebrow. "Uh huh, what color is it?"

Crap. What is this, a trivia test? He looks like a flashy kind of guy, but also artsy. Maybe metallic silver or jet black? I fidget with my fingers and rock back on my heels. "It was dark." Clearly a lame excuse. *Please don't let me embarrass myself anymore.* If he keeps this up I may vomit on him over breakfast.

He walks slowly across the wooden floor. Musky cologne fills the air, more pungent the closer he gets. Oh God, what's he doing? Is he trying to go for round two? There's no way anything more than breakfast is happening today, no matter how good he looks. He continues forward, so close his breath ruffles a few strands of hair across my cheeks. I take a deep breath and hold it in.

He reaches behind me and grabs his keys from the dresser. "Ready?" He holds out his hand.

I nod and take his hand. Yeah, ready for what? I slip on my flip-flops and follow him out the door. Why in the world did I agree to breakfast? Guess I'm not up on my one-night-stand protocol. It's not like he'd believe this was my first one anyway. I'm sure as hell not looking forward to these three floors of steps. I hold onto Tyler's hand and the railing as I make my descent. My head pounds with every snap of my flip-flops. *Please just let me get this over with so I can forget about this mistake of a night.*

My knee buckles. A split second later my foot slides off the edge of the concrete step. It looks like the aftermath of last night continues. He'd never believe I was on the cheerleading squad back in the day. I try and grip onto the railing but miss. Tyler scoops me up with one arm, catching me before I plummet downward.

"Don't fall for me." He chuckles and sets me down onto the landing.

You've got to be kidding me. It'll be a miracle if I make it to the car unscathed. "I'll try my best but no promises." I look down and shake my head slightly. Oh God, everything I say is coming out completely wrong. It's like the alcohol killed every brain cell required for rational reasoning. I raise my head at a snail's pace and gaze into his clear blue eyes.

He slides on his sunglasses, muffling a smirk.

Heat spreads across my cheeks. Well, I guess trying to change his perception of me from last night is off to a great start. Next I'll probably trip and fall on top of him. I navigate the last step safely. Thank God, I've still got money from the coffee shop yesterday. If I had to ask him to pay for breakfast too I might've died of humiliation. The sunlight shines down, illuminating tiny crystals in the sidewalk.

I cup my hands along my forehead to make a visor. The bright California sunshine beats down, blaring through my sensitive eyes. Another reminder of why I should control my alcohol intake in this city. I turn from side to side. Tyler's gone. If he wanted to ditch me he could've snuck out of my apartment before I woke up. I spin around. Tyler leans against a candy apple red convertible Camaro, his arms folded across his chest, accentuating the array of colorful tattoos intricately placed along his toned biceps and forearms. The blood rushes from my face to my toes. Yeah, I couldn't miss this car if we were in the midst of an eclipse. I lower my chin and stomp toward him.

He stands up straight and nods his head toward the car. "Didn't see it again, huh?"

Smart ass! I march along the blacktop and walk around the passenger side. He steps in front of me as I grab for the door handle.

He slides his hand underneath the shiny chrome handle and opens the door for me. "You're quiet today, babe. Where's the Ali from last night?"

I hop into the white leather seat and pull my seatbelt across my chest. "She doesn't appear until she's had coffee." Dear Jesus, what Ali is he referring to? If he's looking for a flirty, easy version she doesn't exist and sure as hell shouldn't have last night.

He closes the door and heads over to the driver's side. "We'd better get you some coffee then."

I'm not that boring. Maybe if the pounding in my head would subside and he stopped acting like we've just come from a sleepover party I'd be in a better mood. Okay, one breakfast and I'll finally be done with this disaster of a night.

I press my body back against the seat as Tyler pulls out onto the freeway. The only thing I miss about living in the country is the two lane roads with little to no traffic. It takes forever to get anywhere in L.A. I pull my hair into a loose ponytail and tuck it into the neck of my T-shirt. Jeez, I could get whiplash from my hair flying in the wind. Note to self, never buy a convertible.

Tyler steers the car with one hand and slides the fingers of his other hand across the seat and onto my thigh. Every muscle in my body freezes except my heart which beats a million miles a minute. He glides his fingers along the length of my thigh and up to my hand. A frenzy of tingles follows the path of his touch, burning up my skin. He interlocks his fingers with mine and pulls my hand toward the center console.

"You have a very important mission if you choose to accept it." He flashes a bring-you-to-your-knees sexy smile.

Please don't let him think I'm doing anything sexual with my hand during this drive to breakfast. I swallow hard, knocking the sour tang in my mouth down into the depths of my stomach.

"What do you have in mind?" I bite at my lip.

He moves my hand forward, releasing it near the radio. "You find us some kick ass tunes while I drive."

Great. It's like he's calling me out on all my weaknesses. The scope of my musical knowledge ends at the songs they play over the loudspeaker at *Entertainment Rock!*'s magazine. I press the seek button until I hear familiar guitar chords. Awesome, *Whole Lotta Love* on the classic rock channel.

"Nice." Tyler turns up the volume and moves his head to the rhythm. "Mission accomplished."

I smile. Why do I even care what he thinks about my taste in music? He could be an ax murderer who plays Zeppelin before he makes a kill.

"Your whole world's gonna change in about five minutes." Tyler turns the wheel and veers off an exit.

I grip the armrest, trying to prevent myself from plummeting into him as the car turns the corner. What the hell does that mean? *Please don't let this world changing event be something that gets me killed or arrested.*

Huh, I've never been to this part of town before. We pull into a small gravel parking lot at the end of the road. My eyes focus on the metal trailer in front of us adorned with a blinking red light on top that flashes Melba's Diner.

Tyler runs his hand through his hair and turns toward me. "Ready to have your world turned upside down?"

Didn't that already happen last night? "I'm up for anything." Crap. Every word coming out of my mouth can be construed as a sexual innuendo. Great way to make him think I'm not a slut. *Please let this breakfast date go by fast.*

"Cool." He winks, gets out of the car, and steps around to my side.

He pulls open my door and holds out his hand. I stare at the intricate tiger on his forearm moving with every flex of his muscle, getting lost in the bright colors of the jungle. He's either a gentleman or doesn't want me to fall on my face. I slide my hand along his calloused fingers and step out of the car.

The warm breeze caresses my skin and sends my flaxen strands dancing along my back. I close my eyes and take a deep breath letting the air invigorate my body. My flip-flops slide along the small rocks of the uneven gravel parking lot. I grip Tyler's hand with both of mine but it's too late, my lack of agility shines through. I plop down onto the ground, ass first, and slide forward. I curl my shoulders over my chest and bow my head, trying to hide my flushed face. Seriously? If it's possible to die from embarrassment I should be in hospice care.

Tyler stops dead in his tracks and bends down next to me. "Can't stop falling for me." He lifts my chin, tucking a stray strand of hair behind an ear. "You ok?"

I nod.

"Only one way to handle this, babe." He scoops me up and trudges forward.

I wrap my arms around his neck and hold on tight. No need to plummet to the ground again. Next time, I'll bury myself in it. It's like my dirty little secret is turning into my Prince Charming.

He heads up the two steps to the door and opens it with a few of his fingers. Dozens of eyes stare. I doubt many girls are carried in here unless they're accident victims. Maybe that's a good summary of the last twelve hours.

"Hey, Jeanie, we need coffee here, quick." Tyler sets me down on the white and blue linoleum.

"You're back in town." A woman rushes forward and pulls Tyler into a hug.

Great, he's a regular. Guess he takes all his girls here for breakfast.

"Just got in yesterday." He turns toward me and slides his arm in the small of my back. "Two Melba's sweet specials."

"You got it, sit anywhere you like. Oh, and I'll bring lots of coffee." She winks.

Tyler guides me to a booth in the back near the window. I slide into the cool pink vinyl booth and adjust my ponytail. It's like I'm in the middle of a puzzle. He just got back to town yesterday and knows the menu by heart. Who the hell am I with?

"Two coffees, the rest will be right up."

I slide the cup toward me and inhale the invigorating aroma of fresh ground beans. Ah, instant relief. I take a sip and let the warm liquid pass along my taste buds. The pounding in my head diminishes to a low thump. An involuntary smile creeps across my face.

"Like magic." Tyler raises his eyebrows and takes a sip of his coffee.

I tap my fingers along the ceramic mug. I've got to clear things up. After last night and this morning, there's no way I can embarrass myself any more.

"Listen, last night shouldn't have happened." Oh my God, I just insulted him. I look down at the table and bite at my lip. My knee bounces. "Wait, that didn't' come out right, I mean..." Coffee sloshes from our cups, spilling a few drops onto the table. I grab a napkin and wipe it with my shaky fingers.

Tyler puts his hand over mine. "I get it."

He lifts my chin so my eyes are staring right into his. My God, he can hypnotize me into doing anything with that stare. I blink repeatedly and will myself back into reality.

"You partied way too much, happens to the best of us." He drops his hand from my chin and runs it through his hair. "Today's a fresh start."

I hold my coffee cup with both hands and take a sip. "Deal."

"What's up with last night's celebration?" He sips his coffee. "I bet I know, you discovered how to prevent the zombie apocalypse."

I laugh mid sip, spilling a few drops of coffee on the table. Amazing, after a year of lame one-time only dates in L.A. I actually found a guy with a warped sense of humor like mine. Didn't think guys like this existed, not since high school anyway. I take a deep breath and shed a memory from my brain. "Well, I'd tell you but then I'd have to kill you." I wipe my lips with a napkin. "I finally got the promotion I'd been hoping for."

He lifts his coffee cup. "Calls for celebration."

I lift my mug and clink it with his. Amazing, my one-night stand mistake is the best date I've had in years. Well, not that I've had many. Funny how things work out. Who knows, maybe last night wasn't the worst thing possible? Of course, he could be an ax murderer for all I know. Time to find out the scoop.

I set my cup on the table and lean back in the booth. "Do you come to L.A. often?"

He slides his cup to the end of the table and nods toward our waitress. "A couple times a year when I'm working at the recording studio."

The waitress plops two plates of fluffy pancakes in front of us. The sweet aroma makes my mouth water. Yum, chocolate chip pancakes with maple syrup and pecans. My God, if this is what Tyler does for one night stands what does he do for a real date? Not that I should be thinking about a real date. From every fairytale I know, the princess doesn't get the prince by banging him the first time they meet. I fiddle with my fingers and grab the fork. Hey, life's no fairytale anyway. I run my tongue along my bottom lip and pop a forkful into my mouth. Mmm, just the right amount of butter and syrup. Pure perfection.

Tyler stuffs a pancake in his mouth, catching a drip of syrup running down his lips with his finger. "Told ya. World changing!"

I slide another forkful into my mouth, savoring every morsel. "You never fail to disappoint." Again? I've got to fill my mouth with food so I'll stop it with these crazy one-liners. It's like I've stolen some sleazy guy's pick-up lines. *Please just get me out of here before I lose every shred of dignity.*

He chomps down the last of the pancakes and stares into my eyes, right down to the depths of my soul. "I'm only getting started."

Oh God, last night isn't going to continue past breakfast. Ok, so the bits and pieces I recall of Tyler's physical talents make every hair on my body stand on end, but this isn't me. I don't do sexy seductress. Conservative and organized is more my style and Tyler is anything but.

I sip the last of my coffee and pull some money out of my pocket as the waitress sets the bill on the table.

Tyler's head falls back slightly. "No way. I've got this. Call me old fashioned." He hops out of the booth to the register before I can even open my mouth.

Yeah, nothing about him is remotely old fashioned. Confident with a touch of white hot molten sexy is more like it.

"Hon, I just have to tell ya. You've got one great guy." Jeanie, the waitress, gestures toward Tyler. "Wish there were more guys like him."

I smile and nod. I'm not really the best judge of Tyler's character. Telling a waitress who adores him that we've only known each other for about twelve hours isn't on my list of things to do today.

Tyler walks back to the table. "Catch ya later, Jeanie." He gives her a quick hug and holds his hand out to me. "Ready, or should I carry you out too?" He flashes a sexy smile. "Can't have you falling for me again."

I bite at my lip and take his hand. "I'll try my best but no promises."

Tyler entwines his fingers with mine. I follow him out of the diner, carefully navigating down the two steps and along the loose gravel. If I fall a third time he may as well just leave me there because I'll die from embarrassment. Small rocks slide under the soles of my flip-flops and the warm breeze glides across my skin. Hot rays of sunlight shine down upon my face, erasing the slight thud in my head. My body is back to itself, I think.

Tyler pulls open the door for me and heads around to the driver's seat. I pull on my seatbelt and prepare for things to return to normal. A dull ache forms in my chest. In a few minutes last night will be all behind me. So why do I want this ride to last forever?

"Think you can handle another mission?" Tyler fires up the engine.

"Huh?"

"Your mission, if you choose to accept it." Tyler runs his hand along my thigh and brings my fingers to the knobs of the car radio.

"I'm up for the challenge." *Please let me find the same channel again.* I've got to brush up on my music knowledge. He must know all sorts of things from working in a recording studio. I've got to stop kidding myself. This is probably my last mission from him. I press the seek button until familiar chords flow through the airwaves. Perfect, *Dream On* by Aerosmith.

Tyler runs a hand through his hair and glances at me. "Mission accomplished once again." He continues down the freeway, swaying to the tune.

I close my eyes and let the wind whip through my hair. The fresh air invigorates my senses. Ah, I am back to normal, somewhat.

Tyler pulls alongside the curb and shuts down the engine. My heart pounds against my chest. Oh God, if I invite him in he'll clearly get the wrong idea and if I don't then he'll think I'm not interested. Great, a catch twenty-two. What happens now?

"Now that your world is turned upside down, I've gotta go." He tucks another stray hair behind my ear.

Yeah, he did tell whomever he was on the phone with earlier that he's running late. At least he's not lying.

"Ah-ha, tempt me and then leave." A meek smile forms across my face. Where the hell did that come from? Oh God, I'm clearly losing my mind.

He runs his hands through his hair. "Huh, I've never been called a tease before." He rummages through the glove compartment and pulls out a pen and piece of paper. "It's only fair to make it up to you. What's your phone number?"

I slide the pen from his fingers and take the piece of paper. Now if I can control my shaky hand maybe there's a chance he'll be able to read it. I write down my number and dot the I in Ali with a heart. So, I'm a little cheesy but it's cute.

Tyler slides his hand along my cheek. "I'll call you soon." He places a sweet kiss on my lips and pulls away.

His soft lips against mine turn my body into a frenzy of pure passion. I step out of the car and carefully walk forward, making sure I have control of my footing. If I fall for him a third time it won't be on the sidewalk.

I wave and disappear into the stairwell. Amazing, the disaster of a night turned into something incredible, or on its way to becoming just that.

I plop onto my bed and grab my cell phone, **no new calls**. What am I thinking, it's only been a few minutes? I close my eyes and drift off to sleep.

My eyes pop open and look at the clock, it's five in the evening. My God, I just slept the day away. I pick up my cell phone, **no new calls.** Jeez, I'm acting like a crazed teenager. Guys don't usually call the same day anyway. I grab a cold slice of leftover pizza from the fridge and turn on the television. Awesome, *The Breakfast Club*, one of my all-time favorites. I check my phone in between commercials but still nothing. My stomach flutters.

I OPEN MY EYES AND STARE AT THE BRIGHT RED NUMBERS SLOWLY coming into focus. Wow, morning already. It's like I slept through the majority of the weekend. I take a deep breath and reach for my phone, staring at the screen as if it's about to tell me something I don't already know, **no new calls.** Emptiness fills the pit of my stomach. What a jerk!

2

NEW BEGINNINGS

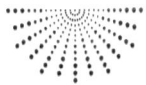

A ROLLING FLUTTER EMITS FROM THE PIT OF MY STOMACH. I glance down at my black shoes with the bright red soles. Christian Louboutin's scream stylish and professional. I've always wanted a pair, so this promotion was a perfect reason to buy a present for myself. Now, if I can only gain the confidence that I'd imagined goes with them. I pick at my fingernails and take a deep breath. *Please let me make a good first impression.* I glance toward the wall to wall windows taking in the breathtaking view of the city. Never in my wildest dreams did I think I'd be here already. Less than a year with *Entertainment Rocks!* and I made it to field reporter.

A buzzing in my purse resonates through the quiet foyer, pulling me out of professional mode. It can't be him, not after two days. I stop dead in my tracks and frantically dig for my cell phone. Damn this purse, it's like everything gets lost in a black hole at the bottom. Ah ha, got it. I pull the phone out. Ooh, a voicemail. I take a deep breath and press play.

"Hey, Ali, just wanted to wish you good luck on your first day. Catch ya at lunch, 12:30 at Café L'amore. You've got to fill me in on the hottie from Friday night. Must've been some weekend. Tootles."

I exhale loudly and press delete. Guess my best friend Chloe thinks I shacked up with Tyler all weekend. Hate to disappoint, but once he dropped me off after breakfast, I hooked up with two guys, Mr. Ben and Jerry. I don't get it. Why would he even bother to ask for my phone number if he had no intention of calling me? I mean, it was a hook-up. We could've just parted ways with no expectations. I toss the phone back in my purse and zip it up. Hope she's ready for a tragic tale full of regrets and mistakes.

I've got to focus and put last weekend behind me. My first day as field reporter starts now. I sling my purse over my shoulder and march forward. My heart beats faster with each step I take closer to the glass door with the words **Jane Reiser, Senior Editor.** I swallow hard and pull open the door. The wall to wall windows showcase a panoramic view of Los Angeles's skyline. Someday, I'll have an office like this one. That is if I can get it together and stop making bad decisions. I bite my lip and take a step forward.

She lifts her eyes from her computer screen and looks me up and down. Oh God, I should've worn the black dress. This so-called power suit is way too outdated. I focus on her dark brown hair pulled into a tight ponytail with every hair in perfect place and stare at the hard line of her lips. She raises an eyebrow.

I clear my throat. "Hi, I'm Allison Whitman, the new field reporter." I hold out my hand and take another step forward to greet her. My knee shakes, causing the heel of my shoe to wobble and send my body into complete chaos. I try my best to steady myself but no such luck. This can't be happening. I fall forward and slide across the sleek tile until my face is at the foot of her desk. Droplets of sweat form across my forehead and a dull ache resonates through my chest. Ugh, this is the worst week of my life. I lift my head at a snail's pace.

Jane stands up and looks down at me. "Nice to meet you,

Allison, we've got a meeting at eleven a.m. in conference room three. Claire, my secretary, will show you to your cubicle." She sits back down and types at her computer.

I work for an ice princess, nothing but business and cold to the core. Maybe it's better to ignore this little mishap, but I've got to acknowledge the incident. I pull myself to my feet and pat down my skirt. "Sorry, new shoes. I'm very excited to be part of the field reporting team." I flash my pearly whites and try to ignore the pain radiating across my chin.

She presses the intercom. "Claire, please show Ms. Whitman to her cubicle." Jane grabs a folder from her desk and leafs through the papers inside.

Great, my new boss wants to communicate with me as little as possible. Guess that's the trend lately. I turn around as the door swings open. A young woman, maybe in her early twenties like me, walks toward me gripping a folder with one hand and extends the other.

"Hello, Ms. Whitman. I'm Claire."

I shake her hand and smile. "Nice to meet you."

"Follow me."

I steady myself and slowly walk out of the room. It's not like I can make a worse impression, but it would be nice if I could make it through the day without ending up in the hospital.

Claire leads me to down an aisle of cubicles and stops at the last one on the left. "Here you are." She sets the folder on my desk. "This is a list of passwords to get you into the computer system and a few forms you need to fill out for personnel. Please let me know if you need anything. Good luck."

I set my purse on my desk. "Thanks, I'll need it."

She smiles and walks away.

I pull out my chair and sink into the soft black leather. Eek! My own office. I lift my feet and swing my chair around. I've got to take a picture and send it to Chloe. I dig in my purse, pull out my phone, and plaster a ridiculous smile on my face to enhance this selfie. I snap a picture.

Deep throaty laughter fills the small space. I jump back against the seat and turn toward the cubicle entrance. Soft brown eyes search my face. Wow, I'm queen of great first impressions today.

"Didn't mean to interrupt, I'm your neighbor." He points behind him and tries to muffle a smile.

I toss my phone on the desk and hide my face in my hands. Peeking out from underneath my fingers I slowly lower my hands. "I'm Ali, and I think I turned into a star struck teenager for the last few seconds."

He smiles and rubs his chin. "Glad you're back on, I'm Jake by the way." He slides a hand from the pocket of a perfectly fitted black suit. "If you've got your inner fangirl under control, how about lunch?"

A mop of dark brown hair with a few sun-induced highlights lies in loose waves ending at the top of his neckline. A perfect combination, the looks of a model and the brain of a field reporter; maybe the day is looking up. *Dammit*, I've got plans with Chloe. I nibble at my fingernails. "Can't today. Rain check?"

"Definitely." He moistens his lips with his tongue. "See ya around, neighbor."

I focus on his broad shoulders, examining the rest of his body as he walks away. The last thing I should be thinking about is guys. Of course, it doesn't help that a Zac Efron lookalike works directly behind me. I'm ready for a fresh start, Ali Whitman field reporter ready for duty. I turn my chair forward and slide it under my black desk. Ok, might as well get settled and fill out my paperwork before the meeting. I slide my purse underneath my desk and fire up my computer. Guess it wouldn't hurt to keep my phone handy. I set it on the desk next to my keyboard and glance at the screen. **No new calls.**

∽

I HOLD MY LEGAL PAD CLOSE TO MY CHEST AND GRIP THE THREE ball point pens so tight it would require the Jaws of Life to pry them from my fingers. I walk slowly, paying close attention to my footing. No need to fall on my face a second time in front of my new boss. Oh, looks like I'm the first one here. I breathe deeply taking in the aroma of leather and fresh coffee. Amazing, it's exactly how I'd pictured it. A wall of large windows reaching from the floor to the ceiling without a single smudge on them, a multitude of black leather chairs seamlessly situated around a table that could barely fit in my entire apartment. I pull out a chair near the end of the table and sit down. Maybe I'll score some brownie points by being punctual. I position the legal pad on the table directly in front of my seat and set the three pens next to it, ensuring they are lined up perfectly.

My heart pounds as footsteps grow closer. Ok, second impressions are just as important as first ones. There's still time to get on my boss's good side. I take a deep breath and turn my chair toward the door. I exhale and sigh.

"Sorry to disappoint, neighbor. Is this seat taken?" Jake plops a manila folder on the table and sips his coffee. "Expecting Brad Pitt or something?"

I'm really nailing the second impressions so far. I grab a pen from the table and chew on the top. "I was hoping he'd be my first assignment."

Jake sits down and flashes a half smile. "Wow, you're aiming high. Mine was a dog wedding."

We both burst into laughter.

I glance at his warm brown eyes and sweet smile. At least I've made one friend, and he's easy on the eyes too.

A small army of people file through the door and take seats around the table. I tap my pen along my lips, waiting for the festivities to begin. Jane bursts through the door and plops a slew of files on the table.

"Alright everyone, let's get started so we can continue with our day. Today I want to focus on *Entertainment Rocks!*'s new agenda. We're going to be shifting our focus from pop culture to music, television, and movies. I want to see up and coming new talent grace our pages before another publication snags the story. I've got assignments for everyone which Claire will be distributing later today. I expect nothing but 110%. I've got a conference call in five minutes. Any questions?"

The room is so silent we could probably hear an ant crawl.

"Good, carry on with your day." Jane rushes out of the room, her heels smacking against the tile like a battle cry.

Claire steps inside and lugs the paperwork out to her desk.

I push my chair back and slide out from under the table, knocking one of my ink pens to the floor. Jake grabs it and stands up next to me. "Brad Pitt interview may be on the table."

I giggle. "Or maybe his dog's wedding." I grip my legal pad close to my chest. "Are the meetings always this short?"

He shrugs. "Depends on the Boss Lady's mood. Always unpredictable."

Great. Maybe my best bet is to steer clear of her until she actually wants to talk to me. Then maybe I can have a conversation face to face rather than floor to face. We all file out of the meeting room, and I retreat back to my desk. I'll try out some of these passwords before lunch. I glance at my phone next to the keyboard, **no new calls.**

"Ahh," Chloe runs at me at warp speed and pulls me into a bear hug. "How's the first day going Ms. Reporter Extraordinaire?" Chloe locks her arm around mine and trots down the sidewalk toward Café L'amore.

"Fell face first in front of my boss and acted like a teenager from back in the day who just met Elvis, you know, typical day." I shrug.

"Ouch." She grimaces. "No worries, nothing a café latte can't fix."

Ah, if only life was that simple. I give her arm a quick squeeze. Maybe I don't have the best luck when it comes to guys, but I hit the lottery when it comes to best friends. The aroma of fresh baked bread and coffee greet me as I step inside Café L'amore. My mouth waters as I walk up to the counter to order.

"No way, I've got lunch today. We're still celebrating." Chloe steps in front of me and leans over the counter. "We'll take two café lattes, two turkey Reubens and two raspberry cookies."

I grab a few napkins and head over to a secluded table by the window. Chloe follows a few steps behind.

I sling my purse over the chair and slide into the seat. "Thanks, Chlo."

She swats her hand through the air. "Oh please, you deserve it." She sets our buzzer on the table and sinks into her seat. "Time to spill it, what happened with the hottie you went home with Friday night."

Ugh, I guess I have to relive this disaster of a night one more time. "We hooked up, he took me to breakfast, then never called me." I look down at the table, then back up at her.

Chloe puts her hand over her mouth, slowly dropping it. "What an asshole. He slipped right under my radar. Plus, he's the only guy who could actually keep up with you on the dance floor." She puts her hand over mine. "I bet he's psychotic."

We break down into a mess of giggles. "They're the ones I usually attract."

Bright red lights dance in a circle, blaring like a beacon. "Order's up, be right back." Chloe hops out of her chair and heads to the counter.

I just don't get it. What was the whole point in taking me to his 'special breakfast spot' if he wanted to ditch me? He could've just said goodbye and left my house, never looking back. Does he think everyone he hooks up with deserves a meal?

Chloe sets the tray on the table and settles back in. She sips her coffee. "Enough about him, so what else happened at work?"

I bite my turkey Reuben and then set it on my plate. "When I was taking that selfie, the guy in the cubicle next to me came over to say hi. He's kinda nice."

She raises her eyebrows. "Is he hot?"

I sip my coffee and set the cup down. "He's really cute but conservative, safe. You know, the kind of guys we should hang out with but never do."

Chloe breaks her cookie in half and nibbles at it. "Yeah, those bad boys are just so damn irresistible, but never worth the trouble." She sips her coffee. "Let's make a pact, no more hot, sexy-as-hell guys who are everything we want and nothing we need."

I bite my cookie and raise my eyebrows. "Wow, don't make it sound so fun." I finish the last bite of my sandwich. "One exciting thing happened, well is about to happen."

"Ooh, do tell."

"I get my first assignment this afternoon."

Chloe drops her cookie and claps. "Oh my God this is big news, any idea what it is?"

I shake my head. "All I know is it's something to do with movies, music, or television."

"This is so awesome. All exciting topics." She wipes her mouth with her napkin. "You've got to call me as soon as you find out what it is. Who knows, maybe you'll get to interview someone famous."

I hold up my hands. "Doubtful, but I'm going to have my name on a byline in a national magazine." An ear to ear smile graces my face. "I might frame it."

"I want an autographed copy." She finishes the last bite of her cookie. "We've got to celebrate, your first byline."

Uh, yeah because our last celebration went down so well. "How about we keep it simple, pizza and wine coolers at my apartment." I slug the rest of my coffee.

Chloe lowers her eyebrows and tilts her head. "What are we, sixteen? We are going to dinner and a club Friday night, and I'm not taking no for an answer."

Lovely, another disaster of a night waiting to happen. Ok, dinner and a club but she didn't mention anything about drinking. I nod. "Deal."

NOTE TO SELF, IF I EVER PLAN ON BEING ON TIME, FACTOR IN THE busy elevator. I get it, the building rivals a New York City skyscraper but I can scale the building faster than waiting for the elevator to make it to the lobby. I stare at the shiny silver doors willing them to open. Ugh, I've got to get to my desk before our assignments are given out. No need to add tardy to the list of qualities branded on me today.

The bell rings, echoing through the foyer like an angel's choir. Thank God. I step inside and press six. It lights up, glowing like a firefly. Footsteps pound against the foyer floor as if a stampede of wild cattle are charging toward me. I step back and press my body against the cool metal wall.

A slew of people step inside, holding the door for more. I'm like a sardine, trapped in a tin box. The crew starts pressing buttons as soon as the elevator doors start to close. I peek my head around a tall man in a pinstriped suit who clearly chose to bathe in cheap cologne. I cover my mouth and cough. You've got to be kidding me. We're stopping at every floor? Figures.

A briefcase slides in between the doors right before they close, sending the steel panels back to their opening position. I let out a loud sigh. Really? It's not like there's an inch of room for anyone else. Great. I'll probably get stuck in here and asphyxiate.

Jake drops his briefcase to the floor and lifts his arm to slide in between Mr. Pinstripes and a woman yakking on her cell phone. "Thanks for waiting."

Low pitched grumbles fill the small space.

He nods toward me. "Claire always starts in the front cubicles so by the time she gets to us we'll be on our third game of solitaire."

My tense muscles relax. "Guess it's not always bad to be last."

The elevator stops, letting a few people out, then stops again, lessening the crowd. I stare up at the large numbers above the doorway, biting my lip. Yes! Floor six. The doors open, exposing the shiny white tiles. I suck in a deep breath and charge toward the doorway, nudging Jake on the way.

He grabs his briefcase and stomps forward to keep up. "Are we racing?"

I slow my pace. "Sorry. Guess I'm over eager."

I turn the corner and gaze at Claire handing out file folders. Jeez, she's already in the middle of the second row. My fingers tremble.

Jake grabs my hand. "Relax, we've got this." He pulls me down the first aisle to a small space between the wall and edge of the cubicles. "Secret passageway."

I hold up my arms and slide in between the small space, grazing my suit jacket against the textured wall. For the love of God, please don't let me rip it. I make it past the first row, now on to the second. I glide by and turn, gripping the edge of my cubicle panel. My breathing slows to an acceptable rate, and I pull down my suit jacket, trying to restore it to its former glory. I plop in my chair and fan my blonde strands around my shoulders. Yes. Made it.

Claire pops her head in my cubicle. "Allison, how's your first day going?" She sets a file folder on my desk.

I flash a quick smile and grab the folder. "Definitely memorable."

"Good luck with your first assignment." She turns and walks toward Jake's cubicle.

I run my fingers along the black letters, **Reporter Allison Whitman**. A kaleidoscope of butterflies flutter in my stomach. My lips upturn into an ear to ear smile, so wide my cheeks hurt. The words I've waited to see are right in front of me.

I SLAM MY SHIFTER INTO PARK AND PULL OPEN THE DOOR OF MY silver Toyota Camry. This is it, my first assignment. I slide my hand across the gray leather and glance at the top sheet of paper in my file folder. Okay, so it's not exactly what I expected, but I've got to hit this one out of the park if I want to make a name for myself. I'm a professional, and I can handle whatever they throw at me. Now, if I can only trick my mind into believing it. I grab my folders and trek toward the tall, red brick building with the large black door.

I close my eyes and take a deep breath. Come on Ali, you can do this. I exhale and walk forward. Why couldn't I have gotten Jake's assignment about the pilot of a new television comedy? I mean, I watch TV all the time. But no, I get an up and coming metal band. The research I'll need to do just to come up with five hundred words may take me weeks. I'm so out of my league.

I clutch my folder to my chest and trudge up the concrete stairway. *Please don't let them be doing anything illegal.* Getting bailed out of jail for any drug offenses is not on my list of things to do today. God knows what a metal band does for fun.

I press the buzzer and wait by the door. My whole body trembles as I stare at the intercom.

"Come on up." A female voice resonates through the air.

My heart pounds. Oh God, there's nothing in this file that

says anything about a girl being in the band. Did they send me the right information? I frantically leaf through the papers in the folder. Come on Ali, get a hold of yourself. Maybe it's a groupie or one of the band members' girlfriend.

"Hello, you coming?"

I clear my throat and press the buzzer. "Yes, be right up."

I pull open the heavy door and step into the stairwell. Well, it's now or never. *Please don't let someone be biting the head off a bat or performing any other equally disturbing rituals.* I swallow hard and head up the steps to 1C. How ridiculous, I'm meeting a metal band, not walking into a prison. I steady my shaking hand and knock at the door. In a half-hour this will all be over, and I'll be on my way to having my first byline published.

The door swings open at warp speed. I gasp and freeze in the doorway, paralyzed. A cold burst travels to my core. This can't be happening.

3

THE INTERVIEW

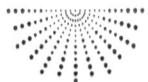

"You plan on coming inside or doing the interview from there?" A gorgeous blonde walks toward me with her arms folded, her black stilettos pound against the hardwood floor with every step.

I shake my head and compose myself. "Uh, sorry" I take a few steps forward and close the door behind me. Last time I experienced anything like this was in a demented dream sequence. I doubt Thor is going to show up, swing his hammer, and whisk me away to Asgard. Nope, I made this bed. Guess I've got to lay in it.

Tyler's eyes widen and his jaw drops. "Ali?" He scrunches his eyebrows.

The blonde huffs. "Looks like I'll be handling the introductions." She holds out her hand. "I'm Jenna Crane, and it seems like you and Tyler already know each other."

I raise my trembling hand and shake hers. "Yes, I'm Ali Whitman from *Entertainment Rocks!* magazine… Umm…. I'm here to interview Devil's Garden." I let go of her hand and step back. Technically, I know Tyler very well, yet he's still a complete stranger.

She looks at Tyler and then back at me. "Whatever, come on, the guys are in the practice room." She heads through the doorway.

I watch her disappear into the hall. What are the chances? Tyler works for Devil's Garden? He mentioned a recording studio. He's probably their sound tech or something. Maybe he'll leave and by some miracle I can pull off this interview.

She peeks her head back in. "Uh, you guys coming?"

Tyler clears his throat and runs a hand through his hair. "Yeah" He looks over at me and flashes a half smile. "Ladies first." He gestures toward the doorway.

I smile and proceed forward. He can skip the gentleman routine. I mean, hello, nice guys call you the day after they've spent the night in your apartment. Not that any of it matters now, I'm a professional, and I'm here to get the story.

Tan walls adorned with a few rock posters lead to the intricate metal ceilings. It's beautiful, just like I stepped backed in time. My shoe catches on the lip of the floor divider, skidding across the hardwood. I step forward, trying to prevent myself from plummeting down. No such luck. My papers fly across the room, and my briefcase slides down the hallway.

Tyler holds out his arm, catching me a few inches before I hit the floor. "Didn't I tell ya not to fall for me?" He winks.

Why am I so uncoordinated? I could probably hurt myself in a cardboard box. Note to self, flat shoes only from here on in. So much for showing off my professionalism. And who the hell does he think he is? He never even bothered to call me after he said he would. Then he thinks we're just going to start back where we left off. Yeah, not happening.

Jenna looks back over her shoulder and lowers her eyebrows. "You sure you're up for this? Maybe I should do the interview and send it to ya."

Wow, she must be a joy to be around twenty-four/seven. I get it, she's beautiful, and guys probably fall all over her regardless of how she acts, but it wouldn't kill her to behave semi-human. I scurry to pick up my paperwork. Great, it'll take me forever to reorganize this mess. *Please let my interview questions be intact.* What the hell, at this point, I'll wing it. "I'm ready, where's the practice room?"

She gestures with her hands like she's landing an airplane. If she had neon lights she'd be in her glory.

I take a deep breath and walk into the dimly lit room. The drumbeat resonates through the air, echoing against the dark carpeted walls. Huh, guess the place is sound proofed. My shoes sink into the soft burgundy carpet as I continue forward, paying careful attention to my footing.

Jenna jumps on the black leather sectional next to a man playing a guitar. I glance at his thick brown hair and watch his fingers move across the strings flawlessly as if they're programmed to do so.

The drummer swings his drumsticks through his fingers and stands up from the seat behind his drums. "Awesome. Looks like the babes are being delivered to us. I love this city."

Jenna shakes her head. "No dumbass, she's interviewing you guys for Entertainment Rocks! magazine." She runs her hands through the guitar player's hair.

The drummer struts forward, still sliding his drumstick along the fingers of his right hand. He runs his tongue along his top lip and raises his eyebrows. "I'm Chaz. Got a name, babe?"

Tyler steps forward and hands me a paper I must've lost in the hallway. "Her name's Ali and forget about it."

Chaz holds up his hands, gripping his drumstick with his pinky. "Didn't know you had dibs, dude."

Tyler shakes his head. "Just ignore him. The rest of us do." He slides his hand in the small of my back and leads me to the couch.

I squirm away from him and sink into the cool leather. No way in hell I'm ever letting him put his hands on me again. And I don't need him to be my hero. I'm more than capable of taking care of myself. Why is he still here anyway? He should be doing whatever it is he does at the recording studio. I set the papers on top of my briefcase and click open my pen.

I lift my head and stare as a man who could easily be mistaken for a Greek God turns the corner carrying a microphone stand and joins us. Maybe Thor is coming to save me. His chiseled body accentuated by his tight black T-shirt could stop traffic, but those emerald green eyes are the most magnificent I've ever seen.

"Hey, Ali." I jerk back, sending my pen rolling across the floor. "Since I'm doing the introductions, this is my husband Marcus, and the guy you're ogling at is Van."

Van nods toward me. "Hey." He sets the microphone stand near the drum set.

Heat fills my cheeks and my stomach hardens. Wow, the only thing that would make this better is if I spontaneously burst into flames. Can it get any worse?

"Oh, and that's Van's fiancée, Lexie." Jenna's voice drips with sarcasm. She waves at a woman who had just emerged in the doorway.

I gaze at the brunette in the doorway. If I don't get my ass kicked by one of these girls, I'll call it a win. Wow, Lexie's not what I expected. She's cute but not a knockout like Jenna. Maybe there's more to Van than meets the eye.

She walks forward toward the couch, her lips in a thin line.

Either this room isn't as sound proof as I thought or Jenna's voice can break the barrier. Except for the drummer who wants to fuck me, I'm pretty much not wanted by anyone else here, and Lexie probably wants to kill me. Great, no one will even be able to hear my cries for help in here.

I close my eyes and take a deep breath. Come on Ali, get it together; you've got a Master's Degree in Journalism and a B.A. in English, no reason to let a few musicians ruin your first assignment.

I exhale slowly, open my eyes, and sit up straight. "If you're all ready, I'd like to get started now." I rummage through a few sheets of my papers and click open my pen.

"Oh babe, I'm always ready." Chaz blows me a kiss and winks.

Tyler reaches around and slaps him in the back of the head.

Jenna rolls her eyes. "Keep it in your pants, Chaz. It won't kill you to be serious for like, ten minutes."

Chaz shrugs. "Never kept it in my pants for that long."

Jenna grabs a gray pillow from the couch and throws it at him.

Jake probably had an easier time conducting interviews for the dog wedding. It's like I traveled back in time to middle school and I'm dealing with a bunch of horny twelve-year-olds. Arrogant rockers might even be worse. How did this band make it? I mean, I get it they're the-rules-don't-apply-to-me rockers, but a certain amount of professionalism needs to exist. Or at least maturity for that matter.

Chaz plops on the couch next to me and slides his arm around my shoulder. "Go for it! Analyze me, babe. I'm an open book." He raises his eyebrows.

The aroma of pungent deodorant burns through my nostrils. Dear God, get him off me. I reach around and pick up his hand, throwing it off my shoulder and move forward toward the edge of the cushion.

Tyler sighs. "Get away from her before she catches something." He kicks Chaz's boot.

"I love it when you babes play hard to get." He winks and heads back to his drum set.

Tyler sits down next to me. He runs a hand through his hair. "What's your first question?"

Wait a minute. I run my pen along my bottom lip. Oh my God, Tyler's in the band. How did I overlook this? I rummage through a few more papers and pull out my detail sheet. *Devil's Garden, an up and coming metal band, is in Los Angeles recording their new album. Originally from Silent Springs, Kansas, the band was founded by four high school classmates, Van Sinclair, Marcus Crane, Tyler Young, and Chaz Nicols, whose unique heavy music along with powerful vocals catapulted the band into widespread success. Their third album will be launched a few weeks before their international tour begins.*

A wave of nausea flows through my body, spewing a sour tang in my mouth. Great, nothing like having a one-night stand with some rocker who probably screws everyone and anyone. No wonder he didn't call me. Guess he can't keep up with his army of floozies. I should take off running and head for a blood test. No more drinking… ever.

I swallow hard, trying to hold my stomach contents inside my body and turn toward Tyler. "What makes Devil's Garden different than other metal bands?"

"Kick ass drum beats, babe." Chaz pounds out a quick drum solo and tosses a stick in the air, catching it in his teeth.

Marcus throws his hands in the air. "Dude, turn it down a notch. It's not the Chaz show."

Van settles in the leather chair across from us. "Lots of different styles influence our music. It's like a mix of blues, rock, and metal."

Finally, a half way decent answer. How the hell am I going to come up with an article that doesn't belong in a letter to Penthouse? I jot down a few notes and flip to a clean sheet of paper. Lexie slides onto Van's lap and wraps her arms around him. Holy hell, that rock is huge. I squint as her diamond reflects off the dim light, casting a rainbow of colors onto the dark walls.

Maybe I can smooth things over with Lexie. I'm sure she's used to girls gawking at her hot piece of man candy all the time. Oh God, now I'm in that category. First, a one night stand with a band member and then getting caught admiring the sexy singer. I've got to learn to get it together or this business will eat me alive. I turn my gaze toward her and smile. "Your ring is gorgeous. When's the big day."

She lowers her eyebrows and then smiles. "Thanks. We're thinking a beach wedding in June."

Ah, my kind of girl. "Beach weddings are beautiful. Make sure you have a sand ceremony. It's really nice." I pull a business card out from briefcase. "I'll leave you one of these in case you need any wedding advice from one of our event planners or fashion reporters."

She twirls her hair around a finger. "I might just take you up on that." She sits up and leans forward. "I know I'm biased, but another thing that separates Devil's Garden from other metal bands is their interactions with the fans." She looks over at Van and then back at me. "Believe me, it's not all that enjoyable for Jenna and I, but Devil's Garden makes sure they spend at least an hour with their fans backstage."

That's pretty cool, spending time with the fans is important. Wait a minute. My stomach turns. I bet Chaz and Tyler spend more time with the fans than the other guys, they are both single. Images of half-naked women flash through my mind. *God Dammit*, it's like I'm a groupie. Tyler just used me and threw me away. Yeah, great way to treat your fans. A few more questions and I'm out of here.

"What can fans expect from album number three?" I tap my pen on my lip.

"Hard, catchy guitar riffs, some pretty heavy songs, but also something new for Devil's Garden, a few ballads." Marcus strums a sweet melody.

"I die a little each time I'm forced to play them." Chaz taps the snare drum with a stick.

"God bless the poor chick who gets you." Tyler shakes his head.

Whatever. Every second I spend listening to Chaz makes me want to blow out my eardrums. I bet women backstage sit and listen to his degrading words as if they're the meaning of life. "What's the best thing about touring the country?"

Tyler runs a hand through his hair. "Freedom. Never being tied down to a boring life where you do the same thing day in day out. Every day is an adventure."

Ah, maybe I'm too boring for him. Glad I could fulfill his daily adventure. Maybe actually calling me would infringe on his freedom. Jerk.

I bite at my pen cap. "Where's Devil's Garden going in the next few years?"

"Straight to the top, baby." Chaz points at the ceiling. "Hell, yeah!"

Cheers fill the small space. Wow, it's like I'm back at high school at a pep rally.

"How about the girls, I know Lexie's planning a wedding. Any plans for you Jenna, maybe kids in the future."

She flinches and wrinkles her nose. "Um, yeah I don't plan on ruining my body, plus the road is no place for kids."

Van turns his emerald eyes toward mine. "We're going to keep rockin' and meeting new fans."

Tyler leans back against the couch. "Heading to new places and living the dream."

Yeah, I'm sure he lives it up every night. Finally, last question. "If you could go anywhere in the world, where would it be?"

"Easy, Tavarua Island, Fiji." Tyler flashes a sexy half smile.

Wow, that's random. He probably saw some chick in a magazine he wanted to bang. I doubt he has any interest in the culture or seeing the landmarks.

"Brazil, baby. They've got hot chicks down there." Chaz licks his lips.

Jenna rolls her eyes. "Yeah, like they'd want anything to do with you." She flicks her hair over a shoulder. "I can't wait to go to Paris, heard the shopping's great and the tour's headed there next year."

Three years of French in high school plus a year in college and I never even got the chance to use it. Maybe someday I'll get there. I slide my hand down to the end of the paper. "What do you want the world to know about Devil's Garden?"

"We're all about the fans, especially the really hot ones." Chaz winks.

Tyler runs his hands through his hair. "The fans are why we play."

So that translates into 'we play so we can bang hot chicks.' Typical. My lips pinch together. Why do all rockers think they're God's gift to women? Like we should be honored to be with them for one night? Damn Chloe and her need to celebrate everything. My life was perfectly fine until I woke up next to him. I inadvertently glare at Tyler.

He scrunches his eyebrows. "Need any more from us?"

I toss my papers into my briefcase and snap it shut. "Nope, I got enough from you." Much more than I needed.

I stand up and take a few steps toward the doorway.

Tyler grabs my arm. "Wait, I'll walk you out." He glides his fingertips along the curve in my forearm.

I pull my arm away and pat my skirt down. Why does he feel the need to see me out? We spent more than enough time together. I guess it would be rude to refuse. I balance myself with each step I take, paying careful attention to my footing. No need to fall yet again. Once I'm out of here, I'm soaking in a bubble bath with a glass of wine and congratulating myself on my first successful interview, if that's what I should call it.

He reaches for my hand and runs a thumb along my fingers. "It was really great to see you again."

Well, it could've been sooner if he knew how to dial a phone. "Yeah, the article should be in Friday's edition." I flash a quick smile pull my hand away. New mission, get as far away from Tyler as possible.

~

THE DOORBELL ECHOES THROUGH MY APARTMENT LIKE A CHOIR OF angels on Christmas morning. I jump out of bed, slide on my fuzzy slippers, and jog to my front door. Oh my God, it's here. I swing open the door like the Incredible Hulk and step outside. The bright rays of the morning sun shine down, temporarily blinding me. I squint and take a step forward, stubbing my toe on the object on my doorstep. My heart races as I focus on the black letters printed across the cardboard box '*Entertainment Rocks!* magazine'. Eek! I snatch the box and hightail it to my kitchen, slamming the door on the way. Oh my God, my first byline. I slide the metal edge of the scissors along the brown packing tape and rip open the box. A glimpse of the cover peeks through the plethora of crumpled up papers and bubble wrap.

Oh my God, here it is. "Ahh" I pick up a copy of the magazine and jump up and down, hugging the periodical. I fumble through the pages as fast as humanly possible, carefully trying to prevent them from becoming bent.

A rush of adrenaline flows through me like I'm about to lay my hands on the Golden Fleece. I peruse the shiny white paper adorned with black letters 'Devil's Garden: Up Close and Personal as they Rock L.A. by Ali Whitman.'

I set the magazine on the table and cover my mouth with my hands, trying to suppress the few tears forming in my eyes from trickling out. I did it. I'm a published reporter. I grab the magazine again, bounce on my feet, and giggle. The sun shines through my window, illuminating the dark script. I trample through the TV room to my bedroom and launch myself on my bed.

Ah, there it is. I grab my phone from my nightstand and slide my fingers across the screen of my contacts. Time to spread the news. "Guess what came this morning?"

"Hopefully you, if you hooked up with that hottie again from the other night." Chloe chuckles. "Just kidding, he was a jerk anyway. Hmm, let me guess. Oh my God, it came? Your magazine proof?"

I grip the magazine close to my chest. "I'm holding it right now." I roll over on my bed and flip through the pages.

"Yay," she screams. "I'm on my way over. We're celebrating, Mimosas or Bloody Marys?"

I wrinkle my forehead. "How about orange juice and pancakes."

"Oh, darling. We're not in pre-school anymore. Now we party like big girls. See ya soon. Tootles."

My phone beeps. I look at the screen 'Call Ended'. Guess she's already on her way. I glance at the magazine and run my eyes over the words 'by Ali Whitman' for the millionth time. My cheeks upturn into a wide smile. Ah, what the hell. If there's ever been a time to celebrate with a few drinks before noon, this is it. I set the magazine on my nightstand and head to the bathroom to primp myself for my two person party.

THE DOORBELL ECHOES THROUGH THE AIR. CHLOE ARRIVES AT WARP speed in one of the most populated cities in America. Sometimes I think she might be a superhero in disguise. I give my hair one last spray of hairspray and skip to the door. Today's just as exciting for Chloe as it is for me. I mean, she's been by my side every step of the way. I swing open the door and bounce on my toes. Chloe rushes inside holding a bottle of champagne and a bottle of orange juice.

We both squeal like two girls who've just been asked to the prom.

She heads to the kitchen and sets the bottles on the table. "Mimosa's are classier for this occasion. So, where is it?"

Oh my God, it's still on my nightstand. I never thought I'd let it out of my sight. I sprint to the bedroom and slide my fingers over the sleek, shiny, cover. It gleams like a diamond. I hold it against my chest, cover outward and march toward Chloe, turning it from side to side as if it's dancing.

She sets down the glasses she just pulled out of the cupboard and charges toward me.

"It's beautiful." She takes it from my hand and flips through the pages. "Ah, lucky number seventeen." She glances at the article and then back at me. "You're a star." She sets the magazine on the table and pulls me into a tight hug.

"I seriously doubt that." I turn toward the table and look at the article one more time.

She fills the glasses halfway with champagne and halfway with orange juice. "You're definitely on your way." She hands me a glass and lifts hers toward mine. "To many more of these celebrations. Congrats!" We clink glasses and take a sip.

She picks up the magazine. "I'm honored I'm the first to read it." She heads to the TV room and sinks into the couch, setting her glass on the table as she holds the magazine in her lap.

I watch her eyes move from side to side, unable to peel myself away. I wanted to get published so badly I never realized there's a change that people might hate it. What if I suck and everyone thinks I'm a horrible reporter? I nibble at my lip. What's wrong with me? This is much worse than someone reading over your shoulder. I take a sip of my Mimosa and savor the sweet nectar gliding along my tongue. *Please let her like it.*

Her eyebrows scrunch together and then relax, she tilts her head to the side. "Wow, great job. You really told it how it is."

I rub my chin. "Huh?"

She sets the magazine down. "I guess these guys are all about partying and one night stands. Good for you for telling it how it is. That's what good reporters do, right?" She sips her Mimosa.

I grab the magazine and bite my lip. Is that what she got out of my article? I read through the column filled with black text. She's got to be reading between the lines.

I PULL INTO THE PARKING LOT AT *ENTERTAINMENT ROCKS!* magazine and shut down the engine. Ah, my first day of walking into work as a published reporter. I grab my briefcase, step out onto the black asphalt, and pat down my gray skirt. The bright sun warms my skin. Everything is perfect today. The birds are chirping a sweet melody, the soft breeze caresses my face, and I'm on my way to becoming a respected reporter. Hey, my first byline is definitely a start.

I take a step forward and walk right into a wall of pure muscle. Pain skyrockets from my forehead to my shoulder like a bolt of lightning. And I've reverted to the first-day-on-the-job Ali. Didn't take long to regain that title.

"You ok neighbor? Hope you drive better than you walk." Jake chuckles and runs a hand down my back.

Maybe I should start a club for people who can't stop embarrassing themselves. I'd clearly be president. Hate to tell him, but I'm not that great of a driver either. "Sorry, new shoes." It's not like he'd notice my Christian Louboutins from my first day anyway. I glance at my watch. "You leaving already?"

He nods. "Yep, I'm on assignment."

I scrunch my eyebrows. "Late for a dog wedding."

He flashes a half grin. "Interviewing the director of that new comedy, Sliced. It's based on a family whose father is a popular chef. Anyway, they film in the morning, so I got to head up to the studio now." He fumbles with his keys. "Hey, congrats on your article. Brutally honest. Good for you." He waves and hightails it to his car.

Why is everyone saying that? I read it like twenty times, and I don't see anything remotely brutal or controversial. Either everyone else is crazy, or I'm missing something. Whatever. Everyone's got an opinion, and I'm only concerned about Jane's. *Please let her be happy with my work.*

I grip the handle of my briefcase and make the long trek from the parking lot to the building, Ali Whitman, reporting for work. I swing open the heavy door and walk toward the elevator. A few people nod toward me as I make my way across the marble floor and to the elevator. For once I'm actually early and I'm the only one waiting. I press the button and wait for the elevator doors to open. I fidget with my fingers. Oh God, what if Jane hates my article? She is the one who decides my fate.

The bell dings, pulling me from my negative thoughts. There's no need to jump to conclusions, and I can't possibly read Jane's mind. I can only hope for the best. I walk inside the elevator and lean against the back wall. Within seconds all the blood in my body rushes to my head. Oh my God, it can't be him. I stare out from the open elevator doors at the man walking toward me, gripping a copy of the magazine, his knuckles white and his eyes cold. I push back against the elevator wall, but I'm trapped, nowhere to run. My heart thrashes in my ears. *Please let the doors close.* The doors start to close at the speed a tortoise runs. I let out the breath I didn't realize I was holding. Thank God.

He holds out his hand, placing it in between the elevator door a second before they're about to close. The sensor notices the movement and the doors open again. I gasp as Tyler steps inside the elevator, staring at me with hellfire in his eyes.

4

REPERCUSSIONS

SIX FEET OF PURE MUSCLE BLOCKS ME FROM ANY CHANCE OF escape. Okay, he clearly isn't thrilled with the article. I'm a reporter, and it's my job to tell it how it is, right? I stand up straight against the cool wall, gripping my briefcase for dear life. Ugh, from the look on Tyler's face I doubt he'd agree with my logic. *God, please let get me out of here unscathed.* Beads of sweat form on my forehead and my body begins to shake. Why is he here? I mean, he knows where I live. Is he trying to make a scene?

The elevator doors close, and we begin our ascent. My stomach flip-flops worse than the time I almost hurled on the Tower of Terror at Disney World. Tyler turns around and presses the stop button. What's he doing? Jesus, it can't be legal to stop an elevator without a legitimate reason. I've got to try and hit the call button. I mean, I hardly know him. What if he has a violent temper? If I was watching this unfold on television, I'd be screaming at the girl for being so stupid. Yet, here I am in another bad situation. I either have terrible luck or need to make some major life changes. He turns toward me and steps forward. Tears fill my eyes as I stare at the vein bulging from his forehead. There's nowhere to run.

He shakes the magazine in front of my face. "What the hell is this?"

Okay Ali, think. No need to piss him off any more than he already is. "You don't like it?" Why did that line sound so much better in my head? Great. Now he probably thinks I'm being condescending.

He holds the magazine up and flips through the pages, crinkling and ripping the edges as he frantically makes his way to page seventeen. "Devil's Garden is all about sex and rock and roll. They love this city because the chicks come to them and love spending time with their fans, especially backstage. Even those of the group who are married or engaged can't get enough of their backstage fans." He throws the magazine on the elevator floor. "What's your problem? Are you trying to use us to make a name for yourself or do you like ruining people's lives?"

Oh God, the words coming out of his mouth burn through me like a firestorm. That's pretty much what I got out of the interview and from my firsthand experience with Tyler; my take on Devil's Garden seems pretty accurate. "I just report what I see and hear." The briefcase falls from my clammy hand.

He runs a hand through his hair and shakes his head. "Guess you need a hearing aid because you got it all wrong, babe. You twisted around everything we said and made us sound like all we do is party and bang girls."

Uh, yeah. Isn't that what goes on? He's no innocent struggling musician. I'm sure I'm not one of his most memorable endeavors, but he should at least remember partying with me and then waking up in my bed. Yep, partying and banging girls. That's pretty much ripped right from Chaz's mouth.

I fold my arms across my chest. "The line stating 'I love this city, the chicks come to us' was a direct quote from your drummer. Don't blame me for using the answers from your bandmates."

He steps closer. His jaw clenched so tight it trembles.

Oh no, I better watch what I'm saying. What the hell am I doing? I've spent one night with Tyler and know nothing about him. He could go crazy and beat the crap out of me. No need to press my luck.

He steps forward so close that his breath blows around a few stray strands of my hair. "I'm going to ask you one more time, what the hell is this about?"

I close my eyes tight and breathe heavy. A stray tear slides down my cheek. *Dear God, please let me get out of here in one piece.* I've got to use my creativity to calm Tyler down. At least enough to have a mature conversation. "Just trying to make you guys sound cool." At least that's an answer he might like better than telling him the truth, that I think they're all a bunch of partying womanizers.

He steps back and slides his hand down the elevator wall alongside my body. "Really? That's what you think is cool?"

I shrug.

"Then you're in the wrong business, babe." He leans against the elevator wall next to me and turns his head toward mine. "This stuff," he kicks the magazine across the elevator floor, "ruins careers."

I bite my lip. "Sorry." Maybe my emotions did get the best of me. I've read that article like a million times before I submitted it and a million more after it was published. I never realized how harsh it sounds until those quotes came out of his lips. I bet Jane is going to rip me a new one when I get upstairs.

He turns my chin toward him. "Is this about me?"

My heart skyrockets into overdrive. No fair, how can he do this to me, especially now? He probably thinks I went all PMS on him like a scorned high school girl. That I made him and his band look like man whores because I'm pissed off from what went down with us. Everything I wrote was taken out of the context of what was said in the interview. He was sitting right there.

I tilt my head. "What are you talking about?"

He raises an eyebrow. "Guess I'm still trying to figure out why you hate me so much." He picks up the magazine from the floor. "You're the one who gave me the wrong phone number."

He clearly has me confused with one of his other conquests. I don't make up phone numbers. If I didn't want him to have it, I wouldn't have given it to him.

I touch the base of my neck. "Hate to break it to you, but I think you've got me confused with someone else."

He slides his wallet out from a back pocket. "Ah, cause of all the partying and banging chicks that you mentioned." He pulls a piece of paper out with my writing on it and hands it to me.

I squint, holding the paper up to the dim elevator light. Crap, he's right. Why the hell did I write a two instead of a seven? Amazing what waking up with a strange man in my bed can do to my brain. A tingle sweeps up my back and across my cheeks. All this time he thought I was the one blowing him off? It's like a verse ripped from Murphy's law.

Heat flushes across my face like wildfire. "I promise that was not intentional."

He smirks. "Yeah, right."

I'm such an idiot. All this time I'm holding a ridiculous grudge over something that's my fault, and I unconsciously let my emotions get in the way of my debut article. I deserve what I get from Jane and Tyler.

He blows air out of his puffed up cheeks. "Maybe you should write an article about chicks who use guys and give them fake numbers." He smirks.

I nibble at my nails. "Seriously, not intentional." Like he didn't admit in the interview that he and the other guys have one night stands with groupies all the time. Why should I be any different? "I figured you only wanted to hang out for one night and that's why you didn't call."

"Not even close."

I try and hold back a smile. *Dammit*, I've got to get over this silly infatuation with Tyler. Maybe it was easier to hate him than admit I have feelings for him. He's an exact replica of everything I need to stay away from, but I can't seem to shake him from my mind. It really doesn't matter. It's never going anywhere, especially now.

He presses the run button, and the elevator begins its ascent. "Not everything is always what is seems." He turns back toward me and waves the magazine. "Hope you can do something about this, or at least apologize to everyone."

I'd rather run a whole new article than face the wrath of Jenna. Psychotic clowns were the scariest image I could concoct in my mind until I met her. I nod.

What am I thinking? Even if Jane hates this article, she's never going to let me write another one on Devil's Garden. If I recorded the interview, then Tyler couldn't accuse me of embellishing. I mean, he was sitting right there, and ninety percent of the interview was about Devil's Garden's need for girls and parties. Right? Note to self, always record interviews in the future.

Maybe the band is blaming him because of what went down with us, and he just needs something done to keep the peace. Apparently, it's easier to blame someone else than take a good, hard look at yourself. Even if I did let my emotions spew into the article, it's not like the band exhibits the most professional behavior. Don't they realize they were hanging all over each other while Chaz bragged about his conquests? Amazing they didn't offer me a shot of whiskey as I walked in the door.

I glance up at the numbers lit above the elevator door, floor two, almost there. Hope his plan was to demand answers from me. I may as well just pack up my desk and head back to the mail room if he plans on taking his concerns up with Jane. It's probably just what she'll want to hear, my debut article sparking all this drama. *Please let this disaster of a day fly by, I've had enough aggravation for the whole week.*

Waves of vibrations spread across the elevator floor. Weird. That's never happened before. I bet I'm off balance from getting myself all worked up. It's probably another Tower of Terror flashback. I take a deep breath and nibble on my lip. I swear it's the longest elevator ride in the history of the world. Why is every second lasting an hour? Ear-piercing screeches emanate through the small space. I hold on to the railing, but it's no use. The elevator sways, and flashes of light blink repeatedly. It's like I'm standing on a bus that just took off at fifty miles an hour. What's happening? Oh God, I'm about to plummet to my death in an elevator shaft with a hot one night stand who's pissed at me because of my article. I can see the headlines now, 'Scorned reporter groupie meets her demise with disparaged bass player.'

I fall forward and smack right into Tyler, who's acting like nothing is even happening. Maybe he's used to these kinds of special effects on his stage show. Hate to break it to him, but this is real life, and we're probably about to die. I might as well make my last seconds on earth memorable. I press myself against him, gripping his shirt for dear life. I don't care what happened between us. Right now, I need him more than anything.

He wraps his arms around me, holding me close. He gets it. At this moment nothing matters but the fact that we're together. Horrible tragedies seem a little better if you're not alone. I've got to do something… anything to get my mind off what's about to go down. I bury my head in his chest and focus on his heartbeat, strong and steady. It's like the world suddenly disappeared and the two of us exist in this safe haven. Everything is silent, like the moment before a nuclear bomb hits. I take a deep breath and let the aroma of his musky cologne flow through my body.

I close my eyes tight and try to balance myself on my heels. *Please God, let us get out of here in one piece or at least guide us to the afterlife.* I rest my body weight against Tyler's rock hard chest. He stands tall and strong, like his feet are rooted to the floor.

In an instant, everything stops. Is it over? Are we dead? I

loosen the death grip on Tyler's shirt but keep my head buried in his chest.

He rubs his fingertips along my back. "You okay?"

I take a step back. That seems like a loaded question. Nothing about this or my life in general at this point is okay. "Yeah." The silver walls are illuminated by dim blue lights. In a strange way, it's kind of beautiful. "What the hell happened?"

He lifts my chin. "You haven't been in L.A. too long have you?"

I gaze into his clear blue eyes like a lost puppy. What is it about him? It's like everything I fear disappears when he's with me. Kind of like he's an angel. Now that image is beyond ridiculous. Even so, never in a million years did I expect to find someone who can do that... definitely not twice. "About a year."

"Looks like you're no longer a virgin. You just made it through your first earthquake."

Oh my God, that was an earthquake. I never thought I'd actually experience one. Sure, the likelihood of an earthquake occurring while I'm living in L.A. is extremely high, but I never thought it would happen to me. Clearly, an immature way to deal with the possibility of being involved in a disaster. I run my hands over my face and tuck a few stray hairs behind my ears. Okay, it's over, I'm alive. Been there, done that, bought the T-shirt. Time to get the hell out of here. I press the button for floor three, but the buttons for every floor are flashing. I press it again. No change.

I turn toward Tyler. "It's not working."

He steps forward, extending his arm. His sculpted bicep brushes against me. "Looks like we're stuck in here."

I lean against the elevator wall. "Oh my God, we're trapped." My heart races and my eyes fill with tears. "We're going to die in here." What's worse, a quick and easy demise or one that lasts forever? Starving to death surrounded by thick metal walls is pure torture.

"Relax." Tyler runs a hand through his hair. "Elevators have cameras. Learned that the hard way." He flashes a sexy half grin.

I stare at the silver walls that seem to be closing in on us. I get it, he's trying to cheer me up, but the best comedian in the world can't shed any light on this situation. I take a few deep breaths, but there's no air. "We're going to suffocate in here by the time they find us."

I slide down the elevator wall to the floor and suck in as many breaths as I can. Oh God, I'm probably using too much oxygen. I cover my face with my trembling hands. *Please find us and get us out of here soon.*

My hands and feet tingle like they're about to fall asleep. I suck in a few more shallow breaths and close my eyes tight. My heart thumps against the walls of my chest like a sledgehammer. I blink repeatedly, and look around my silver tomb. This is it, I must be having a heart attack. It's like I'm dying a million different ways in a matter of seconds.

Tyler kneels in front of me and holds my head with his hands. "You're fine, just relax." He pushes my head down toward my knees.

I take a few more deep breaths and wipe the tears streaming down my face.

"There're vents in here. We're not going to suffocate." He tips my chin up toward the ceiling. "And look, you can see light through the slit in the doorway so we're somewhere near a floor."

I sit back and sweep my hands across my face. Guess I'm not dying, yet. Maybe only of embarrassment. Wait, isn't he pissed at me? Maybe facing a dark fate changed his whole outlook. I must be pretty pathetic if he's pitying me.

He slides over and sits against the wall next to me. "You think this is bad, try waiting out a tornado." He raises an eyebrow. "Now that's some scary shit. Feels like a freight train just ran through your house."

No thanks, those fifteen seconds seemed like it took hours. I had more than enough thrill seeking for the rest of my life plus I've already seen *The Wizard of Oz* and although Emerald City looks awesome, I'm content here. Well, I was until now.

I cup my hands together, making a circle and breathe into my makeshift version of a paper bag, trying to reduce my heart rate to an acceptable level. I close my eyes and pretend I'm on a sandy beach with the warm breeze blowing in my hair while I dig my feet into the gritty sand, gazing upon the open space filled with pink sunsets and soft waves. My brain seems to think I'm in a happy place. The trembling in my hands subsides, and my breathing rate slows. I take one last deep breath and lower my hands.

Tyler places a hand on my thigh. "We'll be out of here soon. Worst case a few hours."

My heart starts racing again. Is it from his touch or the realization I'm not getting out of this anytime soon? Great. What are we supposed to do in here for the next few hours? Thank God Chaz isn't in here with me answering that question.

Tyler brushes my skin as he pulls his hand away. He takes his cell phone out of a pocket and slides a finger across the screen. "What made me think we'd have reception?" He leans his head against the wall of the elevator. "Looks like I'm missing a recording session."

I turn my head toward him. "You've got a pretty good excuse."

"Yeah, the guys are going to freak when they hear I'm stuck in here with you."

My muscles quiver. Yeah, and I'm pretty much Satan to Devil's Garden. How ironic. "Yep, same here."

He flashes a sexy half grin. "Musicians and the press, natural enemies like cats and dogs."

I squint my eyebrows. "Never heard that one before."

"Sad but true." He nods.

Doomed before we even start. Well, if anything would've started. How did one night of celebrating spin off this disaster?

Maybe my next article should be about the dangers of drinking too much, car accidents and health issues aren't the only consequences. Jenna probably has wanted posters with my picture hung all over town by now.

"Let's play devil's advocate. If you were the press, what would you write about Devil's Garden differently?"

He tips his chin. "Seriously?"

I nod. "Looks like we've got some time to kill and since I'm the enemy, I want to know how the other half thinks." I bite my lip, trying to hold back a smile.

He flashes a quick grin. "You're on." He runs a hand through his hair. "Ok... Devil's Garden is a metal band on the verge of stardom with kick ass riffs, edgy songs, and amazingly handsome members destined to become Rock Gods."

I giggle. "Sorry, keep going."

He nibbles on his lip. "Their focus on making awesome music and catering to their fans make them the best band that ever lived."

I start laughing and cover my mouth with my hand. I run my hand down my chin and stifle a smile. "Continue."

He lowers an eyebrow. "Regardless of how big they become they're all about the music and the fans."

I nod. "Nice. Maybe I should take some notes from you." I catch my lip in between my teeth. "Is it possible to be both a musician and its mortal enemy? I think you got the whole press thing down."

He squints. "Huh, a hybrid... we may have to stay in here forever. I can't let this secret get out." He nudges my arm.

I hold up my hands. "Whoa, I'll take a vow of silence before I stay in here forever." I pat down the few wrinkles that formed in the top of my skirt. "Even if there's a zombie apocalypse out there, I'll take my chances."

He turns my chin toward him and locks his eyes with mine.

"So being stuck in here with me is worse than being mauled to death by zombies?"

A wave of tingles flows through my body. There's no one else I'd rather be stuck with, but that's not something I'm willing to share with him... not yet and maybe not ever. I gaze into the clear blue abyss that penetrates my soul. "Wanna be my zombie apocalypse buddy?"

He rubs his chin and scans my body. "Hmm, you can do some damage with those heels."

I shake my head as a smile creeps across my face. "They're definitely deadly." I nudge his shoulder with mine. "Who knows, I might even save your life."

He rests his head against the elevator wall and turns toward me. "Maybe you're not an evil-demon-succubus like Jenna thinks."

Wow, I guess I should take that as a compliment. "Uh, thanks... I think."

I lean back against the elevator wall, letting my muscles relax. Maybe this isn't the worst possible thing that could happen to me today. I close my eyes and take a deep breath, expelling all the negative energy from my body.

A vibration shoots from the elevator walls straight to my core. My heart pounds, about to beat out of my chest. The screech of twisting metal emanates through the air. The elevator sways, and the lights flash. High-pitched sirens ring in the distance, barely recognizable. No, please. Not again.

5

TRAPPED

THERE'S NO AIR LEFT IN HERE, I'M SUFFOCATING. THE JOLT probably blocked the vents. I jump in Tyler's lap and bury my head against his chest, digging my fingers into his rock hard biceps. Oh God, in an instant the elevator cable could snap, sending us plummeting to our death. How can Tyler sit there so calm? It's like I'm the only person who knows life can change in an instant. The tips of my fingers and my toes become numb again. This is it, our short time together is over. I suck in shallow breaths and close my eyes tight. *Please God, save us.*

Tyler wraps his arms around me. "Just an aftershock."

Another aftershock and this elevator can slam into the ground, crushed like a tin can. I take a deep breath and try to compose myself. No such luck. Thoughts of the unrecognizable aftermath and twisted metal flood my brain. I cover my face with my hands as a river of tears flow down. Loud sobs fill the air.

I wipe my hands across my face, clearing the tears. "I've got to get out of here." My hands tremble.

"Never heard that from a girl sitting in my lap." He winks and runs his hands down my sides, settling them on my hips.

I focus on the vibrant tiger on his forearm. It triggers a memory, back to breakfast at the diner. Amazing, I'm in one of the worst situations in my life, and my brain brings me back to a better time. Probably self-defense.

I've got to get it together. First rule in any disaster situation is to the stay calm. I seemed to completely bypass that one so let's move on to rule number two: Assess the situation. Tyler's hand grazes my skin when I move to the side. Okay, maybe being stuck in an elevator with a hot Rock God isn't a total disaster. I lean back and sit next to him.

He places a hand on my thigh, rubbing his thumb in small circles. "Sirens sounded off a few minutes ago. We'll be out of here soon."

My pulse skyrockets. I may have a heart attack before they get here if he keeps this up. "Guess this isn't the best way to find out you're claustrophobic."

He raises an eyebrow. "I can think of a few better ways."

Being trapped in a small space with Tyler is better therapy than any psychologist can provide. Oh my God, it's like I'm turning into one of his groupies. The oxygen levels must be dangerously low in here causing my brain to lose all reasoning skills. I've got to change the subject quickly. "Cool ink. Where else are they on your body? ...I mean, do you have any more tattoos?" I do a quick once over... *Dammit.*

He flashes a half smile. "Yeah, lots." He darts his tongue over his lips. "I'll have to show you sometime."

Oh my God, I'm most definitely the worst conversationalist ever. Especially when I'm trying to divert my attention away from anything sexual. "No ink on me, yet. Maybe if I make it through this unscathed."

He looks me up and down. "I can hook you up."

Yeah, I bet he can, probably in more ways than one. Okay, time for a new subject. I fidget with my fingers. "What's your favorite thing to do when you're in L.A.?" Wow, if his answer to that is a girl's name I'm scaling the walls of the elevator and taking my chances climbing the shaft.

He tips his head. "Guess."

Oh great. This should go well, especially since my brain function is clearly at its best. Hmm, he doesn't seem much like a shopper. I follow his chiseled arms down to his chest, concentrating on the outlines of the peaks and valleys through his thin, dark-green, T-shirt. Butterflies flutter in my stomach. Oh God, I've got to get a hold of myself. Maybe this lack of oxygen in here is making me go into heat.

"Porn star?" What? I cover my mouth with my hand. Where the hell is the filter between my brain and my mouth? My body freezes and a bead of sweat forms along my hairline.

He crinkles his forehead. "Close… I like the way you think."

Tightness forms in my chest. "Listen, I have no idea what I'm saying. I must be in shock from the trauma."

"Whatever, babe." He winks and nudges my arm. "I'm all about the waves."

I scrunch my eyebrows. "Really? Surfing?"

He nods and runs a hand through his hair. "First time we came down here to record I couldn't get enough of Malibu." He moves his shark tooth pendant along the leather strand of his necklace. "I met a few locals who gave me some lessons. Once I caught my first wave, I was hooked. Whenever we have some down time, I meet up with my surfer crew and hit the waves. Nothing else in the world comes close to it."

I've never heard of a Kansas boy turned rocker turned surfer. Maybe there's more to Tyler than meets the eye. "I'm a beach girl at heart, but I've never surfed." I tuck a few stray hairs behind my ear. "I'd probably get eaten by a shark or something."

He leans in closer. "Not if you're with me."

My heart beats faster and electricity flows through my veins. "You slay sharks in your free time too?"

"Only for the right girl." He winks.

I roll my eyes. "You probably say that to all your... um, female fans."

He rubs his chin. "So, you're my fan?"

I nibble on my lip. "Biggest fan in the room."

He looks around at the empty elevator. "Nice, I'll take it." He leans his head on the back wall and turns toward me, flashing those baby blues that could pierce an armored tank. "How about you? How'd you get here?"

"Like the Indians. I headed west following a trail of tears." Why am I telling him all this? This whole near death experience has driven me temporarily insane! I close my eyes and swallow hard, pushing the memories I willed my mind to forget down to the depths of my soul.

"Trail of tears, huh. Sounds like a cool song title." He nods toward me.

Nothing cool about having your heart ripped out and torn to pieces when you're not even old enough to vote. I rub my hands across my face and through my hair. I never even told Chloe everything about Josh and me, no need to share the tragic tale with Tyler.

I plaster on a fake grin and shrug. "I didn't get into Duke, so I went for my second choice, Stanford." More like I ripped up my acceptance letter from Duke and high-tailed it cross-country, leaving everything behind me.

"Whoa, Stanford. Nice."

I nod and fidget with my fingers. "I moved down here right after graduation with my college roommate, Chloe."

"Oh yeah, from the club. She seemed cool."

I turn my head toward him. "She's into the fashion scene. Wants to be the next editor of *Vogue* so we're kind of complete opposites."

"So you're trying to be the CEO of *Rolling Stone*?" He runs a finger along his chin. "You so have to put us on the cover if that ever happens."

"I'm hoping for the cover of *Time*."

"That works too." He winks.

I shift my weight and lean toward Tyler. "So how about you? How'd you get here?"

"In a beat-up Ford pickup." He laughs.

"Sounds like a country song."

He flashes a sexy half grin. "It's kinda like I won the lotto. Made a demo tape right out of high school and got a contract within a month." He runs a hand through his hair. "Me, the guys, and Jenna drove down to L.A. from Kansas to record, and I've been living the dream ever since."

"That must've been one hell of a trip for Jenna."

"Naw, she was a newlywed so not even half as bitchy as she is now."

I stifle a laugh. Yeah, I beg to differ. "You ever miss home?"

He lowers an eyebrow. "Are you kidding me? Being stuck there is like hell on earth. Nothing changes, it's like living the same day over and over again. Yeah, no thanks." He tilts his chin. "How about you? Where are you from, anyway?"

I'd rather travel to Mars and live on a crater with ET than go back to Seamist, Maine. "Small town in Maine. Same story as Kansas... minus the pickup truck."

"Guess we're both kindred souls." He tucks a piece of hair behind my ear.

"Something like that." Kindred souls, huh. Not even close. He escaped to find adventure. I ran.

I bite at my lip. "What if the whole rocker thing didn't work out? What else would you want to do?"

"You mean besides shark slayer and zombie apocalypse partner?"

I chuckle.

He glances around the small space and narrows his eyes. "Probably move down here and work in a recording studio, or hit the road with another band and work with the equipment or something." He shrugs.

If everything went according to plan and Josh and I went to Duke and moved back to Maine afterward, I'd probably be married and working for the local newspaper, or maybe even a local news anchor. Doesn't matter now anyway. Besides, I'm in L.A., the land of opportunity for reporters. Who knows? Maybe I will get an article published in *Time Magazine* someday.

"If you're so good with equipment, what are the chances you can get this elevator working?"

He looks up at the dim lights and barely visible numbers along the top of the doors. "Uh, like zero percent. Sorry, even my kick ass skills can't rival an earthquake."

Of course not, he can't compete with the wrath of Mother Nature. Too bad, I really could use something to drink and maybe a comfy pair of sweats. I slide my toes back and kick off my heels. Wait, my lunch is in my briefcase. The chef salad I made is probably wilted but the bottle of water never goes bad. I crawl along the elevator floor and retrieve it. Tyler's eyes lock onto me, following my every move. If he was in here with anyone else, he'd think they're trying to get some action. After everything that happened between us so far, I think he knows better. Although, it's kind of nice to know he can't take his eyes off me. I pull the leather case toward us and pop open the lock. Yes, success.

I grab the bottle of water and twist off the cap so fast a few droplets spill over the side. It's like I've been trapped in a desert for days. I take a sip and let the lukewarm liquid moisten my cotton-dry mouth. "Want some?" I hold the bottle out toward Tyler.

He reaches forward, brushing his fingertips along mine. "We better save some of this, just in case." He takes a quick gulp.

If he keeps touching me, I may have to pour it over my head to stop any flames from bursting through my body. I take one last

57

sip and twist on the lid. "I don't want to get you too excited, but I've got a chocolate bar in there too."

"Stuck in here with you and a chocolate bar." He winks. "I've only got so much willpower, no promises."

Heat flashes through me. Apparently, willpower is non-existent in the confines of this elevator, or anywhere around Tyler for that matter. The way he can make every inch of my body come alive is nothing short of pure magic. Especially after everything that went down.

I relax my muscles and lean against the elevator wall just as the floor begins to vibrate. Not this again. I close my eyes tight and lean into Tyler. For the first time in ages, I feel safe. Mother Nature can bring it, as long as Tyler's with me, I'll survive. None of this makes any sense. How can it be possible to feel this way when I haven't even known him for a total of twenty-four hours? I run my hand over the hard curves of his chest and wrap my arm around him. If I could stay here like this, bring on the aftershocks.

The elevator sways slowly, like a leaf blowing in a gentle breeze. Everything is calming, everything except every cell in my body which is quickly coming alive. I squeeze Tyler tighter and press myself against him. He whisks a few stray hairs from my face and pushes the flaxen strands over my shoulder, grazing my cheek with his thumb along the way.

I lift my chin and lock my eyes with his. Maybe everything happens for a reason, and I'm meant to be in here with Tyler. He glides his nose along mine as we move in slow motion. It's different this time, and I want to savor every second. I grip his T-shirt tight in my fingers and reach up, brushing my lips against his.

A low-pitched grinding resonates through the air. I gasp and jump back. The lights flash and the elevator jerks. The power's coming back on. Could the timing be any worse? I release my death grip on Tyler's T-shirt and slide to the side.

He lets out a deep breath and runs a hand through his hair. "Looks like we're back to reality."

It wouldn't have killed me, being stuck in the fantasy world for a second or two more. I raise my eyebrows. "Chocolate bar celebration?"

He shrugs. "If that's the only option."

Heat flows through my veins, pure volcanic lava. It's like my body is regenerating itself from its cocoon of safety. Am I ready to be the butterfly? "It's the best one I've got to offer right now."

He licks his lips. "I'll take what I can get."

The elevator bangs and clanks, sending vibrations echoing through the tense air. It's like divine intervention is stepping in. I stand up and press the button for floor three. It lights up, but nothing happens. I press a few more buttons, all lights but no action. Maybe we do have more time together. Tyler stands next to me and glides his fingertip along mine to reach the button. He presses, still nothing.

He steps back and looks around at the silver walls. "I bet the elevator is off track."

"What does that mean?" Is there still a chance we can plummet to our deaths? If there is I need to make up for some serious lost time.

He tucks a few stray hairs behind my ear and bends down, whispering softly. "We're stuck here for a little while longer." His soft lips graze my lobe.

My heart flutters frantically, as if it's going to burst out of my chest and fly around the small space. No reason to waste any more time, it's precious. I run my nose along his cheek, turning toward his lips.

The elevator jerks, sending me flying backward. I hit the back of my head against the wall, and Tyler's solid wall of muscle falls forward, trapping me. Pain radiates through my skull and along my lower back. Great, romance at its finest.

Tyler steps back. "You okay?"

I nod. "Another aftershock?" Jeez, how many aftershocks come from one earthquake?

He moves to the front of the elevator and presses his ear against the door. "No, I think we'll be breaking into that chocolate bar soon."

He tries to peek through the slit in the doors.

The elevator sways again. I brace my hands against the back wall and prevent myself from banging anything else. For once, I actually keep my balance. Tyler stumbles backward.

"See anything?" I bob my head from side to side trying to get a glimpse of the faint light shining through the slit.

"The light is breaking, someone's standing near the door." Tyler bangs his fists against the door of the elevator as if he's King Kong having a temper tantrum.

Jeez, it's like he can't get away from me fast enough. Did I misread everything? I wave my arms in front of the panel where the buttons are located as if I'm about to land a plane. The elevator camera has to catch at least a glimpse of me.

Loud knocks coming from the other side of the doors pull me from my exotic dance. I pat down my skirt and step forward next to Tyler.

He cups his hands around his mouth, making a homemade megaphone. "Hey, we're trapped in here."

Faint muffled voices flow through the air like a whisper and flashes of light and darkness move along the slit in the elevator. Tyler digs his fingers into the metal slit, trying to pry it open. His muscles dance like they're the stars of a choreographed ballet. The colorful tiger almost jumps off his skin. I stare, mesmerized as every muscle in his body expands and contracts. *Dear God, did it just get twenty degrees hotter in here?*

The doors move open, just enough to catch small glimpses of movement. Tyler moves his lips toward the opening. "Hey, anybody there?"

"We're working on getting you two out." A voice calls.

I guess the cameras are working. Good thing the rescuers didn't arrive a half hour later. God knows what footage would be on those tapes. Well, it looks like we'll be out of here soon. I suck in a deep breath and slowly exhale, letting all the built-up tension slowly flow from my body. Seems like I've been in here for a lifetime, but I'm finally saved. Or am I destined for another trap?

6
ESCAPE

"The doors won't budge, safety feature. We need a quarter inch more to use the crowbar," a voice says from above.

How can preventing you from escaping be a safety feature? I've got to look into this elevator company. My next topic "Unsafe Safety Features," that is if I make it out of here.

Tyler paces around the small space like he's about to have an epiphany. I hate to break it to him, but no divine intervention exists in here. Well, I guess that's not entirely true. We're stuck here together for a reason. I doubt it's the universe desperately trying to tell us we're meant for each other. Life is only that romantic in novels and John Hughes movies. On the plus, I learned a few valuable lessons, never let your emotions flow into places they shouldn't, always double check when giving out your phone number to a hot guy after a one night stand, and never underestimate the power of a near death experience.

"Perfect." He kneels and runs his hands down my calf to my ankle.

His calloused fingertips create a sensation that makes me forget about the whole earthquake ordeal. Nothing exists in this instant but the two of us. Okay, not the best timing.

He continues down and pulls off my shoe. "This works." He faces the doors and slams the red heel into the opening like it's a hatchet.

I gasp. The words "noooo" echo in my head even though I can't open my mouth. A tear flows down my cheek. The symbol of my new life as a reporter, as a California girl, as a woman rising from the ashes just died in an elevator with a one-night stand.

"What?" Tyler turns toward me. "We're almost out of here, babe. Thought you'd be happy."

I force a smile even though it feels as though my soul just left my body. I get it. It's a shoe. No harm done. That shoe was my "Hollywood" sign, now it's just another broken piece of me. There's no way in hell I can explain this to him, and he'd never understand anyway.

Tyler wedges the heel back and forth, digging the dagger deeper inside me. "Got it."

A thick crowbar slides in between the doors and like magic, they open. Tyler swings around sporting a grin, but all I can do is grimace.

He shakes his head. "Girls and their shoes."

Yeah, I bet if I had to smash his bass through a window to escape he'd feel the same way. It doesn't matter; we're almost out of here and probably won't see each other again. The story of my life, it's like a fractured fairytale; the only two men on earth who can make me feel alive both destroyed something inside me.

"You guys ready?" A man in a hard hat looks down upon us.

Great, we're stuck in between floors. More complications.

Tyler hands me my tattered shoe. "Ladies first."

I take off my other one and stuff them into my briefcase. Okay, time to put my climbing skills to use. I hand Tyler my briefcase, and he flings it through the doors onto the office floor. I'm frozen, unable to move. I can't wait to get out of here but don't want to leave. It's like I want to savor every last second I have with Tyler even though I know my time has run out.

"Don't be scared. I've got you." Tyler moves me forward by my hips.

Yep, exactly what I'm scared of.

"Grab my hand, Miss." The man in a hard hat reaches toward me.

I grip his hand and attempt to pull myself up, but all I can think about is Tyler's hands on me. Memories of his fingers caressing every inch of skin flood my brain. Clearly, the worst timing ever. I take a deep breath and compose myself. Tyler slides his hands down right under my butt, lifting me. The rescue effort feels more like torture than saving.

Within a few seconds, I'm hoisted onto the office floor like a tuna being pulled up onto a fishing boat. Tyler scales the elevator walls like Spiderman.

He brushes his hands against his jeans. "Just another day at the office." He winks.

I let out a slight chuckle. "Yep, back to work."

The man in the hard hat gestures toward the front door. "I can arrange for medical care if necessary. The building's been evacuated, ma'am. No one is allowed on the premises."

I nod. "Don't worry. We're leaving." Emergency lights illuminate the dark gray walls. Last time I was in a place that looked like this was senior year of high school when we drove to the state line on Halloween to visit the haunted penitentiary. If I could refrain from running out of here screaming like I did then I'll call it a win, no promises though.

"Come on, babe. I'll walk you to your car." Tyler places his hand in the small of my back and guides me forward.

It's funny. If any other guy in the world referred to me as "babe" I'd tell him off in a second and remind him that it's not 1960 and women aren't property. But for some reason when Tyler says it I melt. Why are things so different with him?

I stop in front of my car. "Listen, I'm sorry about the article. I think you're extremely talented and I should've written more about the music and less about what happened during the interview." I fidget with my fingers and look into his clear blue eyes. "And thank you for everything today. No one else I'd rather be stuck with than you." Okay, that didn't come out quite how I planned, but I'm starting to realize it's true.

"That's it?"

I shrug. What else is he expecting? I apologized and thanked him. I'm not going to bow down and worship him. Technically I did nothing wrong. I just want to be on decent terms with him. Who knows if we'll ever cross paths again? "What do you mean, do I owe you dinner or something?" Oh God, I just asked him out. Real smooth, Ali.

He wedges me in between his body and the car door. "You owe me and everyone else a lot more than that."

The aroma of his musky cologne spins another memory of our short night together. A glimpse of Tyler nudging me onto his chest right before we fell asleep floods my mind. Within seconds I'm completely absorbed by his essence.

"You've got to apologize and make this right." Tyler reaches for the door handle, clicking it open.

Just like that, I'm back to reality. I exhale the breath I didn't realize I'd been holding. What is he talking about? Apologizing is one thing, but there's no way the magazine is going to run the story again. It's published and probably already yesterday's news. "Okay." That's all I can muster.

He backs up and opens the door for me. "When?"

Is he for real? I mean, being trapped in an elevator after an earthquake almost causes us to plummet to our death is enough drama for one day. Plus, I think dealing with Jenna is much worse a fate. I'd rather the elevator.

"I think I've had enough excitement for today." I scoot around him and plop down on my seat.

He leans forward, searching my face for an answer.

I guess he's not letting me go until he gets one. "Tomorrow... around 4?" I tap my fingers on the steering wheel. "How 'bout we meet at a public place, you know... lessen the drama?" I nibble my lip. "Olivia's Pasta House?"

"That works." He closes the door and steps back. "See you tomorrow, babe."

IN FIVE SHORT MINUTES, I'LL EAT MY LAST MEAL IN THE BEST KEPT secret in the city if we don't get kicked out before the food arrives. There's no way everyone's going to keep calm and talk politely. Nope, not their style. Knowing I'll never get to indulge the most exquisite eggplant parmesan in existence doesn't make things any better. Like when you give someone a quick peck not knowing it's the last time your lips would ever touch theirs. I tell myself "If I'd only known what was about to happen I would've done things differently." Not true. Expecting the inevitable only causes you to focus on the fact that you're losing something you love. Guess it sucks either way.

I fling my purse over my shoulder and close the car door. Well Olivia's Pasta House, you're the only place in all of L.A. that makes me feel like I'm back at Grandma's eating Sunday dinner. Maybe it's better this way, reminders of home make everything harder.

I spot Tyler's red convertible. Well, so much for being the first one here. I guess I'm walking into a massacre. On the plus, it's early for dinner and late for lunch. Maybe the audience will stay small.

I've never been a fan of being the center of attention. Back in high school when I cheered for the Seamist Tigers, I tried my best to blend into the back row. Of course, when your quarterback boyfriend sweeps you off your feet after every game in front of the crowd it's hard to hide. At least then I walked away happy. Doubt that will be the case this time.

Procrastinating won't change things. It's best to get it over with quickly, like ripping off a Band-Aid. Yeah, it's more like sticking your hand in a snake pit. It's not the bite that kills you but the venom flowing through your veins.

I take a deep breath and march toward the door. No need for dramatics, there'll be enough of those inside. If we can keep the yelling to a minimum and don't end up on the evening news, I'll call it a win. I swing open the glass door and step inside. It's go time.

Jenna sits at the head of a long table at the back of the restaurant. Marcus sits on one side of her and Lexie on the other as if they're protecting their queen. From the way everyone acts, you'd think Jenna was their manager or at least in the band. It's strange how the wife of member has so much power. I guess it's kind of admirable. She's a strong independent woman who looks out for them like they're her baby chicks. I tried to pick up a gosling at my Uncle's farm once when I was eight. The mother goose came charging at me like a freight train and bit me so hard on the arm that I still have the scar. Why do I feel like I'm that same situation all over again?

I walk through the Italian themed restaurant, passing the mural of Venice on the side wall. I breathe deep, trying to savor the aroma of fresh baked garlic bread from the brick oven. If this is the last time I step foot in Olivia's, I don't want to take anything for granted.

I take more time than necessary to reach the table. It's like rushing to an execution... my own. I stand behind Tyler like he's shielding me from the angry energy. The aroma of his musky cologne transports me back to our close quarters in the elevator. The feel of his touch, the way he runs his hand through his hair that makes my heart just about beat out of my chest. Here I go again. My brain turned on its self-defense button. In all reality, facing the threat of suddenly plummeting to our death back in the elevator was a way better scenario than this one.

It's like a showdown in the old west. The melodic tones of the theme from *The Good, The Bad, and The Ugly* plays in my head... louder with every passing second. Jenna's cold eyes stare straight at mine, following every movement. Who's going to draw first?

One of us has to act civilized, and from the sneer on her face, it's not going to be Jenna. Okay, time to get this settled and over with so we can all move on.

Tyler slides into a chair at the foot of the table adjacent to an empty seat. I guess that one's meant for me. At least he's by my side. Maybe that means something. At this point, I sure as hell shouldn't make any assumptions. These guys are all out for my blood.

I pull out the chair near Tyler's and slide into the seat. "Hi."

Jenna throws her hands in the air. "Seriously. Don't you think 'I'm sorry' should be the first words out of your lying mouth?"

I fidget with my fingers. Two seconds in and she's about to jump across the table and attack me, maybe I should've hired a bodyguard. Last time I felt like this was when Brittany Jones cornered me in the girl's locker room for talking to her boyfriend. The fact that I was asking him a question about our lab report didn't change her perspective. I doubt anything said today will change Jenna's opinion either. Jenna and I aren't in high school, she can't turn this into a hair-pulling brawl like Brittany did back in the day, right?

I swallow hard. "I'm very sorry the article wasn't everything you'd hoped."

Twelve eyes glare at me, summoning the fires of hell. Oh God, that came out totally wrong. It's probably the worst apology in the history of the world.

Jenna slams her hands on the table. "It was bullshit." Her face turns bright crimson in a matter of seconds.

"Who the hell do you think you are?" Marcus shakes his head. "You hardly know anything about us, and you print this crap about us partying all the time and banging our fans." He lets out a loud sigh. "You hardly mentioned the music which was the whole point of the article."

"You should write for the Hollywood Star. Looks like gossip articles are your niche." Van taps his hands on a glass full of water.

I get it. I should've focused more on the music and the new album they're recording but they didn't give me much material on that front. Don't they realize whatever they say in an interview can and will be used? They've got to take some responsibility.

I nod. Okay, this is pretty much a business meeting, so I'll act as professional as possible. "Yes, the other pieces of the interview may have overshadowed the new album, and I apologize for that."

Lexie sports a half-grin. "Listen, Ali, I'm in advertising. I know you need to give the public a reason to read *Entertainment Rocks!* but whatever you write is how the public perceives Devil's Garden. They're just coming into the mainstream, and you have them portrayed as a bunch of immature party animals." She sips her cola. "You're branding them with an unfair image. They've worked their asses off, and their music speaks for itself. You should've focused more on the 'small town friends work their way up to hitting the big-time'. Everyone loves a feel-good piece just as much as they do a smut article."

A low growl forms in my throat. I don't write smut articles, but she does have a point. Again, they acted like a bunch of immature twelve-year-olds during the whole interview. Everyone forgot that whole hour of their life. "I'm sorry the article didn't have a feel-good aura."

"You could've mentioned my kick ass drum riffs instead of my other talents." Chaz winks.

Is everyone else sitting at this table deaf? Comments like that are the reason the article turned out the way it did. Not because of anything that went on between Tyler and I and not because I'm scorned from our night together, but because the band portrays themselves negatively every time he opens his mouth.

I sit up straight. "I can only report based on the information you tell me... and you've had a lot to say about your other talents."

"What the hell Tyler? You brought us all here to put up with more of her bullshit? Where's this heartfelt apology?" Jenna smirks.

"Let's take it down a notch." Tyler turns toward me.

That's enough. They just don't get it. Looks like I'll need to tell them exactly what happened and why the article turned out the way it did.

I take a deep breath. "Guys, I'm sorry the article wasn't what you expected. I didn't mean to make you sound like a bunch of immature womanizers. I wrote the article based on the things you told me in the interview. I listened to your stuff, and I think it's great, but I wrote the article solely on what was said in the interview. I'm sorry I didn't focus more on the new album."

Jenna jumps up from her seat. "Bullshit. You wrote that article like a scorned groupie because you hopped in bed with Tyler and couldn't handle the aftermath."

"Jenna, enough." Tyler runs a hand through his hair. "She just apologized."

Jenna shakes her head. "No, she's trying to defend herself. Like she didn't do anything wrong."

The fire builds up inside, like lava flows across my cheeks. "I didn't do anything wrong. Half the article was direct quotes from your drummer." I point at Chaz.

"He's an asshole. No one listens to him." Jenna gestures toward Chaz.

"Hey," Chaz yells.

I stand up. "See... this is the way you all acted in the interview. You should listen to Chaz because believe me, every other reporter who interviews you will. If you want to be portrayed differently, then don't act like a bunch of wannabe rockers who brag about their conquests." Oops, that came out much harsher than I anticipated. Maybe it's for the best. Jenna needs a reality check, and so does the rest of the band.

She walks around the table clicking her black stilettos against the wooden floor and stops a few inches from me. Oh God, this might take a turn for the worse. She deals with sex crazed groupies all the time. Am I about to get my ass kicked?

"Maybe I'll schedule an interview with another magazine." She flashes a quick smile. "The headline: Reporter sleeps with bass player to get her first byline." She shrugs. "If you don't want to be portrayed as a slut who gets stories based on her conquests maybe you should act differently."

That's the kill shot. Jenna can easily ruin my career if she wants. It doesn't matter what really happened or how I was assigned the article. She wins, again. I close my eyes tight but the river of tears bursts through. I turn and flee from the restaurant and the horde attacking me.

"Wait." Tyler is right on my heels.

I open my car door and plop inside but he grabs the door before I can close it. Is he here to hammer the last nail in my coffin?

"Sorry 'bout that, babe. You're right... about everything." He leans over and catches his breath.

I wipe away a few stray tears. "It doesn't matter. Jenna knows what's she's talking about."

"She's a bully. All talk and no action." He bends down so that we're face to face. "You got everyone's attention." He chuckles.

"Chaz will probably be banned from the next interview. Everything you said helped."

"You're the only one who sees it that way."

"I'm pretty much the brains of the operation." He smiles. "Let me make it up to you. Dinner, just you and me. I know this great place."

I need to stay away from Tyler. This is going nowhere fast. His bandmates hate me, last time we were together we almost died, and he's the complete opposite of what I'm looking for. Right now, we'll part ways, and I'll always have a story to tell my friends about how I hooked up with a rock star. We've caused enough drama in each other's lives and luckily learned from the experience.

He runs a hand through his hair. "Saturday at 7?"

"Okay. It's a date." What? I clearly need my head examined. My brain runs on autopilot. The more time I spend with the Tyler the worse it is for my sanity and my career. And to think reporters used to be known as the enemy. The hunter has become the hunted, and I can't seem to resist the chase.

7
BACK TO THE GRIND

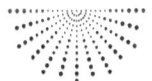

I HOLD MY BREATH AND CLOSE MY EYES TIGHT. WHAT ARE THE chances this can happen again, especially back to back? Probably one in a million, they say lightning never strikes twice. Of course, if it's going to happen to anyone it'll be me. Too bad those odds don't work in my favor when I'm playing the lottery.

The chime of the elevator sounds heavenly. I open my eyes and focus on the office lobby, slowly becoming visible as the doors open. It's like nothing ever happened. Everyone hustles to their offices carrying folders. The secretary mans the phones at her desk. A few people sit on the black leather chairs in the waiting area. No one even misses a beat. I guess I really have a lot to learn about L.A. life.

I make my way to my cubicle and plop into the chair. Huh, not a paper out of place. Even my stapler is exactly in the position where I left it. Amazing, everything is back to its former glory in just one weekend. Everything except me, my first day as a reporter seems like a lifetime ago.

I slide my briefcase under my desk and fire up the computer. I haven't had a chance to check my email since the earthquake. My inbox is probably ready to explode. Thank God Jenna doesn't have access to this account, she'd put out a plea for all Devil's Garden fans to send hate mail. Who knows, there may already be a bounty on my head?

I move the cursor to the envelope icon. The screen lights up with a plethora of messages, the first one from Jane.

Ms. Whitman. Please meet me in my office at 10 a.m. Monday morning. I'd like to discuss your article.

Jane

Oh God. The blood drains from my face. Am I about to get fired? I nibble at my nails. Okay, I can explain myself. I'll tell her about the interview and how I used all the information they gave me to create the article. I didn't realize it's best to filter the information and write an article that's favorable to both of us. It's my first time as a field reporter and my first byline, but I now know what's expected of me in the future. Yeah, that sounds pretty reasonable. She has to understand. She was new once too.

I jump a mile when my phone vibrates across my desk. I glance at the screen. Chloe lights up in red letters. Well, I've got ten minutes before I'm due in Jane's office. Maybe my bestie can give me a bit of encouragement.

"Hey"

"I found this fab new restaurant for lunch. You free?"

"After my meeting with my boss, I may have more free time than anticipated." I sigh. "She wants to talk to me about the article."

"Come on, Al. The article was great. Brutally honest, rockers going wild, just what Hollywood loves."

I didn't think it was possible, but now I feel worse. "We'll see. I doubt I'll have an appetite, so I'll take a raincheck on lunch."

"Oh, darling. I hate to hear you talk like that. Don't worry until you have to. Okay, dinner and cocktails on Saturday, and I won't take no for an answer."

Ah, Saturday. She's going to love this. "Well... I kind of have a date."

"Oh my God, is it that new guy at the office? Do tell."

"No… it's with… the guy from the club."

"You mean the hottie bass player from the band? How the hell did that happen?"

That's an excellent question, one I'm still trying to figure out myself. "It's a long story, but right now I have to walk the Green Mile to my boss's office and face her fury."

"Remember, the story you concoct in your mind is always way worse than reality. Good luck. Tootles."

I don't think Stephen King can create a story scarier than the wrath I'm about to face. I press "end call" on my phone and slide it on my desk. Okay, time to prepare to beg for my survival with this company.

"Hey, neighbor. Heard you shook things up in the elevator?"

What the hell is he talking about? Does he know Tyler was in there with me? No way, no one knows about that other than the firefighters who rescued us.

He scrunches his eyebrows. "You know… the earthquake. Heard you were trapped in there. You okay?"

I nod. "I think I'll be taking the steps from now on." Okay, so it's a lie. I'd be ready for the Olympics if I had to trek up the stairwell every time I needed to get to the office.

He chuckles. "Yep, welcome to L.A., home of the earthquakes."

My phone chimes and a text from Chloe lights up the screen.

Call me as soon as you can. I'm dying to know how you scored a date with the bass player.

Jake smirks. "Guess the band liked the article."

I grab my phone and toss it in my purse. "I've gotta go… Meeting with Jane at 10."

He takes a step back. I fly by him like I'm running from a fire. Who does he think he is? My personal texts are absolutely none of his business, and he has a lot of nerve to insinuate I'm doing more with the band members than what my job requires. I mean, Tyler and I met as a fluke before I even knew he was in the band.

I guess everything happens for a reason but this by far has to be the most twisted fairytale ever invented. Doesn't matter anyway, right now I've got to deal with Jane.

I stare at the glass door that reads **Jane Reiser, Senior Editor.** Those letters look more intimidating today than they did the first time I walked into her office. Okay, Ali, it's go time. I take a deep breath and knock on the door.

"Ms. Whitman. Come in."

I navigate the floor carefully. No need to fall on my face again and repeat history. All I can think about as I make my trek forward is how much I miss my shoes.

"Please, take a seat." Jane tosses a few papers on her desk and adjusts her glasses.

I slide into the hard leather chair. It's much colder than I remember. "You wanted to see me?" I place my hands on my lap, trying my hardest not to fidget.

"Yes, the Devil's Garden article you wrote has been getting a lot of buzz."

Oh God, this is bad. "Yes... I..."

"I think you did a great job. You were honest and told it exactly how it is... a straight shooter. These qualities make a great reporter, especially in the entertainment industry. So many young reporters want to make friends with the celebrities thinking they will somehow benefit but you... you were professional and didn't worry about any repercussions. Well done."

A smile lights up my face. I can't believe it. I'm not on the chopping block, not even close. I managed to impress my boss with my first byline. This may be the greatest accomplishment of my life so far. If all it takes is being brutally honest why aren't more reporters using this approach? I don't get it.

"Thank you."

"Since you've done such a marvelous job with the Devil's Garden interview, I have a special assignment for you. This will be our feature article for the *Entertainment Rocks!* special anniversary edition."

Oh my God, my article is going to be the feature. I sit still in my chair, trying to resist the urge to jump up and down, cheering. I dreamed of this moment a million times in my mind but never expected it to happen this soon. The minute I leave this office, I'm texting Chloe to have some champagne ready.

"I'm honored. Thank you for this opportunity."

She folds her hands together at her desk. Even though she looks a little like Dr. Evil minus the hairless cat, I have nothing to fear.

"After reading your article, I knew you were the right person for the job." She hands me a manila folder. "Your article will be called "Behind the Bench," and you'll be interviewing Elle Crowley. She's the wife of NFL quarterback Nash Crowley. The interview will focus on the true story of what it's like to be married to football royalty."

My stomach turns. I should've known it was too good to be true. Elle Crowley has the reputation of spilling all the gossip on the coaches and other players. It's a well-known fact that Nash cheats on her with anyone from fans to cheerleaders. Maybe the article should be called "Why the hell would you stay married to someone who treats you like that?"

I get it. Now that I have the reputation for telling the brutal honest truth. I guess I fall into the category of "smut reporter." This is not the direction I want my career to go but I can't pass up a feature. Plus, I can't tell my boss I'm not willing to write the article she's assigned me. I mean, I'm a newbie field reporter. Hardly big enough to decide what assignments I'm willing to take and declining others.

"I'm familiar with Mrs. Crowley. I'll give her a call and set up an interview." I stand up and hold out my hand. "Thank you again for this opportunity."

"I know you'll do a wonderful job. Please update me on your

progress. The article will be due back to me in two weeks. Keep up the good work." She turns away and goes back to her work as if I've already left the room.

I flash a smile and head to my cubicle. Ugh, it's like a double-edged sword. There's no way I can pass up this opportunity but I can't write everything Elle Crowley says. I mean, I'd have the whole team and probably most of their fans ready to kill me. Plus, what if she's not telling the whole truth. Sure, I can quote her directly, and I'm definitely recording everything she says, but I don't want to put any untruths out there. Now I see why journalists filter their interviews. Sometimes you just can't write it all.

I'm on the fast track to writing for a magazine in the checkout aisle of the grocery store. I can see the headline now "Woman has Elvis's love child years after his death, by Ali Whitman." I can't do this again for ratings or to get people to read a periodical. I'm right back in high school writing the article about Josh and the tragedy in a small town. Sure, it made the local paper, but I'm not about to let myself go through this again. I'm not putting it all on the line just because it's what the public wants to know.

WHY DOES EVERYTHING GREAT IN LIFE HAVE TO COME WITH A catch? Hard work definitely pays off, but it's like there's a curse associated with success. A dark force refuses to let you be completely happy. Or it lets you have it all and then rips it away after giving you a taste of what total bliss feels like. I'll probably spend the rest of my life trying to get back an ounce of that euphoria just once more. Maybe the devil will show up and offer me a contract for my soul.

"Greasy food and bottom shelf cocktails? Should I even ask how the meeting with your boss went?" Chloe wipes a few crumbs off the booth and slides inside.

I drag a fry through a mound of ketchup on my plate. "I got a feature article."

"Oh my God. You did it." Chloe quietly claps. "Why aren't we drinking champagne? Let's split and head somewhere more appropriate for an occasion like this."

I shake my head. "All I want to do is down this mammoth strawberry margarita and indulge myself in charred beef and cheese."

Chloe sits back against the booth. "Why aren't you jumping up and down and screaming through the streets? Is your article about clogging arteries and you need research?" She snickers.

"Explain to me how Cinderella not only gets her shoe back but also marries the prince and lives happily ever after, no catches."

"Oh darling, Cinderella doesn't have your talent." She sips my margarita. "And I heard the prince is lousy in the sack."

We both burst out laughing.

She puts her hand over mine. "What's up with the article?"

I exhale loudly. "Well, she loved the Devil's Garden piece and praised me for being brutally honest."

Chloe raises her hand to get a waitress's attention and points to my margarita. "I'll have one of those." She props her hand on her chin. "Sounds good so far."

I nod. "And that's when everything went south."

"How does getting a feature upset you? I mean, you wanted this forever."

The waitress brings Chloe her drink.

"Yeah, but now I'm known as the smut reporter of *Entertainment Rocks!* You know, the one who tells all and doesn't sugar coat the truth."

She sips her drink. "A reputation for being gritty and truthful. That all sounds awesome."

"My assignment is to do a tell-all article with Elle Crowley. You know, the one married to Nash."

Chloe covers her mouth and then drops her hand. "The one who called the cops on their coach after he left a victory dinner and ended up getting him charged with a DUI."

I nod. "Yep, best not to piss her off." I gulp my drink. "My boss wants me to be brutally honest and I'm sure the readers are dying to hear what she has to say, but I've got to watch my back too."

If I could do it all over again, I'd scrap the Devil's Garden article and write something everyone involved loves. Repeating history won't make things any different. Not with my career, not with Tyler, and not with me. What would he think of me if I did exactly what I said I wished I hadn't, write another article without taking everything into account?

Chloe steals a fry. "I see it this way. Write the article as you see fit. It's still going to be the feature, you make your own reputation. No one assigns one to you."

Easier said than done. Jane can pull the article or worse, fire me. "I have to get through the interview with her first. Then I'll make that decision."

"Sounds like a plan, don't worry until you have to." She flashes a smile. "Okay, now spill it. How'd you score a date with the hottie?"

Ah, the other half of my complicated life. "The short version. We were trapped in an elevator together when he came to demand answers about the article. Almost succumbed to our animal passions while looking death in the eye, made it out unscathed until I agreed to apologize to the band. And dealt with the wrath of Jenna Crane, the guitar player's wife, and ran out crying. Then Tyler chased me down and asked me out."

"Wow, that's fabulous. Sounds like a Lifetime movie." She taps her fingers on her glass. "So, where's this going?"

I shrug. "It's just dinner. Normally I get that first, but I blame you for shoving all those shots down my throat."

"I can't stand in the way of destiny." She winks. "Seriously, you must like him."

I mean, he's gorgeous, sexy, and the perfect mix of bad-boy rocker meets small town boy. He's the first man that's ever come close to making me feel a hint of what I once did ages ago in another lifetime. Even though I know there are a million reasons to stay away, and an abundance of obstacles, I can't wait to see him again.

"He's fun to hang out with." I hold back a smile.

"Who do you think you're talking to?" She smirks. "It's okay to like a guy. It's been forever you know."

I look down at my plate and then back up at her.

"I didn't mean it that way." She fidgets with her fingers. "You deserve to be happy and if Tyler is fun and cool to hang out with go for it." She sips her margarita. "Plus, he's super-hot."

I chuckle. "And he has a flashy car, very Hollywood."

"Okay, enough of the greasy food and heavy conversation. Let's celebrate your hot article and even hotter date." She throws two twenties on the table. "Time for some shopping. Let's get Cinderella ready for the ball."

Am I ready for all of this? New city, new clothes, new Ali... but somehow it all seems the same. Is the ghost of Ali past about to haunt me?

8

DATE?

HOW CAN TYLER HAVE THE ABILITY TO TURN ME INTO A disorganized mess? I mean, he asks me out, my brain ceases all functioning, and I say yes, and here I am waiting for him to take me God knows where. A girl needs a clue as to where she's going so she can decide what to wear.

I glance at the clock, 6:50 p.m. Great, I'm going on this date naked. I rummage through my closet trying to find an outfit that's appropriate for everything. If I can invent one, I can retire tomorrow.

Okay, last time he took me to a diner, so I doubt he plans on hitting a five-star restaurant. Tyler's low key, casual, more about the experience than the venue. Not the typical L.A. guy even though he can probably fit in anywhere. Is it because he's in a band or just amazingly versatile? He's so different from any other guy I've met. Mysterious yet transparent and can set your soul on fire with one look into those baby blues. I'm in way over my head, like always.

I've got it. I throw on my turquoise sundress and silver sandals. The doorbell chimes through the quiet apartment. I hop on one foot while trying to fasten my sandal and take a quick glance in the mirror. One day I'm actually going to be ready early. I smear on desert rose lipstick and smack my lips together. It's go time.

I rush to the door and swing it open. Okay, so I'm acting a little more frantic than I would've liked, but I didn't want him to think I wasn't coming out.

"Whoa, is the apartment on fire?" Tyler leans against the door jam.

It might burst into flames now. "Sorry, I was running late, and I'm still in frantic beast mode."

"Hope there's a full moon tonight." He winks.

"Be careful what you wish for." Oh God, here I go again. If I keep this up, he's going to expect a repeat of the first time we met. I've got to convince him I'm not "that" kind of girl.

I grab my purse and step outside. "Ready?"

The question is, am I ready for this? Technically, this is the third time we're in each other's company, so we're pretty much dating at this point. I've gone from, *should I bother getting involved with Tyler*, to *how can I keep from screwing this up*.

"I'm always locked and loaded, Babe." He holds out his hand to take mine.

I slide my fingers in between his. An abundance of tingles sweep through my body. The feeling scares the crap out of me. Why am I dying for it to last forever?

We head down the steps to his red Camaro, the metallic specks of paint glisten in the dimming sunlight.

"You know which one it is, right?" He nudges my arm.

"Funny." I guess I'm never living that one down.

He holds open the passenger door, and I slide into the leather seat. The small town Kansas boy always peeks through the rocker façade. He's got that gentleman charm you don't always find with guys in big cities, especially with rock stars.

He jumps into the driver's seat and fires up the engine. He pulls out a few CDs from the center console. "We're going old school tonight. Lady's choice." He hands me the stack. "Choose wisely."

"I always do." If that were even remotely true, I'd have far fewer regrets.

I'm used to satellite radio and iPods, it's been ages since I played a CD, especially in a car. Why does this feel like a test? I peruse the choices and stop at a band I loved since high school. "Here ya go."

"Foo Fighters, nice." He slides the CD into the player and turns up the volume. *Everlong* blasts through the speakers. "You've gained the prestigious privilege of choosing all tunes."

I put my hand to my chest and make my best oh-my-God-I-just-won-an-Oscar face. "I'm honored. Do I get a trophy to commemorate the occasion?"

He flashes a half-smile and digs in the center console. "Here you are, the golden guitar pick."

He's got the best sense of humor. The guys I meet at work, or any of the magazine's executives seem to lack the humor gene. Maybe it's a rare find nowadays. Tyler is definitely one of a kind. Not another person on earth comes even remotely close to him.

"I'll treasure it forever." I smile and slide the pick into my purse.

It's going in my shadow box with the ticket stubs from the first concert I attended, Aerosmith, and the dried rose from the corsage Josh bought me on senior prom. I take a deep breath. Tonight is about fun, no need to dredge up the past.

I sit back and let the warm breeze blow through my hair. The bright lights of the city are slowly lighting up the horizon as the sun sets. Purple and pink hues as far as the eye can see, very picturesque.

Well, we just passed the last exit to downtown, so we're clearly not eating at one of the city's trendy spots. "Are we off to a deserted island?"

"I'm taking you to the depths of my world." He winks.

Hmm, intriguing but creepy, in a serial killer, stalker kind of way. I can see the headlines now, *Reporter slain after dating disgruntled bass player.* Of course, my mind wanders to the worst possible scenario. I know Tyler better than that. What does he have planned? Maybe he's secretly a vampire and about to take me to his lair.

"Should I get ready to have my whole world rocked?" I smirk.

"Every second you're with me, babe."

Butterflies flutter in my stomach. If anyone else in the world said that to me, I'd laugh in their face. Tyler has the power to change my outlook on everything.

"What are you waiting for?"

He moves his hand over to my thigh, caressing my skin with his thumb. "We're almost there."

At this point I don't care where we're going, he can drive off to the middle of the desert, and I'd be happy. Seclusion might be the best date ever. Tyler and me away from the rest of the world for a while.

He pulls onto a dimly-lit road lined with tall grass and an unkempt sidewalk. Salty air floats along my skin. No matter what coast, the scent of the ocean is always the same, salty with a hint of freshness unmatched by anything else. Guess it's just one of the many mysteries of the universe. It brings me back home instantly.

He slowly slides his hand away, sending my body into overdrive. I fidget with my fingers, trying to compose myself. I focus on a small cabana-style restaurant up ahead. Colored lights hang from the orange pavilion and round, picnic tables for two line the boardwalk floor.

Tyler pulls into a parking spot at the edge of the sand and turns down the engine. The crash of waves and faint song of the seagull fill the air. It's quaint and secluded. Only a few other couples sip on drinks on the patio.

"How can you possibly find all these hidden gems when you're in L.A.?"

"Surfer's secret." He walks around to the passenger side and holds open my door.

I stare at the tiger on his arm, dancing with every movement. Whoever placed that tattoo knew exactly what they were doing. I'm mesmerized. I step out of the car.

"Maybe I should hang-ten with you sometime." God, do surfers even say that? I probably sound like an idiot.

He flashes a half smile. "Anytime, babe." He pushes the door shut and places his hand in the small of my back. "Ever have sex on the boardwalk?"

That's random and really weird. "Umm, no." And if I did there's no way in hell I'd be sharing the story, especially on a date.

"I think you'll like it."

I stop and fold my arms. "Excuse me?" Am I on a date with Tyler or Chaz?

He holds up his hands. "It's the signature drink here." He smirks. "Unless you wanted something else."

Heat spreads across my cheeks. "I can definitely use a drink."

We make our way up the few steps to the wooden floor. A blonde, probably around eighteen years old, hops over like she's running on the beach in slow motion. I guess she's our waitress.

"Hey Ty, you're back in town. Want the usual table?"

He nods. "Thanks, Trixie."

How many usual places can a person who doesn't even live here have?

"You really get around when you visit. Maybe I should hire you as a tour guide." I slide into the seat overlooking the ocean.

"All you've got to do is stop for a minute and take a look at what's right in front of you."

Firecrackers spread across my skin. I lean forward and prop my hand on my chin. "Sometimes it's the most amazing view."

Where the hell did that come from? I sit up, willing the filter between my brain and my mouth to regain function.

Tyler runs a hand through his hair. Bright crimson rushes along his cheeks.

Oh my God, I made the rock star blush. Looks like I can cross that off my bucket list. He's right though, so many people neglect to take in the moment, and they let it pass them by. One thing I vow to never do again.

"Do you know what you want?" Trixie smiles, tapping a pen against her lip.

Right now I want to jump across this table and tackle Tyler on the sand. I get it, I've already had my hands on the Golden Fleece, but half of the night erased itself from my mind. Was I really that wasted or was it self-defense?

"Key lime tortilla crusted chicken is our house specialty." Trixie breaks the silence.

"Sounds great to me. House specials are always the best."

"Me too." Tyler winks. "And we both want Sex on the Boardwalk".

Trixie giggles like a 1950's teen who just saw Elvis. She scurries off to the bar.

I raise an eyebrow. "One of your groupies?"

He snickers. "Jealous?"

Is he serious? Just because Trixie has a name reserved for a stripper and thinks she can bring guys to their knees by batting an eyelash. Hell no. And I have absolutely no reason to be concerned about who flirts with Tyler. It's not like he's mine... not yet. Oh my God, what am I thinking? The last thing I need right now is a guy... especially a rock star with an entourage.

"Not my style." I tap my fingers on the table top. I've got to tone down the conversation. It's gone from *let's rip off our clothes* to *is she flirting with you?* "Really, how did you find this place?"

"I met two local guys, Logan and Gavin when I decided I'd buy a board and instantly be able to surf." He chuckles. "Yeah, didn't work out so well. They taught me everything there is to know about surfing, and I instantly fell in love."

"Hmm, with which one?" I smirk.

"Funny." He runs a hand through his hair. "With the ocean, the waves, the way I feel when that board glides against the wave." A half smile graces his face. "It's like the moment when the lights shine down on stage, and I'm in another world. In charge of my destiny for a brief time, nothing in the world comes close."

I stare into his blue eyes, mesmerized. In another hour I'll be giggling like Trixie. "Sounds incredible. I'd probably wouldn't even be able to stand up on the board."

He shakes his head. "It's not about that. It's about enjoying the ride."

Trixie comes back with two mammoth drinks in a glass that looks more like a fishbowl than a cocktail. Two umbrellas hang out of the side along with a gummy crab. If I finish this, I might forget yet another date with Tyler. I've got to pace myself.

"This looks intense." I pull the twisty straw to my lips.

"That's the way I roll, babe." He gulps the drink.

"Anyway, Gavin used to date Trixie so he took us here for drinks after a day of surfing. I've met a bunch of other surfers through them. Been coming here every time I'm in town ever since."

I sip the fruity concoction. It burns my mouth as it passes through. Not a good sign. "Do you surf with Gavin and Logan when you're in L.A.?"

He grabs the back of his neck. "Nah, we had a little misunderstanding about a girl who happened to be Logan's sister. Not my proudest moment."

Of course, it's about a girl. "Spare me the gritty details." Okay, so this was probably years ago, and I'm sure Tyler has matured since then but why would he risk screwing up a friendship over hooking up? Especially when Gavin and Logan introduced him to something he loved. I thought surfers had some kind of unwritten "guy code".

Trixie slides our dinners in front of us. "Hope you enjoy them." She smiles at Tyler, then turns away.

"What about you?" He stabs a forkful of chicken and pops it in his mouth.

"You know I'm a new reporter, haven't been in L.A. that long. Trying to build my career. Listen to kick ass music. What else do you want to know?"

"Everything."

"Not much else to tell." I slug my drink through the straw like I've just emerged from months in a desert. Maybe the alcohol will calm my nerves.

"Mysterious… You on the run from the law?"

"Something like that." I flash a meek smile. I'm making myself sound worse. God knows what crazy thoughts are running through his head right now. I've got to explain, at least a little. "You know I'm from Seamist, Maine. Small town, nothing there for me anymore."

He nods. "I get it, being stuck in bumblefuck anywhere sucks. Would you believe I played football? Not good enough for a ticket out but I escaped anyway."

I chuckle. "I was a Seamist Tigers cheerleader." Oh boy, the alcohol is kicking in. God knows what's about to slip out of my mouth.

"You're hot. I can totally see you at the top of the pyramid. Let me guess, you dated the quarterback?" He chomps on another bite of chicken.

"Guilty." I chow down on my dinner, letting the flavor of the crunchy lime chicken flow across my tongue. "This is delicious."

"Wait until dessert." Tyler finishes his last bite. "So where's this quarterback now? He's not going to show up here and try and kick my ass is he?" He laughs.

I drop my fork. Josh never had to be jealous. I only wanted

him, and no other man existed in my world. I take a deep breath trying to blow off the question. Where the hell's the waitress, I need another drink.

"Hey, you okay?" Tyler reaches for my hand.

"Yeah." I slug the rest of my drink. "The quarterback passed away senior year... car accident."

"Wow, that sucks. I'm really sorry." He runs his thumb along my fingers.

I lift my head. "Ancient history... Now, tell me about this amazing dessert." Thank God the water works didn't turn on. Crying definitely puts the damper on a date.

"Ah. Named after us."

"Ali and Tyler dessert?" It wouldn't shock me if he got the restaurant to let him name a dessert. Especially if it's owned by a female.

"Hot Blondies." He runs a hand through his hair.

"Sounds perfect." I guess I kind of took the cowards way out when it came to talking about Josh. Once you tell someone he passed away they never ask anything else. No one seems to care about what he was like or what we had together. They're always more interested in his death than in his life. Guess I'm still bitter about the way the town acted.

"Hey, Trix, two hot blondies," Tyler yells across the restaurant to our waitress Trixie.

She waves.

"So what's on your agenda next? I mean after the record is finished. You plan on buying a house in every country?"

"Hell no. We're going on tour to promote the album in a few months. I rent a place when I'm here in L.A. I bought a place in Silent Springs right after we started seeing some cash. Now I only go there for family holidays and when I need a place to crash. I don't want to be stuck anywhere."

"Doomed to wander the earth for eternity."

"You say that like it's a bad thing." He crinkles his brow.

Trixie interrupts, setting the biggest blondie I've ever seen in front of me. The mound of ice cream on top wobbles as she slides the plate. "Here ya go, white chocolate blondies with lemon cream." She scurries to another table.

I think this restaurant is located somewhere in heaven. Maybe Tyler missed his calling. He'd be an amazing food critic.

"It all depends on your perspective." I shovel a spoonful into my mouth. They should rename this Better Than Sex. I moan, louder than I'd hoped.

"Told you I'd rock your world." He shoves half the blondie into his mouth in one scoop.

"You delivered." I smile.

He kept his word on everything he's told me so far. I just can't figure out his intentions. Is he looking for a friend to hang out with while he's in L.A., does he feels bad for the way things went down with Jenna, does he want us to be more than friends? I'm definitely not at the point where I can ask.

The melodic tones of a steel drum band flow through the air, harmonizing with the crashing waves. I've always wanted to vacation at an island. In fact, the future honeymoon I planned in my head takes place on Caribbean island, complete with palm trees, frozen drinks, and a hammock for two. I sway in my chair, losing myself for a second.

"Let's dance. I've got moves like Jagger." He stands and holds out his hand.

"I bet." I take his hand and follow him to the wooden dance area in front of the band. "I have the moves of an off balance sloth."

"We both know that's not true." He pulls me close.

Fire scorches my face. It must be a million shades of scarlet. Last time I danced in public was three years ago at my cousin's wedding with one of the groomsmen who had trouble keeping his hands to himself. Luckily that's not an issue this time. As far as I'm concerned, Tyler can put his hands anywhere he wants.

Tyler sweeps me across the dance floor like we're floating. He stares into my eyes like we're the only two people in the world. Right now, we are. I press my forehead against his and slow things down, swaying to the beat. Tyler holds me closer. Nothing can come between us at this moment.

For the first time in forever, I'm safe. His strong arms keep the rest of the world at bay. I close my eyes and lean forward, brushing my lips against his. He slides his tongue along my lip and pulls me into an amazing kiss. Oh my God, I kissed him. I've never kissed a guy first in my life. What is wrong with me? I can always blame it on the drink. Now I'll never know how he thinks of me. Does he just want another one-nighter? We hook-up while we're together and then he does God knows what when we're not?

He pulls away, sucking my bottom lip. "See, you've got moves."

I wrap my arms around his neck and rest my head on his shoulder. What can I say at this point? If I start asking the questions plaguing my mind, I'll sound like a psycho and ruin our date. No reason to put the cart before the horse. I'm going with the flow and not worrying about anything. It seems to work for Tyler.

If I want to avoid any other uncomfortable situations, I need to get my hands off him. "Wanna hit the beach?"

He pulls away. "You read my mind. Let me take care of the bill quick and don't argue. You know I'm old-fashioned."

"Yep, just like Humphrey Bogart."

"Here's lookin' at you, kid." He winks and pulls his wallet out of his jeans.

My heart erupts into a frenzy of radical beats. And he knows Casablanca, too. Tyler surprises me every second we spend together. It's like a blessing and a curse. I meet someone who brings out things in me I haven't felt in years, but he doesn't want to settle down, ever. What the hell, I'll enjoy it while it lasts.

I hop down the few wooden steps to the edge of the sand. The soft breeze and salty air instantly frees my mind. The beach is so therapeutic. Like all my troubles wash away with the crash of a wave.

"Come on, I want to show you something." He entwines his fingers with mine.

"Is it Jaws?" Not that it matters. At this point, I'll pretty much follow him anywhere.

"Better."

We walk through the gritty sand to the shoreline. The almost full moon lights up the night sky, casting golden shadows on the dark water. I stop and take off my sandals, letting my feet sink into the soft sand.

He stops near a jetty made from rocks and plops down onto the sand, pulling me into his lap. I wander back to junior prom. When the dance was over, we all headed to the beach for an after party. The moon looked just like this one. Josh pulled me into his lap as the fire crackling in the fire-pit took away the chill in the air. One of the best times of my life.

"Look out ahead." Tyler points to the ocean, bringing me back to the moment.

"What? All I see is water." I sweep the beachline.

"Exactly. See how the wave makes a wedge shape from hitting off the jetty?"

"Yeah, the waves are pretty high."

"Makes for great surfing. We surfers look for those breaks."

Ah, I heard about surfers protecting breaks like it's their territory. I guess that's what it's all about. Keeping the best waves for their crew.

"What beach do you like best?" I turn toward him.

"The one you're on." He tips my chin and presses his lips to mine.

I lean in, following his twisting tongue like a moth to a flame. He eases me down onto the sand and hovers above me.

Tingles sweep my body. A slew of memories hit me like a freight train. Josh, setting me down on blanket on our most secluded beach. I stole a bottle of pink champagne from Chateaux Blanc after my shift in an effort to make the night special. He delivered. The first time we were together was more exquisite than fireworks shooting from every mountain in the world simultaneously.

My stomach drops. I pull away. "Maybe we should go. There's some places not meant for sand to get into."

He jerks his head back for a moment, then rolls over. "Okay, I guess you've got a point." He stands up and brushes the sand off his jeans.

I shake a few grains of sand from my hair and join him. He probably thinks I'm a tease. I mean, I want to be with Tyler. But not here, not like this. There's a few memories I'm not willing to recreate. Plus, I really don't need a fuck buddy, and I'm starting to think that's what this whole deal may be all about.

He takes my hand and walks along the water line. Cool water rushes across our feet. I sink into the gritty sand with every step. It reminds me of quicksand. Am I about to be swallowed?

Pain radiates through my big toe like a bolt of lightning just hit me. I jump like a startled cartoon character. Oh no, did I step on glass?

Tyler bends down to assess the damage. "You've got to be kidding me."

Oh God, what is it? Did I step on some poisonous creature and now I have seconds before it's venom kills me? Maybe I shouldn't have stopped Tyler from having his way with me. It might've been my last chance.

"What? Do we need to go to the hospital?"

He pulls something from my skin. "Nah, but you're the first person in the history of the world to be bitten by a shark on land." He holds up a white shark tooth.

It looks beautiful glistening off the moonlight, like a treasure from the sea. Of course, I wouldn't feel that way if it was still attached to the shark. "I'm a shark attack survivor."

Tyler slips the tooth into his pocket. "Yep, barely made it out alive."

I cringe when the salt water flows over my fresh wound. Never in my wildest dreams did I think I'd get hurt like this on a date with Tyler.

He stops and scoops me up in one quick swoosh. I instinctively wrap my arms around him. It's kind of romantic in a twisted way.

"You don't have to carry me. I can walk."

"Are you kidding me? Next, Moby Dick will show up and swallow us both whole. Better safe than sorry, babe."

I chuckle. "Yeah, better not take any chances."

Tyler marches along the sand like I'm weightless. The soft breeze flows sending the faint scent of salt and Tyler's musky cologne through the air. Everything about him screams sex. From his looks, to the way he talks, to the way he can drive me wild with one glance. I'm in serious trouble, and it has nothing to do with the shark bite.

He sets me down onto the pavement near the car and opens the passenger side door. "I think you're safe now."

"My hero." I blow him a kiss.

He swings around faster than the speed of light and slams his lips into mine, pressing me against the car. I weave my fingers into his hair and put all the passion I've been holding back into the kiss. A low groan escapes from his throat. He moves forward, so close that not even air exists between us. Ah, he wants me now more than ever.

What am I thinking? We're in the middle of a street. Okay, so it's deserted, but still public property. I slide my hands down and slowly pull away. "I think I better get home, you know, tend to my wound."

He exhales loudly. "Whatever you want, babe."

What I want is usually never what I need. At least when it comes to guys. I hop into the seat, swinging my legs around so I don't put any pressure on my toe. It hurts, pretty bad. Of course, a few seconds ago I hadn't noticed.

I fidget with the radio trying my best to impress Tyler with my musical tastes. He's quiet, not his usual self. It's not like I can blame him. In his eyes, I'm probably some tease that doesn't know what she wants. Could he be right?

I crank up the volume letting *Detroit Rock City* blast through the airwaves. "Kiss fan?"

He nods. "Saw them back in Kansas. Best stage show ever. Tons of fireworks."

"I know what you mean. I saw them once in Maine." The summer after junior year Josh's brother Trent insisted he introduce us to "real music" and bought us third-row tickets. The energy flowed through me, showing me the passionate combination of kick ass rock matched with an amazing stage show. It was life-changing. Kind of like the last few weeks.

"Let's say I had some face paint, who would you be?" Tyler nibbles on his lip, holding back a smile.

"Definitely Paul Stanley. Gotta love that star. How about you?"

"The demon, Gene Simmons. You know I'm a bass player."

"The demon, huh. Is there something I should know?"

He pulls the car to the curb in front of my apartment. "Yeah, lots but it's more fun if you find out on your own." He steps out and pulls open my passenger door.

Am I going to get the chance to find out his secrets? I step onto the sidewalk and hobble on my wounded foot. I should really win some award for being the most accident-prone person on earth.

Tyler shuts the door and swings me up into his arms. His strong biceps, decorated with intricate artwork are turning into my safe haven. I can't let him go. Not tonight.

"Thanks for the lift." I nuzzle into his chest.

"You know I'm a sucker for a damsel in distress." He marches up the steps and stops outside my apartment. He sets me down slowly. I quickly slide the key in the lock and open the door. It's the last moment of our first official date. I turn back toward Tyler.

Whatever comes out of my mouth next can make or break us. "I don't want to get hurt again." *Dammit*, where's the filter from my brain to my mouth?

"I'm all about the pleasure, babe. Not pain."

I nudge the door, opening it a bit more with my heel. I'm at a crossroads. Should I listen to my rational mind or trust my heart? Just like that, my brain shuts itself down like my defense mechanism has lowered the shields. Nothing exists but passion for the man standing in front of me, searching my face.

"Then why end the night here?" I grab his shirt and pull him toward me, backing us both into my apartment.

Is this the end or just the beginning? I guess I'll find out if Tyler is really about the pleasure or if I'm destined for pain.

9

BLISS

Every touch sparks a vague memory of our first night together. It's all familiar but completely new. Was it really the alcohol that erased my memory or did my brain go into self-defense mode? Right now, it's just about shut itself off.

Tyler bends down and grabs the back of my thighs, hauling me up. I wrap my legs around his waist, squeezing him against me. Ah, he really wants me. It's been forever since I was an object of desire… all my own fault. That changes tonight.

He navigates through the kitchen and into the bedroom like he's got a schematic of my floor plan etched in his mind. Just one of his many talents. Still lip-locked, he slides his fingers underneath my sundress. The hard callouses create an invigorating sensation, like little electric shocks shooting energy down to my core. I squeeze my legs around him tighter, desperate to feel him pressed against me.

His instincts kick in like he can read my mind. He maneuvers the dress up and over my head, pulling away from my lips for only a second. He's probably done the move a million times and been deemed an expert. What other skills does he excel in?

He lowers me on the bed and hovers above me, tearing

through my soul with his stare. The intensity of the moment hits me. For once, I don't care about the consequences or what happens tomorrow. Right now I want Tyler more than I've ever wanted anything and I need to have him.

He slips a finger underneath each side of my bra straps and lowers them down my shoulders. I move forward to allow him to unhook the back and release my breasts, along with my pent up desires. Every move he makes is perfect, like something you'd see in a movie. Josh was rough, and awkward, probably why I went through six bras one month. Not Tyler, he knows exactly what to do and when to do it. Maybe this is the difference between being with a boy to being with a man. Tyler is quite the man.

He runs his tongue from my neck to my breast, circling the nipple and sucking hard as he pulls away. I let out a slight moan. I can't stand it anymore. I need him. Patience is a virtue that doesn't exist at this moment. Time to give Tyler a taste of his own medicine.

I grab the hem of his shirt and rip it over his head like it's on fire. He scoots up on the bed, flexing every muscle of his chest like he's a peacock spreading out his feathers. I'm way out of my league in the seduction category. Time to step up my game. I slither my fingertips along the curves of his chest and down his abs to his jeans.

The timid Ali who always lets the guy make all the moves is no longer in existence. The caterpillar has shed its cocoon and turned into a lustrous butterfly. I pull the dense denim fabric to release the button, almost ripping it off. Tyler's heartbeat pounds in his chest so strong it vibrates his skin. No more playing games. I shove my hand down his pants and take hold of all I desire.

He lets out a moan and kicks off his jeans and boxers one smooth motion. My pulse races, like my heart is about to escape and flutter around the room. All of sudden, nervous energy surrounds me. Self-defense? I won't let it ruin things for me, not this time. Even though we've already been together, tonight is truly the first time. It's the first time I've let a guy take me home on a first "official date", the first time I'm with someone I'm not in a relationship with, and the first time I'm ignoring my rational brain and letting passion run the show.

And just like that, all the doubt and fear erases from my brain. Tyler reaches down into his jeans pocket and pulls a condom out. Was he expecting to get lucky or is he always prepared? Either way, I'm glad he has one.

He hooks a finger on each side of my panties and moves them from side to side, slowly slinking them down my legs. I arch my back to help him with the journey. He rips the condom wrapper with his teeth and eases it on. Am I ready for this?

My breathing increases and heart rate triples. Tyler crawls up, hovering above me and leans down. His hair tickles my skin, creating an amazing sensation. He runs his tongue along my bottom lip before pressing his lips against mine. Dear God, clearly the best kiss of my life. I'm in store for quite a ride.

He traces his fingers along my thigh, spreading my legs open just enough for him to press against me. Slow and steady, he enters. I gasp as his impressive body fills my core. We move in a perfect rhythm like our bodies were meant for each other. I thought this kind of connection only existed between Josh and I. Thank God, that's not the case. We mimic each other's movement, increasing the passion between us. I dig my fingers into his back as energy builds inside me. I've never felt like this before. Every ounce of my body tingles, like electricity sparks through all of me simultaneously. I thrust forward and gasp as my body surrenders to Tyler. I grab onto him like he's my lifeline, providing the most amazing pleasure I've ever experienced. He's definitely all about the pleasure. My body relaxes as if I've just run a marathon.

He continues moving his body inside me, building up more passion with each passing second. His heart beats like a drum, creating a unique song. I match his movements, desperate to give him the same pleasure. Within seconds, he thrusts hard and lets out a loud moan. His body pulsates inside me as he releases the energy we generate together.

He exhales loudly and eases himself out of me. I squirm, the motion causing electricity to shoot through me once more. Tyler is truly a talented man. I mean, I've heard of earthshattering sex that makes you beg for more. I just never thought I'd experience it... ever.

When I was with Josh things were different. We were two kids in love, destined to be together for the rest of our lives. When we made love it was all about expressing our emotions to each other. Soft touches, sweet caresses, and it was perfect. I would've been happy if it was the only sex I had the rest of my life. Of course, toe curling insane pleasure is a close second. One I can't wait to experience again.

Tyler rolls over and lies next to me on the bed. He turns toward me and props himself on his elbow. I catch my bottom lip in between my teeth, replaying the last half-hour in my mind.

He tucks a stray hair behind my ear. "Best first date ever."

I playfully slap him. "Um, definitely not our first date."

He crinkles his forehead. "Yeah, I'm pretty sure it was."

I shake my head, holding back a smile. "Nope, not even our first time." Why did that sound so much better in my head?

"You got me there."

Why do I suddenly feel like a groupie? "I get it. This is all part of your one-night-only show."

"Not even close." He runs a hand through his hair. "I think it's more like a tour."

Yeah, not funny. "How do you do it?"

He holds back a smile. "I think you know the answer to that and you seemed to like it, babe."

That's the understatement of the year. More like dying to have more if it. "Not what I mean." I prop myself up, facing him. "How do you go from show to show, hooking up with random girls you'll never see again?" Oh God, did that just come out of my mouth. *Please don't let him refer to the article.* "I mean, you're a great guy and care so much about your fans. How can you use them?" Yeah, that might sound worse. Definitely not the best after sex conversation.

"I see it as giving the fans what they want."

"No one wants to be tossed out like yesterday's trash." For the love of God, Ali, stop talking. "I mean…"

"Think about it. Half-naked girls do just about anything to come backstage in the hopes of banging a guy in a band that they hardly know. For what… bragging rights? I'm not the one doing the using, babe."

Okay so he's got a point. It still just seems so wrong. "But these girls listen to your music like it's gospel and feel so strong and passionate about the band. It's like they're in love with you before they even meet you."

He nibbles at his lip. "I guess I never thought of it that way."

"You have fans that worship you. If you use the love 'em and leave 'em attitude they're bound to get hurt."

"The whole point is so no one gets hurt." He rolls over and sinks his head in the pillow.

Great, now I'm hitting a nerve. It's not that I expect him to change or declare his love for me. He needs to know what it's like from the woman's perspective. I guess this is some of the spice I added to the article that made him want my head on a platter. He may feel that way now.

"I wish it worked that way." I roll over and stare up at the area of chipped paint on the ceiling.

He turns his head toward me. "You know I don't think of you like that, babe. Right?"

I have no idea what he thinks of me or what the hell we're doing. He's made it more than clear that he never wants to settle down or be in a relationship. He wants to be free like the wind. Maybe he should be a Hell's Angel instead of a surfer.

I nod.

He pulls me close, and I lay my head on his chest. I really don't care about what the future holds. Maybe we'll never see each other again after he's finished recording and leaves L.A. Right now, I want to stop thinking about the future and burrow myself in his strong body that makes me feel like I did forever ago... happy.

"ALI." A SOFT TOUCH CARESSES MY CHEEK.

I barely muster enough energy to open an eyelid. "Hmm."

"We need to get up."

I blink a few times, willing my eyes to stay open. The dark room only lets in the slightest bit of moonlight from the window. It's probably the middle of the night. Is he trying for round two?

I jump up from the bed into a sitting positon. The clock radio reads 5:00 a.m. I search the room for Tyler. He stands by my dresser pulling a T-shirt over his head.

"Is something wrong?" *Oh no, please don't let my building be on fire.* From the heat sizzling off Tyler, I wouldn't doubt the whole town could burst into flames.

He sits next to me on the bed. "I want to take you somewhere."

I guess I should explain to him I'm not a morning person. I'd much rather party into the depths of the night than wake up before the sun. A rocker who's up before sunrise without partying all night. He's clearly full of surprises.

"If it's a diner for breakfast they'll still be open when the sun comes up." I lie back on the pillow.

"Nope, not that. Come on, it'll change your life." He runs a calloused finger from the side of my belly to my thigh.

Well, that did the trick. What's with all these life changing experiences? I mean, every time he's said those words something in me did change so it's not like he's lying. I never realized one person could change your life all the time. Then again, there's only one Tyler.

"Okay, I'm up." I stretch and turn toward him.

"Right back atcha." He leans over and smacks his lips against mine.

Hmm, maybe there's more to this early morning wake-up than I anticipated. I'm ready for more life-altering love.

He pulls away. "Trust me. You'll love it."

No doubt I will. So far his surprises are awesome. I hop out of bed. "Okay, should I wear anything in particular for this secret adventure?"

"A bathing suit." He grabs his keys from the nightstand and heads to the kitchen.

Oh God, please tell me he's not taking me to a photo shoot for his new album or something crazy like that. Models get up at all hours of the morning for shoots, and although that would be life changing, it sure as hell wouldn't be something I'd love.

"Where are we going?" I need to prepare myself for this… whatever it is.

"I'm sacrificing you to the shark that bit your foot," he yells from the kitchen.

Funny. At least I know I'm heading to the beach. Maybe we're heading to Cabo or some gorgeous beach that's a few hours away. Sipping on frozen drinks is a great way to spend the day. I slide on my swimsuit and throw a T-shirt and shorts on over it. "I'll bring my shotgun like Chief Brody."

He chuckles. "That only works if you've got an oxygen tank handy."

I toss a few towels into a beach bag and sling it around my shoulder. "Ready when you are, Captain."

WE PULL UP TO A SECLUDED STRETCH OF BEACH. THE SUN IS JUST rising over the horizon, sending golden specks along the dark blue water. Everything is serene, calm. The song of the seagull fills the air.

"Is this your favorite place to watch the sun rise?" I step out of the car, pushing the door closed.

"It's my favorite place to surf." He flashes a half smile. "Ready to hang ten with me?"

Is he serious? I can barely walk down the steps without falling, and he wants me to stand on a surfboard in the middle of the ocean without killing myself? Plus sharks swarm the water. "Are you trying to kill me?"

"Don't worry, I know CPR." He chuckles. "I'll show you the ropes... or the waves." He winks.

Oh well, I guess I've lived a pretty full life. A burial at sea wasn't what I expected. I'll probably go right into shock when the cold water hits me. I'm more of a lay-on-the-beach-and-watch-the-surfers kind of girl. How can I get myself out of this?

"Maybe I can just watch you... you know, get a feel for what it's all about before I try." At least that'll buy me some time.

"I know you're a doer, not a watcher." He takes my hand and guides me to a small cabana near the sand.

A tanned man with shoulder length brown hair and abs that look like they've been carved from a washboard nods toward Tyler.

"Hey, Dave, got a newbie to the break. Can you fix us up with some gear?" Tyler runs a hand through his hair.

"Hell yeah. Good to see you, bud. We'll have to catch some waves before you head back." Dave grabs two boards and a pair of black wetsuits. "What level is she at?"

"A zero." If there's a board with training wheels I want that one.

"Nice, a virgin." Dave hands Tyler the gear.

"Ready to be de-flowered." I smirk. The closest thing I've

come to doing something like this was when I decided I could man the sailboat by myself. Josh told me I wasn't strong enough to handle it without him so of course, that sounds like a challenge to me. When I forgot to duck and was knocked off the boat by the boom, Josh laughed so hard he almost rolled into the ocean with me. If I can avoid a repeat of that fiasco, I'll call this a win.

"Some nice waves out there." Dave forms a hang-ten with his fingers.

"Catch ya later." Tyler takes the boards, and we head to the water.

I stomp along the beach like I'm walking through quicksand. The cool, gritty grains twist into my shark-bite wound. Great, going in the ocean with an open wound, it's like the first rule of what not to do on every episode during shark week. I'm clearly losing my mind, or someone else is controlling it.

Tyler plops the board on the sand. "First lesson."

"I know this one, always put the board in the water." I smirk.

"Maybe you should quit writing and become a comedian." He sets his board next to mine. "Will you please give it a chance? You might even like it. It's happened to you before." He winks.

Giving him a chance isn't quite the same thing. As far as I'm aware, I wasn't in any danger of death by being with him. He's right. I should at least try it. Then if I hate it I'll never have to do it again. If I even get a chance to surf with Tyler again. A pit forms in my stomach. Not this again. We're just having fun that's all. No need to try and plan a future.

"Okay, I'm ready to hit the waves. Teach me, oh wise one." I kneel down on the board.

"First you need to learn how to stand." He lays on the board and gestures for me to lie on mine.

There's no way in hell I'm going to be able to stand on this flimsy foam board when I'm fighting the ocean's waves. Hope he enjoys watching me get dunked a million times. I lie flat on the board.

"Perfect, now stay in the center and pull yourself up to a kneeling position with your arms, like a gorilla." He moves from a lying position to standing in a second flat.

Really, a gorilla. I'll try to hold back the sex appeal. I use all the strength in my arms to pull myself to a kneeling position. A split second later, I lose balance and topple over the edge onto the sand. "I'm off to a great start."

"I know you can move better than that, babe." He runs a hand through his hair, flashing a half smile.

Heat creeps across my cheeks like a blaring sunburst. "Totally different scenario. I'm better in some than others." Holy crap, where did that come from. At this point, anything goes. I follow Tyler's instructions and plop up to a standing position on the board. "Oh my God, I did it."

He nods. "Try again. Practice makes perfect."

Logic to live by, we should put those words to work in other areas. I follow the steps three more times and hit the mark like a torpedo locking onto its target.

"You got it, babe. Ready to try it in the water?" Tyler grabs his board and heads toward the water line.

Butterflies swarm in my stomach. Maybe I should've written my own obituary before I got out of the car. At least I know it'll be grammatically correct. We slip on our wetsuits. Great, now I look like a seal, more appealing to the sharks. I take a deep breath and follow him to the water.

"We're starting out slow, babe. Staying in the white water." He drops his board in ankle deep water.

Oh God. This sounds so bad. White water rafting knocks dozens of people unconscious every year... or worse. I don't want to be anywhere near the white water. "Maybe we can start where it's calm."

"Trust me." He grabs my free hand and leads us to knee deep water.

The frigid ocean stuns my body. I can barely move a muscle.

If it was up to me, we'd be floating in a tube in the Caribbean. How does he have this hold on me... already?

"Stay here, in the water after the waves break. After you can stand up on the board in the white water, we can try catching a wave." He looks out to sea and lies on his board.

A wave crashes and breaks off into a ripple of white foam. Tyler jumps up as soon as the board moves and takes a standing position. He makes it look so damn easy. How could he do everything so... perfectly? No one should possess that much talent.

Okay, maybe I overreacted. Looks like the worst that can happen to me is looking like a drowned rat. I can deal with it. I lie on my board and wait until the white water pushes it forward. I follow the steps and pop up. My foot hits the edge of the board and I plunge over the side, face first into the salty water. How the hell is this fun?

Tyler straddles his board. "Good first try. Keep going."

I try at least a hundred more times with the same result. Balance seems to be key and when you're clumsy and uncoordinated, surfing is not for you. One last try before I bail. A big wave crashes behind me, sending a mist of salty water along my skin. I grab hold of my board and pop up, just like I did on the beach. My feet hit the foam board and I stand. The wave pushes me forward while the breeze blows through my hair. I'm flying. It's like I'm floating on air, part of the wave guided by the moon. Totally free.

I ride the wave to the knee-deep water and jump off. I get it. It's exhilarating, unmatched by anything else. A completely unique experience.

"What'd you think?" Tyler floats next to me.

"Life changing." I slick back my hair. "You always deliver."

"That's my motto." He winks. "You ready to catch more waves."

I shake my head. "I'm lucky the shark didn't finish me off. I'm ready to get out of this wetsuit and watch you impress me with your superior skills."

"I didn't do that last night?" He raises an eyebrow. "Kidding. I'm ready to catch some waves. See you on the beach, babe."

I yank off my painted on wetsuit and sit on the board. Tyler paddles out to the deeper water and floats on his board, waiting. The anticipation of holding out for the right wave requires the patience of a saint. How do you know if you should take what comes your way or wait for something great?

Tyler lets three waves go by, and then he spots what he's looking for. A massive wave lifts the ocean. He paddles forward, then pops up just in time to catch it. He glides across the surface like he's a feather floating in the wind. He bends down allowing the curl to engulf his body just before the wave breaks.

Is that what Tyler's looking for? The wave that he can't resist. He enjoys every second of it and then leaves right before the crushing blow. Am I destined to be left floating in the white water or carried off to sea?

10

REALITY CHECK

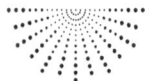

"You know this is all your fault, right?" I tap my fingers on my glass of iced tea.

"No need to thank me, darling." Chloe blows me a kiss from across the table.

"I wasn't going to." I sigh. "No more celebrating with you. All it leads to is hooking up with random guys who etched their way into my brain and now it's driving me crazy." I take a minute bite of my turkey sandwich on rye and toss it back on the plate. "It's like you gave me a brain tumor."

Chloe laughs, almost spitting her sparkling water all over the linen tablecloth. "Maybe you can turn the drama down a notch."

"Sorry... I'm ultra-stressed today. I've got that interview with Elle Crowley this afternoon."

"Ah, the drama continues." Chloe chuckles. "You'll do a great job, like always."

My first feature article and my brain is twisted into knots. I've got to focus. If I don't get every quote correct she'll probably sue me or something. Jane wants me to write a juicy gossip column and call it a feature article, so I need all my ducks in a row. Why did I agree to this?

"If you don't eat you're going to pass out on Elle's lawn, and she'll probably mistake you for one of the cheerleaders her husband bangs." Chloe raises her eyebrows.

"Funny." I take another bite of my sandwich.

If I could stop thinking about Tyler for a minute maybe, I'd be able to create some intense interview questions. So far, I'm doomed. I need to know where I stand with him. Life was so much easier a month ago. It's my own fault. I should've never agreed to go out with him. Sure, the first time was an alcohol-induced mistake, but everything afterwards was all me.

Deep down I know where I stand. He's been crystal clear about the fact that he doesn't want to be in a relationship... ever. He's free as a bird. I guess we do our thing until he leaves and then it's over. I'm not that girl, though. Of course, I'm pretty much breaking my number one rule, focus on work and stay away from the complications of love. How can he keep his feelings from interfering with his plans? Maybe I should take a lesson from him.

"He was so hot. After they finished playing their set I snuck around backstage," a girl brags from the table caddy-corner to us.

"Don't be ridiculous, you know it's not about him." Chloe tips her chin and gives me the famous get-a-grip stare.

I shrug. "No, but I'm sure it will be from some other girl in some other town."

"Are you looking for a marriage proposal or something?"

I drop the rest of my sandwich on the plate. "Yeah, 'cause rockers are the most faithful people on the planet. Once they're married, they stop their wild ways."

"I think you'll do just fine with your interview with Elle. You're two peas in a pod."

No need to get nasty. "That's a low blow."

She puts her hand over mine. "You know I love you, but you're turning into a bitter bitch for no reason." She sits back in the chair. "I won't let you do this to yourself. It's bad for your complexion."

I let out a chuckle. "The salt water is bad for my hair too."

"Ah yes, now you're a surfer girl." She sips her water. "Never thought I'd see that happen."

"I'm sure it's short lived. I'm probably one of many."

"Enlighten me. First, you want nothing to do with him, and now you don't want him with anyone else. What exactly do you want?"

And that's the million-dollar question. My heart knows exactly what it wants—to be safe from pain. If only my body and brain would follow suit I may have a chance of getting out of this unscathed.

I LEAF THROUGH THE STACK OF PAPERS ON MY DESK. TEN YEARS isn't enough time to prepare for this interview. Elle's probably seeing this as an opportunity to bash God knows who in *Entertainment Rocks!* magazine. My questions mean nothing, she'll push this in whatever direction she wants. I need to wrangle her enough to keep us both out of trouble. Ugh, but Jane wants something juicy. That's it. I can't win no matter how hard I try. I'll record our session and wing it. I drop the papers on my desk and rub my temple.

"Let me guess, hungover?" Jake stands near my desk, sipping coffee.

"More like my brain is ready to explode. No alcohol involved." I sit back in my chair.

"Hardly worth it. You out partying like a rock star... or with them?"

What's his problem lately? Ever since he discovered I was meeting Tyler outside of work, he's been acting like some jealous frat boy. I've got enough complications at the moment. No need for unnecessary drama. "Partying like a nerdy college girl during finals."

He snickers. "I heard about those nerdy girls."

"Yep, hanging out with a bunch of paperwork. Very wild. I don't think you can handle it." Hate to break it to him but whatever I do outside of work is none of his business.

My phone vibrates, jumping across the desk. Tyler lights up in red letters across the screen. I swear he has Jake radar.

Jake leans over and smirks. "Another interview with the band or do you guys stay in touch now?"

I press the ignore call button and send him to voicemail. "I've got something in the works."

"I bet you do." He raises an eyebrow. "See ya later neighbor."

He shows up when I'm at my worst and then brings me down a level lower than that. What happened to supporting each other? He never showed any interest in me, so it's not like he's jealous. He seems to want to compete like it's a game of who has the best assignment or who screws up the most. I've played enough games, so he's out of luck.

One more quick check of my email and I head out to meet Elle. My stomach flip-flops. *Please don't let me say anything she can use against me.* It's like I'm the wallflower invited to the prom by the heartthrob football God, way out of my league yet again.

ALI,

Please have a draft of your article to me by Friday. Remember, you are a professional. Although we want to be friendly to our clients, we are reporters, not their friends. In their eyes, we are the enemy who can break them with the written word. Record everything and document all direct quotes. I look forward to seeing your work.

JANE

. . .

WHAT IS JANE GETTING AT? OTHER THAN STUMBLING INTO HER office I've always been professional. Heat flashes through my body. Unless she knows about Tyler and has misconstrued our relationship. Only one person could've told her. Jake.

I SLAM MY CAR INTO PARK IN FRONT OF THE INTRICATE WROUGHT iron gate boasting the words *The Crowley's* directly in the middle of the magnificent structure. How could Jake go and tell Jane about Tyler? I mean, it's not like they're both vying for my affection. Jake is a friend, nothing more, or so I thought. I just don't get how he'd benefit from sabotaging me. If we were both trying to get the same piece at least he'd have a reason to act like an immature tattle-tale, but we each have our own agenda. Plus, he has no idea about my relationship, or whatever it is, with Tyler. I've got to shake off this negative energy and kill this interview with Elle. Success is the best revenge.

An intercom set into the brick column on the left blinks. Of course it's secure, fans can get crazy when it comes to football. Yeah, kind of like the way groupies act at a concert. My stomach drops to the floor. Maybe Tyler has a similar system, although L.A. and Kansas might as well be on different planets. What's his demeanor with the fans? I mean, all the entire band does is talk about how much they love the fans, and give them as much of their time and attention as possible. So exactly how much love does Tyler give his fans? As much as Nash does?

Oh God, I sound like some jealous girlfriend. First of all, I'm not even sure where we stand at the moment. Second, it's his career and meeting fans is part of the deal. Third, Nash and Elle are not me and Tyler, so I'm not destined to fall into their train-wreck of a relationship.

I step out of the car and walk toward the intercom. Okay, time to clear my head of anything not related to this interview. I take a deep breath and press the button.

"Ali Whitman. I'm here to interview Elle for *Entertainment Rocks!* magazine."

"I'll buzz you in." A voice crackles through the intercom.

The gates slowly open, causing *The Crowley's* emblem to separate. How symbolic I jump back into the car and follow the driveway to a monstrous home that can rival the white house. Huge white pillars, probably made of marble, adorn the front porch of the two-story mansion. Tan bricks lead up to a carved wooden door that looks like an entrance to a castle. I pull around the circular driveway, with a mermaid fountain in the middle, and park my car.

Everything about this place is over the top. I can't help but think of Elle as a princess trapped in a tower. Sure, she can leave anytime she wants, but that would be like being banished to the dark forest. Maybe that's part of the reason she stays with Nash despite his... downfalls. Why else would she stay with him?

I guess that's what I'm here to find out. I grab my briefcase and march up the marble steps. Alright Ali, get your game face on. Whatever happens with this feature paves the way for future offers. I've got to keep a level head and leave all emotions far away from the paper. I pat down my black pin-striped skirt and ring the doorbell.

Heels click, louder by the second. I take a deep breath. The last time I felt this nervous was when I trudged through the aisle of the church, half blinded by tears as I stepped on the altar to give Josh's eulogy. I knew I'd never be the same person after I left. It's kind of ridiculous. There are so many times in my life I should've felt this way and didn't. Does my brain know something I don't or is it back in self-defense mode?

The noise subsides. Elle pulls open the door and flashes a million-dollar smile. Her long brown hair falls down her back in perfect loose curls, flowing onto her pink sundress. She's the epitome of beauty, exactly who you'd expect a famous quarterback's wife to look like. If you put her in a Victorian dress, she can grace the cover of a romance novel with Fabio. Deep blue eyes sweep my body.

I hold out my shaky hand. "Ali Whitman. Nice to meet you."

She shakes it and takes a step back. "Elle Crowley. Please, come in."

The inside of the house is something you'd see on *Lifestyles of the Rich and Famous*. A crystal chandelier, about the size of my car, hangs in the foyer reflecting prisms of light all around. A double staircase leads to a huge hallway, adorned with numerous colorful paintings and a dark red oriental rug. I scan the room like I'm in a museum, taking myself out of the moment.

Elle clears her throat. "I have some refreshments set out on the patio for us."

I blink a few times and pull myself back into reality. Great, I'm making the same impression as a star-struck fan. "Please lead the way." I fidget with my fingers and follow her out to the veranda.

An oval shaped in-ground pool adorned with a waterfall sits in the middle of the property, surrounded by a pool house that is almost the size of my apartment building and landscaping that probably cost more than my college education. An enormous screened in gazebo with lights and a television is to the right of the pool. The cobblestone walkway continues to tennis courts, a basketball court, and an area of pristine grass that Nash might use as his own personal football field. The Playboy mansion has nothing on this place, although from what I hear some of the stories may be similar.

Elle stops at the fanciest picnic table I've ever seen overlooking a pond and gardens. "Make yourself at home." She pours two glasses of lemonade.

I nibble my lip and pop open my briefcase. "I'll be recording our interview to make sure everything is quoted accurately." I know I put it in here, where the hell is it? My body temperature rises at least fifteen degrees as I search for the little black tape recorder that will serve as my saving grace. A bead of sweat rolls down my hairline.

"You're new at this, right?" Elle crosses her legs and sits back in her chair.

And there goes all hopes of taking the professional approach. No matter how hard I plan every last detail of an interview, I wind up dropping the ball somehow. Maybe I'm not cut out for field reporter, or maybe my brain realizes that what Jane wants me to do and what I want to do are on opposite ends of the spectrum. Everyone's got to start somewhere so I've got to go as far as I can with *Entertainment Rocks!* and get my name out there. The name I make might stick with me forever, so I've got to decide what I want it to stand for.

I glance over at Elle. It's like she's a lion, watching the zebra prance through the field before taking it down. I've heard all the stories and know exactly what I'm dealing with. Now, I just need to survive this interview and write a feature that wows the world. Yep, nothing like setting a nearly unattainable goal. I bump my finger against hard plastic. Thank God, here it is. I pull out the tape recorder and set it on the table, along with my pen and legal pad. I press record.

"I've recently took the field reporter position at *Entertainment Rocks!*" I click open my pen and grab my pad.

She puts her hand over mine. "I was new once too. I get it." She sips her lemonade. "I like you. You remind me of myself another lifetime ago."

Wait, where's the smart talking succubus that spends her time ruining other people's lives until they mimic hers? Maybe she acts like your friend and cuts your throat in the end, like half the horror movies I've seen. The killer ends up being the last person you expect. Or maybe it's all a publicity ploy. Is Elle really the person the media makes her out to be? Probably not, the truth always seems a little less interesting. When Josh had his accident, there were stories floating around from all angles. Anything from he was wasted on pills and booze to he was getting a blowjob while driving. Bastards. I'll never forgive the people who insisted on tarnishing his reputation... never. I won't let anyone else go through that either. Today, the world finds out about the real Elle Crowley.

"The piece I'm featuring is titled Behind the Bench: The Untold Story of Elle and Nash Crowley." I sip my lemonade, trying to steady my hand as I lift the glass. "So let's start at the beginning, how did you and Nash meet?"

She leans back and flashes a small smile. "Back in college." Her face instantly lights up, like it's Christmas morning and Santa left a puppy. "Freshman year we ran into each other at Evans Hall... literally ran into each other while we were both trying to find English 101." She chuckles. "Hard to believe Nash was uncoordinated. It's amazing how things change over the years." She clears her throat. "Anyway, we pretty much didn't leave each other's sight from that day on."

"I haven't seen that story in any other interviews before. It's a cute way to meet. I'm probably the clumsiest person on earth, but it didn't benefit me in the love department."

She nods. "No one's ever asked how we met before. They're not interested in those kind of stories." She taps her fingers on her glass. "How about you, are you single?"

Oh boy, this interview is certainly taking an interesting turn. Hey, whatever keeps her talking about things that have never been published in an interview before. It looks like I'm on my way to getting an exclusive interview. "I'm dating someone right now." If what we're doing is dating.

"Is he a reporter too?" She raises an eyebrow.

I shake my head. "No, he's a musician." Okay, when I hear it out loud it sounds like a conflict of interest. A reporter dating a musician, based on the rules of entertainment we are supposed to be mortal enemies.

"Back in college I didn't have to share Nash with anyone. He was all mine. Now... I share him with the world. I think you're about to find out exactly what that's like."

What is she doing? It's like she thinks we're kindred souls or something. I hate to break it to her, but I'm not her. There's no way in hell I'd put up with a guy who's unfaithful.

I leave through my papers. "What's it like to be married to a famous athlete?"

She smirks. "There's a question I'm used to. I'll give you my honest answer this time. It's great, a dream come true, and at the same time it's a nightmare." She locks eyes with me. "You probably know exactly what I'm talking about."

No, but I may very well be on my way to finding out. Her words mimic something Jenna and Lexie might say. Very philosophical, now if I can translate that into English. "I get it, good and bad, just like anything else."

Sadness clouds her face. "I can have anything I could possibly want, but nothing I need."

What the hell does that mean? It's like she's talking in riddles. I can't print that without a clear explanation. Maybe she's trying to tell me some topics are off limits. "Do you want to move on to the next question?"

She flashes a meek smile. "Let me see your list."

I hand her the paper and fidget with my fingers while she peruses it. Barbara Walters sure as hell wouldn't conduct an interview like this. I might as well have Elle come up with her own questions and write the interview herself.

She sets the paper on the table. "How about we nix the questions?"

"Okay, we can try a different approach." Oh God, I'm way out of my league. How the hell am I supposed to conduct an interview with no questions?

"What's the one question you are dying to know but don't want to ask?" Elle sits up straight. "Throw it at me."

"Why do you stay with Nash when you know he cheats on you?" I cover my mouth with my hand and quickly drop it. The blood drains from my face. Did I just say that out loud? I look down at the table unable to lift my eyes. She's probably going to throw me out. I mean, if someone said that to me I'd clock them. It's no one's business what she does in her marriage other than her and Nash's. I get it, and I'm here to find out about their life together, but some things are better left unsaid. The subscribers can read between the lines and come up with their own theories.

I take a deep breath. "I'm sorry. It's really none of my business. Just tell me what you want the public to know about you, Nash, and the reality of being married to a star football player." I slowly lift my head.

She sighs. "It's a fair question, and you're the first reporter to actually ask it." She pulls her chair closer to the table. "You want to know the truth? Here it is. When I met Nash he was a real guy; nervous, unsure of where life was going to take him, and full of passion. If I could dream up my perfect man, it was him. We had it all those four years and they were the best times of my life. We shared everything, and it was almost like we were the only two people on earth. Nothing else mattered. I never met anyone like him, completely unique in every way yet familiar, like we were made for only each other."

"It sounds like you found your soulmate. How can anything change that?" I don't get it. If you find the perfect person wouldn't everything else in life take second place? I mean, when you find the "right" one you can get through anything together.

"He turned into Nash "the crusher" Crowley. Once there was buzz about him going pro everything changed. It's like a switch flipped inside him, and he went from a man to a God. Fans crowded him after games, pushing me far into the sidelines. He started spending more time off the field with the team than he ever had. I was almost like one of his frantic fans, trying anything to get his attention. It was like I took a backseat to the pigskin. I was okay with that at first, I mean it's his career. Everything he worked so hard for." She gulps her lemonade. "One time when he had a girl on each shoulder for a picture, I couldn't take it anymore. I walked away, swearing I'd never come back."

I can understand a little of what she's going through. Josh didn't have hopes of going pro, but he was the "Golden Boy" of our small town. The cheerleaders hung on his every word, and just about every girl wanted to date him, but he never made me feel like I was his silver medal. "What made you change your mind?"

Her lips upturn to a smile. "He must've left at least two dozen voicemails on my phone and sent flowers every week. I ignored him for two months but when he had a singing telegram sent to my door inviting me to meet him at the 50-yard line I thought he was turning back into the Nash I fell in love with. I trudged down to the 50-yard line, wrapping my scarf around my face to protect me from the frigid wind, but he wasn't there. My heart sunk, and just as I was about to walk off the field, the PA system started playing *I Don't Want To Miss A Thing* by Aerosmith which was our song since the sophomore homecoming dance. I turned around and Nash was on one knee in the middle of the 50-yard line, holding the most beautiful diamond ring I've ever seen."

"That's so romantic. Your life sounds like a movie." I jot down a few notes onto the pad. The woman readers are going to fall in love with Nash again once I get this story out there. But, that's not how the story ends.

"We got married, Nash signed his first pro contract, and it all started again. Only this time, I was pregnant in a new city and couldn't just walk away hoping he'd stop and see what he's missing. Then it got worse. The more popular Nash became, the more attention seeking fans appeared, especially the female ones. They acted like half-naked prostitutes, hanging all over him for pictures, asking him to sign their breasts. And I had to stand by and watch because the coach insisted it's all a show, part of the package. Well, then Coach started spending more and more time with Nash, taking him to strip clubs, and God knows where else. He was coming home at all hours of the night. And then he was on the road with the team, and I was home with my daughter Shana." Her eyes well with tears but she quickly wipes them away.

"The rumors started, tabloids published pictures of him with other women. Every time I confronted him, he swore up and down it wasn't true, but I can't trust him anymore. He's not that handsome guy that ran into me trying to navigate to class. He's someone I never see, and don't even know anymore. The bitterness starts to take over. First, it's little jabs or sarcastic remarks, then it's hoping he loses the game after seeing something in a tabloid. Hell, there's even times I wished he'd get injured so he can come home and we can be the Nash and Elle we once were again." She lets out a deep breath. "So I guess to answer your question. I stay because I don't want to let go of the Nash I fell in love with and I believe he still exists."

Why does this scenario seem all too familiar? Half-naked fans hanging on his every word, being separated and letting your mind concoct scenarios that you're not entirely sure are false, growing apart because your life suddenly takes a backseat to the rising career of your spouse. It's like the future is mapped out in front of me and it's looking pretty bleak. I'm on my way to becoming Elle.

11
OPPORTUNITY

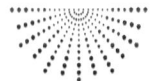

EARTHQUAKES, SHARK ATTACKS, READY FOR ANOTHER DISASTER, BABE?
Interesting choice of words and they always seem more powerful in print. Am I ready for what's next? Even though Elle pretty much told me exactly what it's like, full of heartache and regret, I still can't stop my heart from fluttering every time I see his name flash across my cell phone screen. I text Tyler back.

I draw the line at ritualistic sacrifices;)

Hmm, no promises. I can't control myself when I'm with you.

Footsteps pound from behind me. I flip my phone over face down on my desk. No need to show anyone else my personal discussions. Especially after the stunt Jake pulled. What an asshole. Whoever said girls fight dirty never worked at *Entertainment Rocks!* I mean, there's really no benefit to him other than getting on Jane's good side. Big deal, she's got a heart of stone so once he's no longer useful to her, he'll be right back here, except alone.

"Hey neighbor. Read your article. Interesting take, you went all girl power with this one." Jake sips his coffee and walks to his cubicle.

He has no idea of what girl power can accomplish... yet.

Dammit, I left Tyler hanging. I glance the length of the hallway to make sure Jake isn't in view of my phone and quickly snatch it up.

Yeah, I know what that's like. Is this your way of asking me out?

Ready to have your world rocked... again?

What did you have in mind? I'm starting to think he doesn't write lyrics. He tends to be a one-liner, of course, it's a good one, and it always works.

Let me give you a glimpse into my world. Pick you up Saturday at 10 a.m.

So what's up his sleeve? His world is a universe full of so many activities. Most people choose one thing and stick to it but not Tyler. He's kind of like a renaissance man, a master of many trades. God knows what I'm in for Saturday.

It's a date ;) Okay, maybe I should stop with the winky smiley faces. I mean, it's like I'm a slutty teenager.

Great article by the way. Lexie really loved it.

Tyler read my article? And Lexie read it too? No way in hell I'd think anyone from Devil's Garden would read anything I wrote again... ever. If Lexie loved it, then that means she can relate to everything Elle said. Normally, it's amazing to connect with readers but knowing that Lexie found the story remotely interesting scares the crap out of me.

"You've got mail," blares from my computer.

I click on the link.

Ali,

Please meet me in my office in fifteen minutes. I'd like to discuss your Elle Crowley piece.

Jane

Great, she didn't even include a salutation. Not a good sign. I get it, it's not what she expected since it's the complete opposite of my debut article but it's real. Plus, she's the one who left for assignment and put her assistant in charge of handling the feature.

I take a deep breath and shut off my cell phone. Okay, no more distractions. I need to prepare myself for the epic battle I'm about to face. I slug some water and pop a piece of spearmint gum into my mouth. Maybe I can choke on it as my means of escape if things get too out of hand. I glance at my watch. Being late on top of everything else might push her over the edge. I pat down my skirt and high-tail it to Jane's office.

Every time I'm within twenty feet of Jane's office it's like I'm on another planet. Everyone scurries, clinging folders to their chest and refraining from speaking. The only sound is the clicking of shoes against the tile. Fear can make people do crazy things. Why do I feel like I'm about to learn this firsthand?

Claire spots me and trots over, opening the door. I smile. For some reason, I can't bring myself to thank her. Maybe because I know what's about to happen.

Jane looks up from her desk. "Ali, have a seat."

I fidget with my fingers and plop into the hard leather chair. It's almost as cold as her stare. "What would you like to discuss?" Like I don't know the answer to that one.

She takes off her glasses and sets them on the table. "The feature wasn't at all what I expected."

Her eyes peer into me. A chill runs down my spine. Dear God, she's more intimidating without the glasses. "Is something wrong?"

She shrugs. "You tell me. Is this the piece we discussed?"

I nod. "I was completely honest and wrote everything that was described." I nibble at my nails. Well, she wanted me to write a brutally honest piece without sugar coating any of the details, and that's exactly what I did.

"The piece portrays Nash as the villain and Elle as a victim. Is that what you think she is?" Jane pulls out the article and scans the pages.

Yes, she and Nash were both victims. Their lives killed their love, and that's the bottom line. It seems you can have extreme success or extreme love but not both. "I recorded the entire interview and wrote the brutal, honest truth she told me without leaving out anything… just like last time."

Jane taps her pen on her desk. "Just keep in mind that you need to leave your personal life out of your writing." She slides on her glasses. "Claire will hand you your assignment on your way out."

Jane was much easier on me than I thought. Maybe she couldn't argue with the facts. I wrote an honest piece and recorded the interview. It just wasn't the controversial feature she was hoping for. Plus, she's kind of a hypocrite. The Devil's Garden interview went sour because my personal feelings inadvertently got in the way, which is exactly what she liked about the article. I guess if it brings in better ratings, she can overlook what sparked the story.

I bolt out of her office before she finds more discussion points about the article or being a field reporter for *Entertainment Rocks!* Once the door closes behind me I let out the deep breath I didn't know I'd been holding. Okay, that's over, and I'm happy with the outcome. Now, on to the next project.

I stop at Claire's desk. "Hi. I'm here to pick up my next assignment."

Claire nibbles her lip. "Let me know if you have any questions."

I grab the manila envelope and sneak into the elevator right before the door closes. So far I hit the music scene, then sports, maybe this time it'll be someone in television or movies. I open the file and leaf through the pages. Wait… this can't be right. I slam the file shut and double check the front of the folder. I scan the tab and make sure Claire hasn't handed me the incorrect file. Ali Whitman blares in red ink across the tan tab. Yep, no mistake here. It's mine.

~

CHLOE STABS A CUCUMBER WITH HER FORK. "YOU'RE JOKING, right?"

I shake my head and tear into my double cheeseburger. "Wish I was." I slug a gulp of cola. "Next stop Foo Foo's Pet Spa." My stomach turns as I hear the words leave my lips.

"Look on the bright side, maybe you'll meet a celebrity and can fire up your own interview." She drops her fork in her half eaten salad. "It's not the end of the world, darling."

Yeah, easy for her to say. She's not the one trying to become a respected reporter. "Nope, just the end of my career, which barely started by the way." I shovel a load of fries into my mouth.

Chloe pushes my dish away. "Getting fat won't make things better."

I shrug. I need something… anything to give me some sort of pleasure. Memories of my night with Tyler flash through my brain. Tingles sweep through me. "A little indulgence never hurt anyone."

She chuckles. "Sounds like famous last words." She slugs her water. "You can make any article great, no matter what it's about. Do your thing. Write an awesome Ali Whitman piece."

"The subject matter makes a hell of a difference. What am I supposed to report on, the most popular dog shampoo fragrance?"

"Add a little spice… like Nash Crowley spends ten thousand dollars a year on manicures for his dog but won't buy his wife the car she always dreamed of."

My lips upturn to a smile. "That's ridiculous… and I've had enough of the Crowleys for one lifetime."

"What I'm trying to say is that you can turn this article in any direction you want." She blows me a kiss. "Tootles, I've got to head. Keep me posted on the pooch pampering."

"Funny." I slug the rest of my soda and wave.

She's right. I've got to make the best of this. What other choice do I have? If only Jake didn't see that text on my phone. If there's anything I learned in my time on this earth, it's that the past can't be changed and dwelling on it only makes things worse. I'm going to rock this article and hit Jake where it hurts, on the printed page.

THE AROMA OF WET DOG AND OATMEAL SHAMPOO FLOW THROUGH my cubicle. So Foo Foo's was not at all what I expected. Actually, it pretty much mimicked a regular spa except the patrons were furry and probably nicer than the ones I sit next to when waiting for a manicure. Everything was spotless and extremely professional. The pricing was outrageous, but then again, pets are family and should get to enjoy the best life has to offer. Of course, no celebrities showed up. They send their assistants to handle these types of occasions. I should've known.

I fire up my computer. If there were a pet salon back in Seamist, I would have taken Josh's Golden Retriever, Buddy there and given him the works. If any dog in the world deserved to be treated like a king for a day, it's Buddy. Whenever I'd go to Josh's house Buddy's tail wagged so vigorously I heard the thump of it banging against the wall all the way at the end of the driveway. No creature in the world was more loyal. Josh's parents even took Buddy to the funeral, and he laid right beside the casket the whole time, staring down as they lowered his best friend into the ground. A dull ache fills my chest. The few times I left my house after that, I'd see Buddy sitting on Josh's porch staring into space and when he saw me, the thump of his tail echoed like a distant memory of happiness. My walks became less frequent. It was just too hard. Josh was everywhere, and I couldn't handle any more pain. But then I couldn't get Buddy off my mind. He lost his best friend and rather than console him, I left him too. A stray tear runs down my face. He's probably sitting on the porch right now staring off into space and wondering what he did wrong to make everyone leave him.

"You okay?" Claire stands in the opening of my cubicle clutching a stack of folders.

I wipe away a few more tears. "Yeah, just missing an old friend."

She hands me a paper. "You got a message." She gives me a quick once over and slowly walks away.

Why is Claire hand delivering a message instead of calling or emailing me? My stomach drops to the floor. Oh God, Jane must have something up her sleeve. I mean, a handwritten note is probably the most private way to give a message. Hackers can get into emails, and phone calls can be traced, but a handwritten note is one of the only things that can be completely destroyed without any evidence of it ever existing. I run my thumb over the post-it.

Wow, if my mind would only wander like this more often maybe I could write fiction novels rather than interviews. Claire was probably on her way back here and it was just easier to stop at my desk. Jane already told me exactly how she felt about my feature and punished me with this dog spa story. What else could she possibly do to me? Ah, note to self, never ask that question.

I set the note down on my desk and gently scan the blue ink. The words slowly come into focus.

Ali,

Kate Winters from Newswatch Weekly Magazine would like to speak with you. Please call her back at 555-200-3070.

A kaleidoscope of butterflies flutter in my stomach. Oh my God, *Newswatch Weekly* wants to talk to me? I've sent out at least a dozen applications to them but was rejected for every position. There's no way they'd be interested in the stories I've written so far. *Newswatch Weekly* is on their way to being the next *Time Magazine.* I look over the note again.

I get it. This is one of Jake's little jokes, and he managed to get

Claire in on it. Asshole. He knows my dream is to write for a magazine like this. It's my own damn fault for telling him. Now I see why Claire didn't want to send an email, no proof of this nonsense on the company server. I'm sure calling this number will send me to some stupid message saying, "You got punked." Way to act mature, like a professional. Well, I'll play along with his little game. Girls invented this type of warfare, and he's about to get annihilated.

I grab my cell phone and dial, tapping my heels against the floor as the phone rings. Maybe if Jake were a little more creative, he'd do better in this business. I mean, in 7th grade Rachel Higgins sent me a letter that was supposedly from Justin Timberlake asking me out to prom. At least she put in a little more effort and mailed the damn thing. Plus, it was well-written, unlike Jake's cheesy articles. I guess I'm stooping to his level for even calling, but I need to get this settled once and for all.

"*Newswatch Weekly* Magazine, how can I direct your call?" A voice says.

Oh my God, it's the real number for *Newswatch Weekly.* Great, I'm about to make a fool of myself. I glance at the note. "Kate Winters, please."

"Thank you. Please hold."

My heart thumps like the woodpecker back in Seamist that always seemed to wake me up at six in the morning every single day. I know, I'll just tell Miss Winters that Jake gave me a message that she called. Then he'll look like the irresponsible, unprofessional, asshole that he is.

"Kate Winters."

Oh God, this was so much easier in my head. I clear my throat and swallow hard. "Hello, Miss Winters, this is Ali Whitman. I received a messaged that you'd like to speak to me?" My voice shakes.

"Ah, yes, Ali. I heard you went through quite the ordeal."

Which one? My life this far has been a series of ordeals, most of them unfavorable. "What do you mean?" It's all I can say.

"The earthquake. I was stuck in an elevator once for three minutes, and it felt like an eternity."

How does she know I was stuck in an elevator? I wasn't interviewed by the news and no one made too big a deal about it at work. "Not the best scenario for those of us who are claustrophobic. Did the rescuers tell you about the aftermath?"

She muffles the receiver for a second. "No, my brother owns Sunset records. Tyler's band is recording their new album, and he told everyone about the earthquake. He also mentioned you were a reporter."

Oh my God, Tyler's almost as connected as the mafia. And this phone call, it's real. Not a prank but genuinely real, and Tyler's the reason Kate is talking to me. After the article and the meeting with his band that went sour, Tyler stuck his neck out for me knowing everyone else with him at the studio wants my head on a stick. Heat flashes through me like wildfire.

"Yes, I'm currently writing for *Entertainment Rocks!* magazine, which is how I met Tyler." Okay, so it's a lie, but it sounds so much better than the truth.

"How would you feel about writing a piece about the earthquake for us? Of course, it would be an informative piece about the effects of being trapped in an elevator during a natural disaster. The fact that you were trapped in with a rock star is an interesting twist."

Oh my God, am I stuck in a dream? I press my lips together, desperately trying to prevent myself from screaming YES into the receiver. I swallow and take a deep breath. "Yes, I'd love to write for *Newswatch Weekly*. How long of a piece would you like?"

"Wonderful. We'd need the story in one week. Around 2000 words is a good length. Oh, and run through your contract with *Entertainment Rocks!* quickly to make sure you're able to freelance. Most contracts for new reporters allow that option." She muffles the phone again. "Please give me a call later this week and we'll set up a lunch meeting. I'm looking forward to working with you."

"Yes, me too, Kate. Thank you."

I drop the cell phone on my desk and lean back in my chair. It's really happening. I've got my once in a lifetime shot, all courtesy of Tyler. Normally I'd find a million reasons why I should work my way up on my own and never take charity from anyone... especially the guy I'm currently hooking up with, but it's different this time. Tyler might have gotten me the big break I've been hoping for, but the rest is up to me. Time to start researching everything I can about near death experiences, earthquakes, claustrophobia, and the power to resist the hero standing right in front of you. I guess I need some help with the last one.

An ear to ear grin bursts through. I can't help it. For the first time since I can remember my will power is at an all-time low and I love it. The stars aligned and turned my life into a glimpse of what it once was... perfect. I gaze around the rows of cubicles, watching the few people staring at me while they're pretending to do something else. The office staff probably thinks I'm way too excited for my pampered pooch article. Who cares? For once, I'm savoring every second. Oh, but first I need to thank a certain someone.

Maybe he tossed my name to Kate for some publicity for Devil's Garden or he could've wanted to help make my dreams come true since his already have. No matter, the result is still the same and if it helps us both in some way, even better.

I tap the buttons on my cell phone and dial Tyler.

"Tyler's phone. Speak to me."

A chill runs through my blood. My luck just ran out. The condescending tones from Jenna's voice rip through me.

"Hello, I haven't got all day." Her voice drips with sarcasm.

Of course, my name's probably flashed on his screen once the phone rang so she knows exactly who's she's talking to.

"Tyler please." I sigh.

"Umm, I think you and Tyler spent enough time together for one lifetime. The rest of us have certainly had enough of you for eternity."

Looks like we're off to a great start.

"Listen, Jenna, we all got off on the wrong foot. I understand your hatred for me, but I really need to talk to Tyler. Can you please put him on?"

She taps her fingernails on the receiver. "Naw, don't think so. On either case."

"What's that supposed to mean?" Okay, so that came out a little harsher than I wanted.

"Umm, you have no idea how much I despise you, but the fires of a thousand hells comes to mind. And I'm not putting Tyler on. If you really care about him, stay the fuck away from him. All you do is bring him down and if you don't realize it, re-read the article you wrote. We've all had enough of the Ali Whitman experience." She ends the call.

In a split second the joyous euphoria turns to utter disgust. I get it, I screwed up and it affected Tyler's career yet he's trying to help mine. I've got to make this right, with the article, with the band, and with Jenna. Is it even possible to do anything to melt Jenna's cold heart or am I about to make a deal with the devil?

DECISIONS

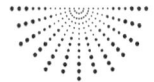

ETHICS, MORAL VALUE, INTEGRITY... THEY'RE PRETTY MUCH IN THE eye of the beholder. Okay, maybe I shouldn't have hacked into the *Entertainment Rocks!* files to find Tyler's address but what other choice did I have? Jenna managed to highjack his phone like some deranged ex-girlfriend. Except for the fact that she's never dated Tyler and has this "mother bear" complex. I get it, they all watch out for each other, but she takes it to a whole new level. Time to break out the claws and finish this once and for all.

I sigh. Why do I let her do this to me? I'm right back in Seamist walking with my head held high and Josh at my side right after I'm crowned Homecoming Queen, sneering at Krissy Brown. Of course, Krissy's plot to steal Josh by walking into the boy's locker room and snapping a selfie with him was so asinine. When she posted it with the caption, *Look Who I Intercepted,* my heart shattered. I knew Josh would never cheat, not in a million years, but I hated her for making me doubt him for that one second. She turned me into someone I don't want to be, just like Jenna's doing now. Josh got her back by posting a pic of the whole football team giving a thumbs up with the caption, *Krissy intercepted us all.* She gained the reputation she deserved, dirty slut. Even though Jenna is astronomically more diabolical than Krissy, she'll get what she deserves eventually, from our good friend karma.

Things don't get easier when you're out in the real world. People mature, but they take the conniving and deceit to a whole new level. Everything's magnified. People are smarter and want to bring you down worse than they did back then. It's like going from the farm team to the big leagues.

I grip the steering wheel and glance at the GPS Almost there. Thank God Tyler has a place of his own when he stays down here, and Santa Monica is the perfect spot, close enough to L.A. with the ocean in your backyard. Living with a group of people day in and day out must be pure hell sometimes, especially when they're cramped in a tour bus together and one of them is an evil demon from hell. Privacy lines get crossed on a daily basis. He probably doesn't even realize Jenna had his phone and I'm sure she deleted the call log so there's no evidence of me trying to get in touch with him. She's like a serial killer, covering her tracks to hide her path of destruction. Of course, I'm acting like a stalker at the moment.

The GPS sounds, "Pull to the right to your destination."

I park the car and glance over at a cute blue bungalow. A surfboard leans against the second floor white railing, adding to the breathtaking view of the beach. Yep, everything about this place screams Tyler. I made it... now what?

This whole scenario played out much better in my head. What's gotten into me? I never rush into anything without a plan. It's like I'm running on pure adrenaline, letting passion take over and stopping at nothing to reach my goal. What happened to calm, cool, conservative Ali? Tyler turns me into a whole different version of myself, one I hardly know.

Okay, time to get back to reality. I'm not in some rom-com about to hold up a boom box and expecting Tyler to come running out professing his love to me. I'll just tell him the truth, or at least a version of it.

I step out of my car at a snail's pace and walk up the steps to Tyler's door. A warm breeze of salty air caresses my face, taking some of my nervous energy with it. I lift my hand but can't seem to will myself to knock. More self-defense or does my brain realize I approached this situation the wrong way?

I take a deep breath. Nothing about Tyler and I is rational. None of it makes sense, but I know that if I walk away right now, I'll regret it. There's nothing worse than wishing you could change the past. I knock on the door and take a step back. My heart thumps against my chest, louder than the crash of the waves.

Tyler pulls open the door and leans in the door jam. "Ah, you heard about the 15-second tube I rode and rushed down for dibs on the story." He scrunches his eyebrows. "Should I grab my board for a picture?"

A drop of water falls from his hair, sliding down his shirtless body. I follow the droplet down his sculpted pec right down to his six-pack abs. It slides underneath the elastic of his board shorts. No need for a picture, the image etches itself into my brain. The sun glistens off his still-wet body, sending sparkles of light across his skin. Wait, why did I come here again? Oh right. Sticking to this surf story might help break the ice.

I nod. "The locals called up the magazine. Said we'd be crazy if we missed this story." I nibble my lip. "I told them I'll take it, I owe you one." Great job, Ali. Nothing like conjuring up bad memories of the recent past.

"Yeah, I'll need to sign off on this one before it goes live." He runs a hand through his hair. "Did you have to pay off the mafia to find me?"

I flash a half smile. "Something like that." Okay, he's dying to know why I showed up at his house uninvited. Here goes nothing.

"I wanted to thank you. I tried to call, but that didn't work out so well so I did some investigating on my own." Kind of the truth. I fidget with my fingers.

"Maybe investigative reporter is more your thing, babe." He steps to the side. "Come on in."

I step into the small, tiled foyer. Ah, a beach lover's dream, from the light blue and green motif to the paintings of the ocean gracing the walls, right down to the fake palm tree in the corner of the room. A tan couch sits in the middle of a large living room across from a huge television. Seashells and coral decorate the end tables. It kind of reminds me of home, except every house back in Seamist has at least one lighthouse knick-knack. Tyler brings on more memories of home than anyone I've ever met since I left. This place had to come furnished; no way would Tyler omit band posters or rock and roll paraphernalia.

"You've got a great place here." I do a quick once-over and focus on Tyler.

"Thanks. Best of everything, the beach and only a half-hour from L.A." He plops on the couch. "So you said something about thanking me." He winks.

Our eyes meet, and I drift away into an amazing place where everything's perfect, and the only thing that exists is Tyler and I. A plethora of ways to thank Tyler flow through my brain, all of them requiring full contact and no clothing.

I sink into the couch cushion next to him. "Kate from *Newswatch Weekly* called." I shift my hand over to his thigh. "I know you set this up. It's my dream project. Thank you."

"Least I could do." He presses his forehead against mine. "Especially after the whole earthquake incident and the shark attack."

Okay, I stepped on the shark tooth because of my own clumsiness and if I didn't write the article about Devil's Garden the way I did, Tyler would have avoided the earthquake completely. Everything that happened is completely my fault, but when he's this close to me, none of that matters. I take a deep breath, taking in the essence of Tyler. "None of those things were your fault."

"Maybe I know what's it like to have a dream, and I want yours to come true." He slides his lips over mine, sucking on the bottom one as he pulls away.

Electric shocks flow through my skin. Making my dreams come true is an understatement. Tyler pulled me from a place I never thought I'd leave and turned off the part of my brain that prevents me from taking chances, living for the moment, and letting myself be happy. And he did it effortlessly like it's destiny's plan for us. Of course, someone else is trying to ruin it all.

I move back and let out the breath I didn't know I was holding. "I tried to call before going all stalker on you."

He leans back into the couch. "Left my phone at the practice room. No worries, you can stop here any time, babe."

Yeah, and God knows what or who I'll find if I come here unannounced. First things first, take care of my Jenna problem. "Jenna answered… it didn't go well."

He turns off the charm oozing through his pores and sits up. "What are you talking about?"

Okay good, so he doesn't know. This would go much worse if Jenna told him she let out the monstrous bitch she keeps locked up inside and warned me to stay away.

"She answered your phone when I called to thank you." I nibble at my lip. "Listen, I get it… you guys are close, like family. But I'm not going to stay away from you just because she told me to."

Well, that came out like something a kindergartener would tell to her five-year-old friend. That's the thing, Jenna acts like an immature bully and has the ability to make others stoop to her level. Am I more disgusted with her or myself for buying into it?

"Jenna can go fuck herself. Come on, we'll take care of this right now." He leaps from the couch, pulling me with him.

Alright, I've clearly made things worse. I'm not looking for a fight or for Tyler to pick me over Jenna. Although it says something that he wants to rip her a new one. I just want to be honest with him. She's trying to sabotage us and he has a right to know.

I put my hand on his forearm. "Listen. She can say whatever she wants. It doesn't matter. She's not getting her way this time."

"I don't give a shit what she does." He grabs my hips and pulls me closer. "As long as I get my way with you."

And just like that, the rest of the world disappears. I slam my lips against Tyler's. The sweet flavor of his peppermint gum with tiny hints of salt invigorates me. I weave my fingers through his hair, gripping the strands near his scalp and pulling him even closer. All inhibitions erase from my mind; nothing but primitive passion left.

Tyler slides his fingers under the hem of my tank top and rips it up, leaving my lips for only a split second. I hold up my arms, and he flings the skimpy white top into oblivion. A few strands of his damp hair tickle my face, adding a gentle touch to this inferno of desire. He slides his hand down my back and unhooks my bra with a snap of his fingers. Ah, he's bringing out the rock star moves tonight, or what I'd expect being with a rock star is like.

I've been with Tyler before, no new territory here but everything's suddenly different. Jenna's stunt turned on a switch inside Tyler. He's a man on a mission, almost like he's showing me I'm his with no words. Actions speak louder anyway, and if this is his way of claiming me, I'm all in.

He moves his hands to the front and grabs my breasts. I gasp as his calloused fingers stroke my nipples. The soft touch mixed with a hint of roughness drives my body insane. It's torture not having him inside me right now. He sends kisses from my neck to my chest, sliding his fingers down as he encircles a nipple with his tongue.

Oh God, I'm on the verge of tackling him like the Incredible Hulk. So, I haven't been with a slew of guys, but Tyler's talents extend beyond the music world. He hooks a finger on each side of my elastic skirt and pulls it down, along with my panties. His kisses continue down my stomach as he makes his descent. My heart rate triples. Okay, enough. I need him, and I need him now.

Before I can say or do anything, Tyler grips each of my thighs and pushes me backwards onto the couch. He kneels in front of me, continuing to glide his tongue down. I moan with pleasure as his tongue twists and turns along my nether regions. I breathe a mile a minute, almost panting. Complete new territory for me here, he took the only piece left of my virginity so to speak. Damn, I've been missing out. He knows exactly what to do and how to do it. Desire builds within. I let out a loud moan and grip the throw pillow next to me as I release my passion.

Tyler sends kisses along my thigh as I catch my breath. He's clearly the most amazing man I've ever encountered. Rock God, Surf God, Sex God… does it get any better? I need him. Not just right this second but always. Right now is what I've got so I need to show him.

I leap from the couch like a frog on steroids and tackle Tyler to the floor. I straddle him, slamming my lips against his. I've never been much of the seductress type, but Tyler brings out things in me I never knew existed. He grabs my hips, pushing me against him, grinding his impressive body against me.

He sits up and whispers, "Let's take this to the bedroom, babe."

"I'll take it wherever I can get it." Where the hell did that come from?

By the time I jump to my feet, Tyler's already standing in front of me. His eyes lock onto mine, piercing my soul. He grabs onto the back of my thighs and lifts me up. I wrap my arms around his neck and my legs around his waist, pressing against his length. In a split second we're lip locked.

Tyler walks forward, placing me onto the bed. I can't stand the wait any longer. It's pure torture. I latch a big toe around each side of his board shorts and pull them down, releasing him from the damp fabric. Finally, skin to skin contact. I maneuver myself, trying to ease him inside me. Tyler moves forward and digs in his nightstand.

Oh my God, what am I thinking? Sure, back in the day condoms weren't always on the menu. I was on the pill and Josh wasn't a rock star. Tyler's hotness factor and sex appeal are clearly clouding my judgment. Never in a million years did I think he'd be more responsible than me.

He rips open the packet with his teeth and slides on the condom in one quick swoop, like he patented the move. He slams his lips into mine, sliding his fingers down my breast and stomach. My breathing increases, like I'm about to hyperventilate. Maybe I am.

He glides his calloused fingertip down my thigh, and then thrusts himself into me. I moan, sucking in breaths in between kisses. Sparks ignite from every cell in my body as he fills me. He thrusts forward, filling every inch of me. I grab his ass, pushing him deeper inside with every movement.

The headboard slams against the wall, creating rhythm to our music. Tyler lets out a moan and pushes deeper into me. My toes curl as a wave of passion floods through me like a tsunami. I moan and dig my fingernails into Tyler's back, unable to contain the desire. He holds himself up and stares into my eyes, saying more than words ever could.

I catch my breath and gaze into his baby blues, an involuntary smile gracing my face. In this moment he's mine, completely. The mind-blowing intense passion only exists between the two of us. A special combination made by destiny. Could he be my soulmate? He eases himself out of me and slides off the condom. I pull him close, needing to feel his skin against mine once more.

He lies flat on the bed and pulls me onto him so my head rests just under his shoulder. "You need to visit more often, babe."

I raise my head and shoot him a quick glare even though I can't hide my smile. "Maybe you should just trash the cell phone so I have no other choice but to stalk you."

He glides his fingers along my arm, making figure eight patterns. "She's not getting away with this shit. She's way outta hand."

"Who cares what she thinks. It's not like you're staying in L.A. forever."

He shifts his weight to make eye contact. "What's that supposed to mean?"

Of course, after the single best sexual experience of my life, I'm managing to ruin it by thinking ahead of the game. It is the truth though, once he's done recording, he's gone. It's ridiculous to think he's still planning on being with me.

I fidget with my fingers. "Once you're done recording she won't have to worry about me anymore." And that sounded much better in my head.

He slides to the side and props himself up on his elbow. "Is that what you think?"

I shrug. He's been more than clear that his goal is to live it up and never settle down.

He tucks a stray hair behind my ear. "Sorry babe, can't get rid of me that easy."

Okay, he's not great at sharing his feelings. For some reason guys must think talking about their emotions decreases their testosterone levels. I get it. But right now he's talking in circles. I need to know where I stand.

I prop myself up so we're eye to eye with each other. "What exactly happens with us when you leave?" I brace myself. No matter what his answer, I need to know.

He lifts my chin. "Ali, you're not some chick I'm banging." He sighs. "I'm sure Jenna said something like that."

I shake my head. "Nah, she's way more insulting." Even though that's probably the worst thing I could hear right now. Please don't let him change the subject.

"I've never met a girl like you. You tell me exactly how it is. You're not afraid to try something you never thought you'd do. You're smokin' hot with a brain like Einstein. Hell, you even wrote smut about my band in a national magazine and I still can't get you off my mind." He presses his forehead against mine. "Don't you get it? I want you and not just for the few months I'm in L.A. You've survived an earthquake and shark attack with me. You're the one I want by my side in a zombie apocalypse, babe."

Heat flushes through my body like wildfire. Never in my wildest dreams did I think the most romantic thing I've ever heard would involve the terms shark attack and zombie apocalypse. I'm in, much deeper than I've ever imagined. I want this to work with Tyler, but the obstacles aren't easy to overcome. Yeah I know, nothing great is ever easy, but being together requires Tyler to change his whole outlook on what he wants. Is he ready to do that? I'm finally getting to a place in my career where I want to be, too. I'm not ready to give it up before it starts. We need to think with our brains rather than our hearts. Is there really a chance for us?

"That might be the best compliment of my life." I flash a quick smile. "It might take an apocalypse to make this work."

He backs away. "It's not rocket science. We want to be together, so we'll be together."

Yeah, if life was only a fairytale. "Except that I'm here and you're... everywhere. I can't give up my dreams and neither can you."

"Sometimes dreams change a little, babe. I'm not giving up mine, you're not giving up yours, and I'm not giving up *you*."

I run my hand along his cheek. "I love it that you're a hopeless romantic even though you'll never admit it. How are we supposed to be together if we're miles apart?"

He moves forward and brushes his lips over mine, kissing me softly before pulling away. "My tour won't last forever. Then after that, we'll figure things out."

In his head, we all get everything we want. If only life was that kind. "How?"

"You'll find a way, just like you always do." He sits up. "Hell, if I have to buy a plane and fly back to you every night I'll do it. If we want to make it work, it'll work."

Oh my God. Just think, a few hours ago I thought we were done before we started and now Tyler's moving heaven and earth to be together. He's saying everything I want to hear. It's got to be the truth, right? There's no reason for him to say anything he doesn't mean at this point. Dating Tyler is a wild ride, more twists and turns than I ever expected.

I jump on top of him and press my lips against his. If there was ever a time in the history of the world for a round two, it's right now. I run my fingertips down the peaks and valleys of his sculpted torso.

He pulls away. "I hate myself for doing this, but I've gotta go."

Jeez. I burst into his house, uninvited and disrupt his plans. Although he didn't seem that upset about it. "Oh, sorry I would've called before coming, but you know how that went down."

He sits up. "Ever been to a recording studio?"

I shake my head.

"Today's your lucky day. And we can take care of this bullshit with Jenna."

Jenna is going to murder me, and it'll all be recorded. She'll probably promote it until she gets a platinum record. If Tyler is willing to put it all on the line, then so am I. Time to put on my big girl panties and face the wrath of Jenna.

13

RECORDING STUDIO

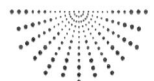

WHOEVER INVENTED SCAVENGER HUNTS DELVES IN EVIL RITUALS. I scan the living room for any remnants of my tank top. Showing up to the recording studio topless would only solidify Jenna's opinion of me. I mean, she already thinks I'm using Tyler for dirt on the band. Hate to tell her, but she's dead wrong. That story's over, but Tyler's and mine is just beginning.

I spot a piece of white fabric hanging from the edge of the kitchen table across the room. If music ever fails him, Tyler can profit from his athletic abilities. I rush over and grab the crinkled up shirt. Great, nothing like showing up disheveled and wrinkled. I guess I'll look the part of a desperate groupie. One smirk from Jenna and I might clock her.

"Ten minutes before we leave. I gotta jump in the shower," Tyler yells from the bedroom.

I glance in the hallway mirror. You've got to be kidding me. My blonde strands resemble a bird's nest that was recently caught in a hurricane and my sweaty skin screams we-just-had-sex. Last time I looked this bad was when I got caught in the midst of a thunderstorm running through the grocery store parking lot. Once my umbrella turned inside out, I waved my rhetorical white flag and gave up the fight. I can't walk in to the recording studio like this. Maybe I should just head home.

"Listen, Tyler, I can't go without showering. I'll head home and catch up with you later," I yell through the hallway.

Tyler emerges from the bedroom with nothing but a white towel wrapped around his waist. "There's room for two."

My jaw drops to the floor. The light shines off his glistening body, accentuating every muscle from his bulging biceps to perfectly sculpted pecs. My brain freezes as if kryptonite paralyzes me. "Okay." *Dammit.*

I follow him through the bedroom and into the master bath as if I'm a Stepford wife and robotically programmed to do whatever he wants. I fling my tank top on the bed and continue forward. He turns on the water and drops his towel.

I scan his body from the multitude of tattoos to his six pack abs, stopping at his impressive length. I quickly look away. Jeez, what's gotten into me? It's not like I've never seen him naked before. I just can't seem to get enough. *Please don't let him notice.*

He takes a few steps closer and pulls me toward him by my hips. "No one will die if we're a few minutes late."

Oh no, I'm not getting blamed for this too. I already have enough going against me when it comes to his band mates. No need to give them another reason to hate me.

"He who hesitates is lost." I step into the shower. Okay, my brain turned to auto-pilot and refuses to let me curb all desires.

He winks. "I like the way you think, babe." He joins me in the shower and positions the shower head so it pulses on his chest. "Ready to get wet?"

Way ahead of you. I grab the bar from the soap dish and slowly rub it over the mountainous terrain also known as Tyler's chest. The slippery suds build, and I drop the soap. "I got it."

I bend my knees, sending a multitude of bubbles down Tyler's body. He stands tall, perfectly chiseled like a sculpture from the romantic era of Rome. I glide my fingers down, tracing every muscle in his abs until I'm kneeling on the shower floor in front of him. Time to give Tyler a hint of the pleasure he gives me.

I lean forward, gliding my tongue around him. *Please don't let me choke on the water or anything else for that matter.* Last time I was in this position was in another lifetime, and there wasn't running water involved. I suck hard, twisting my tongue in an array of circles. Tyler leans back against the shower wall and moans. The glass walls steam, creating a sauna of pure passion. I continue to move, taking in as much of Tyler as I can.

His breathing becomes erratic. "You're killing me, babe. Dear God, don't stop."

Maybe I'm not as rusty as I thought. I slide my hands up, cradling him, and move faster, tucking my teeth underneath my lips. Tyler lets out a loud moan and finds his release, filling me.

I lower my head and let the remnants of our sexy shower flow down the drain. He opens his eyes and pulls me to my feet.

"You destroy me."

Okay, not what I expected to come out of his mouth. "What?"

"You can bring me to my knees in a split second. Scares the hell out of me."

I guess it's kind of a compliment. "I think I was the one on my knees."

"Not the way I see it, babe." He runs a hand through his hair. "Our ten minutes is now negative two... and worth every second."

Dammit. I squeeze some shampoo into my hair and take the fastest shower in the history of the world. We jump out of the shower and towel-dry ourselves at mach speed. I twist a quick loose bun into my hair and search for the remainder of my clothes. Tyler emerges from the bedroom in about two seconds, looking like he could grace the cover of a surf magazine.

I throw on my skirt, pat down my wrinkled-to-hell tank top and slide on my flip-flops. "I'm ready." Biggest lie I've ever told.

"Time to get a glimpse into my world, babe."

Why is it every time I hear that phrase my stomach drops to the floor? Ah, because his world contains more evil than the deepest depths of hell and her name is Jenna.

~

I FOLLOW TYLER ALONG THE BURGUNDY CARPET, CLINGING TO HIS hand like it's my first day of kindergarten. An eerie feeling takes hold of me with every step through the long hallway. Flashbacks of *The Shining* pop into my brain. I'd probably have a better chance of surviving at the Overlook Hotel. Nope, I'm in my very own horror story this time.

We turn the corner and continue through a gray steel door. Tyler pulls it open, and the gates of hell unleash themselves. If I didn't care about Tyler so much, I'd never put myself through this aggravation.

Jenna stands tall, her hands on her hips. She looks me up and down. "Umm, time is money. You're twenty minutes late."

What the hell's her problem? It's not like it's coming out of her pocket. If she was the band's manager I'd understand her excessive involvement in their affairs, but she's not. I just don't get why they let her act like their keeper. She's way out of control, from a business perspective.

"Traffic was a bitch." Tyler takes his bass out of its case.

"Yeah, not the only bitch here." Jenna shoots a death-to-you glare in my direction.

"Enough, Jenna. I'm really sick of your shit. Who the fuck do you think you are?" Tyler's face turns crimson.

"Alright, we're here to record. And she's right… time is money." Marcus swings his guitar strap over his shoulder.

"You better do something about your woman. I'm done with the bullshit." Tyler steps forward and points a finger in Marcus's face.

"Are you kidding me? First, she writes a smut article about

your band and then you have the nerve to bring her here. You're the problem, not me." Jenna taps her foot and sneers.

"I don't care if she posts naked pictures of you on a billboard with a 'Bitch of Devil's Garden logo next to it'. She's with me, and that's how it is. If you don't like it… I'll leave right now, and you can all go fuck yourselves." Tyler flings a chair on wheels and it rolls into the drum set.

"What the fuck!" Chaz runs to his drums as if his child was just thrown from a bridge.

Okay, now everyone's getting crazy. Tyler is not leaving his band because Jenna's a bitch to me and they can't ruin a recording session just because I am with him. This is really insane and immature. How did I ever get that impression before?

"Please, me naked on a billboard would only help the band." She flashes a half-smile.

Lexie walks across the room and stands between Tyler and Jenna. "Let's all calm down. Jenna, you need to back-off. Tyler can date whoever he wants whether you like them or not." She pulls Jenna into a side hug. "This scene seems a little familiar, don't you think."

Jenna folds her arms over her chest. "Not even close, you didn't try and sabotage the band in a national magazine."

I swallow hard. "Listen, that was not my intention, and I apologized. I got your message loud and clear." I sigh. "Taking Tyler's phone is really immature and an invasion of privacy."

She throws her hands in the air. "Oh, I get it. Trying to prove your article was accurate. By the way, I didn't take his phone. He left it here, and I just answered the call. Thought I was doing him a favor."

Marcus covers his face and drags his hands down to his chin. "Jenna, you gotta stop getting involved and you sure as hell shouldn't touch his phone. What the hell were you thinking?"

She turns toward him. "I was thinking about the band and

protecting you guys from this bullshit reporter, but Tyler can't stop dancing with the devil."

"I've never danced with you." Tyler glares at Jenna.

"You should all perform a one-night only show for the ladies like I do. None of this drama bullshit." Chaz adjusts the stool of his drum set.

"Yeah, not helping." Van shakes his head and fiddles with the microphone.

Tyler runs a hand through his hair and then rushes toward Jenna, stopping about an inch from her face. "This bullshit stops right now. I'm with Ali. You'll be seeing her a lot. Get used to it." He takes a step back and nods toward Marcus as if to say *Sorry I'm in your wife's face.*

"Whatever." She swings around like a supermodel and leaves the small room.

Lexie gestures toward me. "Come on, we can watch from the control room."

Great, a confined space containing both myself and Jenna, how can anything go wrong? I flash a quick smile at Tyler, even though his face screams I-want-to-murder-someone. He winks.

I follow Lexie up a few stairs and into another room. A multitude of lights in a variety of colors shine across a wall to wall board with hundreds of dials. Jeez, it looks like the inside of a very sophisticated space shuttle. I'm sure Jenna wants to shoot me into outer space. Above the control board is a glass wall. If Tyler wasn't staring straight at me, I'd think I was in a safe room, separated by a two-way mirror. Like the ones you see in just about every cop show. Of course, this room is far from safe.

I stand near the sound tech, a young guy, probably in his early twenties with long brown hair any woman would kill for and a tattoo of a dragon on his forearm. He presses a button and speaks into a microphone. "You guys ready?"

"Yeah, Jay. We're good," Van talks into his mic.

Jay slides back and forth in his rolling chair adjusting the dials of the insane setup. Everything around me fades away, and I lock onto Tyler. He stands tall holding his bass guitar, a few strands of damp hair falling along his cheek. Every part of me wants to leap through this glass barrier and tackle him to the floor. Sure, he's sexy as hell when he's riding the waves, but Rock God trumps all.

"Drool much?" Jenna huffs. "Aren't reporters supposed to be professional?" She holds up her fingers, making quotation marks in the air.

She's not getting a rise out of me this time. "I'm off duty today." I stay locked on Tyler, barely acknowledging her existence.

Marcus strums a soft melody that turns hardcore within seconds. Tyler closes his eyes, losing himself in the music. They're on another wavelength, almost like they all exist in between our world and notes they create. Van grips the microphone and belts out lyrics, telling the story of a girl who stole his heart. No doubt it's about Lexie, sure to be a hit. The passion oozing from their pores is nothing short of magical. Seeing Tyler in this light makes me want him even more.

"What do you think of the song, Ali?" Lexie takes a few steps toward me.

She must have dealt with Jenna's nonsense before because it's almost like she has sympathy for my situation. God knows what happened when Lexie met Van and he introduced her to Jenna. There's clearly more to this Mother Bear complex. I bet Jenna's threatened by an intelligent woman. Sure, she's got the looks of a supermodel, but they'll eventually fade, and when that happens, she'll be left with nothing but a bitch attitude.

"It's amazing." I turn toward her and smile. "Let me guess, Van wrote it for you."

She nods. "Yep, right after we got engaged."

Even in the dim light, that enormous rock turns this small room into daylight. "My offer still stands if you need any wedding planning help."

Jenna rolls her eyes. "Who are you, Jimmy Hoffa?"

"Hope not, he seemed to disappear never to be found." I nibble my lip.

"Like we could be that lucky." Jenna smirks.

What's it going to take to get her to stop her bullshit? "Jenna, what do you want from me? I get it, you're all about the insults, but it's getting really old... you can call me whatever you want; I'm not staying away from Tyler. Whether you believe it or not, I really care about him."

She folds her arms across her chest as if she's closing me off from the world. "Yeah, I saw how much you cared about him in that article."

"Give it a rest." My blood boils in my veins. "I made a mistake, apologized, learned from it. It's over. He's forgiven me, why can't you. What's it going to take?"

"A lot more than two words." She shakes her head. "He has some weird obsession with you now, but what if it goes sour. You gonna write about how he's abusive, or worse?"

"Are you insane?" How could she even think I'd slander someone? Um, hello, there are laws against that kind of stuff.

"You can't be trusted, and you have the power to tear us all down... it's a really bad combination." She holds up her head and stands next to Lexie.

Is she trying to build an army? "I never thought of it that way. You'd think you'd be nicer to me if that's what you're afraid of."

"I don't make friends with my enemies."

"Listen, I don't need to be friends... or even acquaintances for that matter. All we have to do is tolerate each other. Do you want Tyler to be miserable?"

"Of course not." She taps her stiletto against the floor.

"I really need to start wedding planning... and you probably have great connections here in L.A." Lexie flashes a meek smile at Jenna.

"Have fun, you two." Jenna returns to her resting bitch face.

"I guess I can plan things without my maid of honor helping through every detail, but it would be tough. Especially since I don't have her amazing fashion sense." Lexie twirls her hair around a finger.

Great use of reverse psychology. Last time that tactic worked for me was when Gretchen Vale wanted to wear the same prom dress as me. I tried on a horrid orchid halter and everyone bragged about how great I looked. Of course, she tried that one on too and immediately bought it, leaving the pink dream dress for me. I bet Lexie rocks the advertising world.

"When are you free?" Even though the question is aimed at Lexie, I guess I have to accommodate Jenna too.

"How about Saturday afternoon? I was hoping to start with the dress. My sister says once you've got the dress down you're halfway there."

"I can make myself available." Jenna stares at the guys through the glass as if wedding dress shopping is no big deal.

"Perfect. I'll get us an appointment at Bridal Couture. Is eleven good?" Please let me be able to get this appointment. The last thing I want to do is look like I'm fake. Plus, Jenna's probably dying for me to slip up.

"Works for me... now that we've got our girls day planned, let's listen to our guys rock out the rest of this album."

I want this day to go perfect. If I can win over Jenna, at least to the point where she only insults me once an hour, Tyler and I will have one less obstacle to overcome. There's only one person who can make sure this goes off without a hitch, and I'm lucky to call her my best friend.

14
FEMALE BONDING?

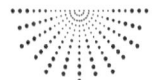

"LESSON NUMBER ONE, STAY AWAY FROM PUFFY SLEEVES AND BIG bows on the ass." Chloe chuckles.

"What ever would I do without you?" I roll my eyes.

"Seriously, I have zero experience with wedding dresses and need to hit this one out of the park. It's my one chance to get these girls to like me." I sip my peach tea.

Chloe bites a croissant. "Please, you sound like some geeky high-schooler vying for the attention of the popular girls. You know nerdy girls are really the cool ones, darling."

I tap my fingers on my glass. "Not quite the same situation." Dating a guy in a band turns more complicated by the minute. It's like I'm dating all of them. Well, not in a slutty-whore kind of way but it seems like everyone's approval is needed, like they're some crazy deranged close-knit family. "What happened to the good ole days when you move away, bring a guy home, tell your parents you're getting married, and everyone joins in one big group hug?"

Chloe lets out a laugh, almost spitting out her croissant. "Those situations only exist in Hallmark movies, my dear."

"Okay, now honestly. Any advice on this shopping trip from

hell?"

She finishes the last bite of her croissant and folds her hands together. "First, find out her plans for the venue. If it's a beach wedding she won't want a ball gown and if it's at a castle she'll want something over the top. I take it budget isn't a factor. How about body shape?"

"Perfect. She'd look great in a garbage bag."

She wiggles her pinky like Dr. Evil. "That's half the battle."

I sigh. "I need to find her something rocker chic yet classy like Grace Kelly meets Gwen Stefani."

"And that's exactly what you tell Rochelle at Bridal Couture." Chloe claps quietly.

"Thanks again, for getting us in. I didn't realize people make appointments a year in advance."

"What are besties for?" She slides out of the chair of the small sidewalk café table.

"You've always got my back, love ya." I blow her a kiss.

"Don't worry, I'll cash in on all these favors one day." She winks and tosses two twenties on the table. "Have fun and call me later. Tootles."

I wave and suck down the last few drops of my peach tea. The girly gene, used for things like important shopping trips and interior decorating doesn't exist in my body. I mean, if the lady at the make-up counter didn't help me choose shades I'd be running around like either a whore or a clown.

I glance at my watch. Okay, an hour until D-day. Maybe I'll get to the shop early and come up with a game plan with Rochelle. Since I've met Lexie all of two times, I have no idea what she likes in general, let alone in dresses. I'm sure this'll be a breeze. *Dammit*, did she mention a wedding venue? When I questioned the band in that disaster of an interview, everything she said to me fell on deaf ears. I'm doomed.

I gesture for the server. According the GPS, I should arrive at Bridal Couture in twenty minutes so that roughly translates to an hour when factoring in parking and time to prepare myself mentally. My stomach flip-flops as I start the car. Waves of nausea pass through like tidal waves. Great, I guess I forgot to factor in time for mental freak outs. Déjà vu floods me, bringing me back to Speech 101 and my heartfelt memoir of Josh. Sure, I had the room in tears and ended up with an A plus, but I'd like to keep the crying to a minimum today.

I SHIFT THE CAR INTO PARK AND TRUDGE THROUGH THE SMALL parking lot. The Victorian building bursts with old world charm. I scan the gingerbread woodwork along the porch, admiring the peaks and valleys of the witch's hat roof. The quaintness of the surroundings is very exclusive, like you need an invite to walk through the large wooden doors. Chloe never name drops, but I bet a ton of celebrities come here to find a gown for their special day.

I mosey to the front of the building and step inside. The foyer gleams like a mansion back in the golden era of Hollywood. A gold-trimmed crystal chandelier, half the size of my car, hangs from the vaulted ceiling. Burgundy and gold curtains decorate the walk out windows, and intricately designed moldings finish the look. It's like I took a step back in time to a really rich friend's house.

I continue forward and walk up to the front desk, containing more state of the art computers than we have at *Entertainment Rocks!* "Hi, I'm here for an eleven o'clock appointment. The name's Ali Whitman."

A girl with dark hair in a severe ponytail taps away at the computer keys. "Yes, Chloe's friend. Is the rest of your party here?"

"Not yet, I thought maybe I could come early and get

acquainted with Rochelle until the bride gets here." More like, come up with a game plan.

"Sorry, we run a tight ship here. Rochelle won't arrive until two minutes before your appointment time. Feel free to have a complimentary glass of lemon-infused water. You can sit right in the waiting area."

The waiting area consists of two couches that look like they belong in a museum. My Aunt Nancy would have plastic all over those babies. A beautiful glass table, covered with perfectly placed bridal magazines sits in between them. I pour a small glass of lemon water and plop onto the couch. Okay, maybe I can browse the magazines and get a few ideas. God knows why I'm stressing over this. Lexie probably knows exactly what kind of dress she wants. I mean, girls dream about their wedding day forever. I used to... before it all ended.

Heels click along the marble, pulling me back into reality. Ah, maybe Chloe has more influence here than I thought. I lift my eyes hoping to see Rochelle, but a blond bombshell stands before me.

Jenna slides off her sunglasses and tosses her hair over a shoulder. "Nice place."

Okay, that may be the best compliment I'll ever get from her. She eyes the store like she's purposely looking for a flaw. For once, she's speechless.

Lexie strolls in behind her. "Ali, this place is amazing." She scans the room like a kid in a candy store.

At least I'm making some headway. I've got to find out more about the wedding without asking too many specifics. The last thing I want is for Lexie to think I wasn't listening to her the first time we met.

I rise from the couch and set my water down on the table. "How far have you gotten with wedding planning?"

"I have a few venues in mind, but we haven't chosen one yet.

We're getting married on the beach in June, after the next tour." Lexie picks up a magazine and leafs through the pages.

Reality hits me. Tyler's going on tour shortly. I know he said we can make it work, but can we really? Being apart is the biggest obstacle in any relationship. Add in women crawling all over you, and alcohol, and you've got a recipe for disaster. Maybe this shopping trip can give me a little more information about what's about to happen.

"Beach weddings are beautiful. You should look into a sand ceremony. It's a great keepsake." The mixing together of colored sand in a vase to signify unity stands out in my mind from the last beach wedding I attended back in Maine. That's probably the extent of my knowledge on the subject, but at least I sound like I know what I'm talking about.

"I saw that on an episode of "Say Yes to the Dress." Lexie folds the magazine in half. "What do you guys think about something like this?" Lexie flashes a photo of a beach bride in an ankle length white strapless gown embellished with silver crystals. The dress gathers to the side with small silver crystals scattered along the length of it, adding bling to the classic look. "I think I'm in love with this dress and I haven't even seen it in person."

Wow, this was a million times easier than I thought. "It's an amazing choice, classic meets rocker chic." Okay, not sure where I pulled that from but her smile could light up the room.

A woman who resembles Zsa Zsa Gabor struts in wearing a champagne sequined dress. Ah, I bet she's Rochelle. I walk up to her holding out my hand. "Rochelle, Ali Whitman."

She shakes my hand. "Yes, Chloe mentioned you were stopping by with a friend."

I gesture toward Lexie. "This is the lovely Lexie and she's getting married in June on the beach."

"Ah, darling. Beach weddings are fabulous. Congratulations. You are gorgeous. Let's see if we can find something in here as beautiful as you."

Lexie blushes. "I like this one." She shows the magazine picture to Rochelle.

"Yes, it's brand new from Vera Wang. We just received it yesterday. Let me start a dressing room for you and bring it in." Rochelle scurries off.

"I can't believe they have it." Lexie practically jumps up and down.

Jenna puts her arm around Lexie. "Try on a few, when you find the right one you'll know... just like your man."

"Everything is finally coming together. I mean, we haven't really done anything other than say we want to get married at the beach. Now, it's... real."

Nothing seems real until it's actually happening. You can imagine it in your mind a million times and think about how it's going to go down and what you'll do in that moment but it never truly hits you until you're in that moment. I get to share this moment with Lexie. It's like the epitome of female bonding.

"It's the best day of your life." I flash a smile.

Jenna squints. "Who knows, maybe you'll even be there."

Okay, here we go. I brush it off and pretend I didn't hear her.

"Of course she'll be there." Lexie sets the magazine down. "I've never seen Tyler like this before. You'll be stuck with us more than you think."

An involuntary smile forms. Tyler and I are going strong, and everything is great at the moment, but Lexie seems to know something I don't. Of course, I've never seen how Tyler acted before we met but if he's changed since we've been together that has to mean something. Maybe the same thing happened for Lexie and Van.

Rochelle returns with another bridal associate. "Come, girls, I pulled a few dresses and set them in the fitting room."

We follow Rochelle to a room which is more like a small house than a fitting room. A round platform surrounded by mirrors sits in the middle of the pink carpeted room. Two tan

Victorian couches face the platform as if you have the best seat to watch the stars grace the red carpet. A large dressing area is off to the right, separated by a thick gold curtain. A table with lemon-infused water, a small fruit tray, and cheese and crackers sits between the couches.

Jenna's eyes widen as she peruses the room. It's like she's in disbelief that I could arrange an appointment at a place like this. Her snide comments have been to a minimum so far so maybe that's her way of saying she's impressed.

Jenna and I plop down on the couch while Lexie and Rochelle enter the dressing area.

I pop a grape in my mouth. "Do you think she'll find the dress of her dreams?"

Jenna turns toward me. "Hello... she already did."

Ah, there's the sparkling Jenna attitude I'm used to. "You never know until you try it on, right?"

"Please, anything looks good on Lexie. When you've got that going for you, you can pick whatever you want." She nibbles on a cracker.

And that statement right there tells me everything I need to know about Jenna. As long as you're hot, you can get anything you want. I hate to break it to her, but life doesn't work that way. It's not my job to enlighten her about reality. I just want to be civil enough to be in each other's company without World War III breaking out.

"How about your wedding? Did you find your dream dress right away?" She seems to like talking about herself and she has more experience than me in the wedding department. Maybe we can put her knowledge to good use.

"I had my wedding dress picked out since I was six. Once I found my prince charming it was a done deal." She lowers her eyebrows. "Why? Did Tyler propose or something? He's acting like aliens took over his body so I wouldn't doubt it."

What the hell is that supposed to mean? From what I've seen

on earth, Tyler acts like a guy who cares about a girl, totally normal behavior. I'm the one who did a whole 360, muting the tiny voice in my head that's been telling me the same thing for years, stay away from the complications of love. Okay, so I have no idea how Tyler acted before he met me, but there's no way he turned into another person. Control freak Jenna needs to step down. I'm done with the bullshit. I've tried everything, and I'm sick of walking on eggshells. This ends now.

"What's your problem?" My hands inadvertently clench into fists.

"Excuse me?" She sneers.

"Let's lay it on the line, Jenna. I've had enough of the digs, and the bitchy attitude. Let's settle this." I hop up from my chair. Dear God, what am I doing?

She stands up and sarcastically chuckles. "Are we going outside to rumble?" She folds her arms across her chest.

Okay, maybe I'm being a little dramatic. "Tyler and I are together. End of story. You're causing all this unnecessary friction between us, between you and Tyler, and amongst the band. It needs to stop."

"Who the hell do you think you are? I've been here since the beginning, honey and I'm sure as hell not letting some smutty reporter ruin Devil's Garden's reputation because she's banging Tyler." She waves her finger in my face.

It takes every ounce of my self-control to stop me from punching her in the face. Doesn't she get it? I'm not some groupie using Tyler for sex. Wait a minute, that's it. She thinks I'm worse than a groupie. In her warped mind, she thinks I'm using Tyler for articles and to further my career. I get it now. If we have a torturous break-up and I write something negative about the band where does that leave her? Lexie has her own career and can support herself, but Jenna has as much invested into Devil's Garden as the guys who are on stage. Without Devil's Garden, she's lost.

"Jenna, that's not happening. I've told you this before." Am I talking to the wall? Everything falls on deaf ears.

"Yeah, and your word is good as gold. Please, I've seen it a million times. A woman scorned is more dangerous than a nuclear weapon." She shakes her head.

Actually, that would've been a pretty good line for my interview with Elle. What a thing to think about at a time like this. Looks like my brain turned back into self-defense mode. I've got to settle this now.

"I made a mistake and believe me... I learned my lesson." I let out a breath I didn't know I was holding. "I care about Tyler, and I don't want to lose him. But I can't have everyone fighting because we're together. It's like some screwed up version of Romeo and Juliet."

"So you're both going to off yourselves?" She smirks.

Yeah, I bet she'd like that. "I thought I'd try another approach. If Romeo's family got to know Juliet, maybe they would've been okay with the relationship and everyone would've lived happily ever after."

"Or they would've started a huge war and everyone dies."

Demons are easier to make deals with than Jenna; at least they only want your soul. She devours every speck of hope.

I throw my hands in the air. "I tried to apologize, I'm helping Lexie with her wedding plans, and putting up with all these digs you throw at me to try and make things better for Tyler. I'd rather rip my ears off than hear another one of your insults, but here I am... trying again. What's it going to take, Jenna?"

"A hell of a lot more than that." She taps her foot.

"Name it... at this point I'll do whatever you want so we can be civil." I regret those words the second they slip out of my mouth.

"For starters, drop the, *I'm-so-important* attitude. I get it, you've got connections. That doesn't win any of us over...

although I could use a massage and a mani/pedi." She flashes a smile.

Is she joking or insulting me? Maybe both, with Jenna you can never tell what she's thinking, which is probably a good thing because if I could read her mind I might want to take Juliet's way out.

"Can we start over, fresh?" My stomach drops as she stares at me.

"Listen, I'm doing something I never do… giving you another chance. It's best for the band." She drops her arms to her sides. "Now, we're not BFF's or anything, but I'll tone down the drama."

That's the best I can expect from Jenna. Who knows, maybe we will become friends. Yeah, and maybe the sky will fall, and hell will freeze over, and I'll win the lottery on the same day.

A split-second later Lexie walks out of the fitting area. The dress looks amazing. It flows with every step she takes, like she's floating. The material follows every curve of her body as if it was tailor-made just for her. She walks onto the platform in front of the three-way mirror.

My eyes tear. I'm not sure if it's a stress release from the altercation with Jenna or if my mind is thinking back to a time when my dreams matched Lexie's. I take a deep breath and blink repeatedly, suppressing any impending tears from falling.

"It's perfect." I know it's not my place to say anything but it just slipped out.

"This is it… the dress I'll be wearing when I promise forever to Van." Lexie's smile lights up the room.

Jenna turns toward me. "You hit this one out of the park… nice start."

And somehow the compliment makes me feel more uneasy than happy. Sort of like when you've given 110% and nailed your goal greater than you expected, and then someone tells you *I expect great things from you* or *you're off to a great start.* Everything I do seems like it's part of test, the Jenna test. But has anyone ever passed?

15

RED FLAG

"So you pretty much made a deal with the devil... for me."
Tyler leans in toward the center console of his Camaro, gliding
his thumb along my thigh.

"Better with the devil you know." I place my hand over his,
interlocking our fingers as he drives down the boulevard.
"Underneath all the hostility, and general evil bitchiness, Jenna
knows causing unnecessary tension doesn't help anyone."

"I think I could use a little tension relief, babe." He turns
toward me and winks before stopping at a red light.

"Hmm, maybe I can help with that." I slide my hand over his
board shorts. The siren deep within comes to the surface, ready
to unleash her song of seduction.

A white Corvette pulls up next to us, lining up perfectly with
Tyler's Camaro. I quickly pull my hand away. One of the
downfalls of riding in a convertible, complete and total lack of
privacy. Heat creeps across my cheeks like wildfire. No doubt
they're as red as Tyler's flashy car. A young guy, maybe around
eighteen, with buzzed cut hair, looks directly at Tyler. He lifts his
chin, in a 'what's up' kind of way and revs the engine. Tyler nods
and tightens my seatbelt.

"What are you doing?" My heart thumps against my chest.

"Getting ready to kick this guy's ass." Tyler revs his engine and stares straight ahead at the light.

"You can't be serious." Is he insane? I try and reach for the door handle and escape from this disaster of a situation but I'm frozen… paralyzed. A green hue flashes and Tyler floors it. I sit back against the seat, bracing myself with my feet. Wasn't one near death experience with me enough for a lifetime? I suck in a breath, but there's no air. My body shuts itself down, almost as if I'm in shock. I close my eyes tight.

The wind whips through my hair like the time I rode The Twister back in Playland on one of our class trips. I squeezed Josh's hand so tight he had small bruises the size of fingertips on the top of his hand for a week. Once I stepped onto solid land, I barely made it to the garbage can before puking up my lunch. And that was on a state inspected ride, nothing like what's happening now.

Doesn't Tyler get that he can kill us both… or worse turn us into vegetables. Once a little testosterone flows, all sense and rationality disappears. Doesn't he get a rush from surfing, and playing in front of thousands of people? No need to speed down the road like a maniac and for what… to beat this idiot next to us, who we don't even know, in a street race with no benefits other than bragging rights?

The car screeches to a halt, sending the aroma of burnt rubber through the air. I pry my eyelids open. Both cars stop at the next red light. Thank you, God, we're still alive. I try to calm my body from end-of-the-world hysteria to please-make-me-a-strong-drink panic. The white Corvette speeds away, and Tyler takes the right hand turn toward my apartment.

I take a deep breath and try and control my trembling hands. At this point, I'm not sure if they're shaking from intense rage or the near-death experience. Tyler turns into a fearless teenager whenever the opportunity presents itself. I get it, his sense of adventure dominates but there's a hell of a big difference between having fun and putting your life in danger. He thinks he's invincible like bad things happen to other people, not him. I hate to break it to him but life doesn't work that way. No one knows that better than me.

Maybe I'm the one who's crazy. Why on earth would I put myself in this position again? It's like history repeating itself. This stupid drag race stirred up memories as if they happened yesterday. For a split second, all the pain and devastation flowed through me. Am I a glutton for punishment with a deep psychological need to torture myself? I've got to get away. I won't go through this... not again. I lost it all, the love of my life, my family, my friends, my home. I finally built up another life for myself here in L.A. and I'm about to lose it all again, like a vicious cycle. Well, I'm jumping off this ride before it crashes and burns.

Tyler pulls up alongside my apartment building. "You're quiet, babe. Still reveling in the victory?"

Like I give a shit if he won the race. I wipe my sweaty palms against my jean shorts and turn toward Tyler. Hot lava flows through me as I study the smug smile on his face. I unhook my seatbelt and turn toward him. All I want to do is talk some sense into him. Let him know that everything he lives for and loves can change in the blink of an eye. I open my mouth, but nothing comes out. Just a river of tears flows down my cheeks.

He reaches over to wipe them away. "What's wrong?"

I push his hand away and hightail it out of the car, bounding up the steps like an Olympian. So much is wrong I don't even know where to start.

I bolt into my apartment and close the door behind me, shutting out the world. Maybe that's half my problem. I lean against the door and take a deep breath. I mean, the stunt Tyler just pulled was ridiculous and dangerous but I may have overreacted a bit. I guess I could chalk it up to PTSD from our near death experience with the earthquake, but my past trauma runs much deeper.

Loud knocking vibrates the door. I stand tall and run my hands along my cheeks, trying to make myself semi-presentable. I've got to explain this to Tyler, but I really have no clue where to start. I pull open the door.

Tyler runs a hand through his windblown hair. "Did you want to hold the checkered flag?" He flashes a small smile.

I let out a quick laugh, probably to hold back anymore tears. "Sorry I freaked." I take a step back. "Come on in."

Tyler grabs my hand and leads me to the couch. We both sink into the cushions. He turns toward me and flashes those baby blues that set my soul on fire. Only this time, they're full of concern.

"What happened back there, babe?"

I shrug. "A momentary lapse of sanity."

He nods. "Yep, I've been there... now how about the truth."

I fidget with my fingers. "Remember when I told you the quarterback passed away in a car accident."

"Yeah, were you in the car?" He places his hand just above my knee.

I shake my head. Believe me, there were times I've wished I was in there with Josh. Not to end it all with him but who knows, maybe I could've done something... anything to save him.

I take a deep breath. "Listen, you don't always end up in the victory lane."

"I get it. Take no chances, and you won't get hurt."

"Exactly." Tyler does understand.

"Except then you're not really living are you, babe?" He takes my hand. "I promised myself a long time ago I would never let fear hold me back."

Yeah, that's because he has no clue what it's like when tragedy strikes and your whole life crumbles. Living life recklessly doesn't mean you're defeating fear, it means you're acting idiotic.

"Easy for you to say." I pull my hand away. "You don't get it. One moment... one lapse in judgment can ruin everything."

"Running away is worse."

Who the hell is he to judge me? "Sometimes it's for the best." A stray tear rolls down my cheek. "Waking up every day to something that triggers a memory of what could never be... a whole life planned... a life I wanted and then, poof, it's gone. So I tried to pick up the pieces and move on, just like everyone tells you. Well, they forget the part where everything around you, the trees, streets, cars, people... even the air reminds you everything you once had is all a distant memory. It's like the movie *Groundhog Day* set in hell. I couldn't stand the torture anymore, so I left it all behind and started over." The levee breaks, sending a river of tears streaming down my face. I quickly wipe them away and swallow hard. If I don't get this out now, I never will. "Then I met you, and everything changed. The shattered pieces of me molded themselves back together." I steady my trembling hand. It's now or never, time to lay it all on the line. "You're sexy as hell, funny at the exact right moment, bad-ass with a hint of hopeless romantic, and still a dreamer. You make every part of me come alive. I want to feel the way I feel when I'm with you forever... and you never want to settle down, which scares the hell out of me because now I can't imagine being without you." I breathe deep. "Tyler, I don't want to lose you."

He wipes my cheek with the back of his hand. "You won't." He pulls me on top of him and wraps his arms around me. "You rock my world, babe."

I chuckle.

"Yeah, I know how it sounds. That's why I write the music and not the lyrics. I've never been the best with words." He runs his fingertips along my back. "You completely blindsided me... took me by total surprise. You're hot, but you don't realize it, smarter than anyone I know and can bring me to my knees with one look. You're it... everything I want."

He's much better with words than he thinks. "Tyler, I think I'm falling in love with you." Holy shit, the words just slipped out of my mouth. Oh God, he's probably going to spring up from the couch and catapult me into the kitchen on his way to run out the door.

"Me too, babe."

Okay, so he didn't say those magic words exactly, but I heard them. I rise from the couch and take both Tyler's hands, leading him to the bedroom. I walk backward, refusing to break eye contact. His intense stare radiates through me. Whoever said "a picture says a thousand words" hasn't seen the look in Tyler's eyes right now. They say more like a million.

Once my feet hit the soft bedroom carpeting, I instantly hunger for his touch. I drop his hands and pull his shirt over his head only breaking eye contact for a split second. I toss the shirt and press my lips against his, softly at first but quickly gaining intense passion. Everything's different now. Like it's the first time all over again.

I need to feel him, be close to him. Show him the things I can't express. I untie his shorts and let them fall to his feet, sliding his boxers down with them. I take a step back. His tanned skin glows like a lantern, showing off his perfectly chiseled body. He's flawless in every sense of the word. I take an extra second to admire him. He's everything I desire in every way, and by some weird twist of fate he's fallen in love with me.

Tyler pulls me close by the waist of my jean shorts, ripping the button open. He slides his hands along the skin of my hips. In a split second, my shorts and panties fall to my ankles. He yanks off my tank top, throwing it into oblivion and presses himself against me so close that not even air can fit between us. He throbs against my belly, showing me just how much he wants me but it's nothing compared to the desire that lurks inside of me. I'm stripped of everything right now, no worries about what will happen, no what if's, nothing exists right now but the passion I have for this man.

I walk backward, still lip-locked, and pull him toward the bed. I reach into the nightstand and rummage through the contents until I feel a condom from the box I bought last week. I fumble with the wrapper and rip open the paper. My heart pounds inside my chest. It's been a hell of a long time since I've done this but that stands true for almost everything going on in my life right now. I slide the sheath over his impressive length.

He lifts me, and I wrap my legs around him, pressing against him as hard as I can. He lets out a low moan. Animal instincts kick in, turning me into a seductress with no inhibitions. I sway from side to side until he slides inside me, wrapping my legs around him like a python. Electric shocks flow through me.

He slams us down on the bed and thrusts himself even deeper inside. I groan as the intense passion builds within, letting out a release of pure pleasure. My God, his talents are endless. All the walls between us fall down, and we find a place where anything goes, dirty rock star sex turns into amazing love making.

He flips us over, and I sit up straddling him. The uncomfortable almost embarrassed feeling from my lack of experience that normally dominates when I'm the one in control has completely disappeared. I rock back and forth, locking onto his intense stare. He bites his lip and breathes deeper. I pick up the pace, refusing to lose eye contact. I need to see him, to know that I'm giving him the pleasure he desires. He lets out a loud moan and releases his passion.

I fall on top of his chest, easing myself off him. The earth shatters every time Tyler and I make love, but today... the universe crumpled sending me into hyper-speed. I tilt my chin toward his face. He lies still, catching his breath. His blond locks spread across the bedsheets in a perfect mess. His skin glistens from the droplets of sweat formed on his hairline. I meet his gaze and lose myself in the blue hue. He's never looked better.

We stare at each other, sweaty and satisfied, neither of us feeling the need to say anything. The last twenty minutes said it all... we're in love. The weariness of the day takes over, and we drift off.

THE CRISP COOL AIR CUTS THROUGH, SENDING AN ARRAY OF golden leaves across the far end of the field. I glance at the scoreboard. Unbelievable, we're one touchdown away from winning the final playoff game. It's been like twenty years since the Seamist Tigers made it to state.

I turn toward the squad. "Ready... Go-Fight-Win." Clearly not one of our best routines but it seems to get the crowd on their toes.

We grab our pom-poms and psych up the fans. Oh God, Josh is probably ready to puke. Everyone's counting on him to bring it home. Doubt I could handle that kind of pressure. It's not that I'd care if we lost, I mean it's just a game but letting everyone else down is a tough burden to bear.

I glance at the huddle out of the corner of my eye. Only twenty yards for a touchdown. Josh takes his position and gives me a quick Miss America wave. I chuckle and do the same. It's kind of corny, but I love how we have these little things, just between us. That's our signal, we've got this. The ball snaps into Josh's hands. He backs up... looks from side to side but no one's open. I stop, mid-cheer, and stare. He cradles the ball and heads toward the sideline, running the play. The time ticks down on the scoreboard, only ten seconds left. Josh moves like a gazelle being chased by a lion. He leaps toward the goal line with only seconds to spare. I close my eyes, peeking through the lids. The clock winds down. Josh lands inches past the goal line. Touchdown! The Seamist Tigers are going to state!

Everyone rushes the field, but my feet refuse to move. The

cool air douses my fiery cheeks. Today he's everyone's hero, not just mine. The players lift Josh up, carrying him across the field. I stand still, taking in the energy of this moment. He spots me and gives me "our" wave. A smile spreads across my face like wildfire. I wave back.

He jumps from the huddle and marches toward me. I finally will myself to head onto the field. Our eyes lock, and we both move toward each other, like missiles on a path to their targets. He flings his helmet and wraps his arms around me, pulling me into a knock-your-socks-off kiss. A few fans slap him on the back or shoulder to congratulate him, not even realizing they're interrupting the most romantic moment of my life.

He pulls away. "We did it, Al. You said it would happen and it did."

I press my forehead against his. "I didn't do anything. This is all you."

He shakes his head. "Not even close." He gives me a peck on the lips. "Don't you get it? As long as we've got each other, we can do anything... rule the world."

"I'll shine up my tiara."

The crowd dissipates. I take a step back and take hold of Josh's hand. "Shana's having a party. You up for it?"

"Hell yeah. Let me hit the showers, and I'll pick you up at your house."

I slam my lips into his one more time. Who knows, if we win state, I might be kissing Josh on television next week. "Hurry up. I need to congratulate my hero in style."

He walks backward. "Looking forward to it." Within seconds, he runs toward the locker room.

I head home and slip into a red sweater and black flirty skirt. Sure, the rest of the cheerleaders will stay in uniform, but since I have to make a pit stop at home to give my mother her car, I might as well use the time wisely. So working the graveyard shift at the hospital is no picnic, I get it. Still, it would be nice if I could have the car just once on the weekend. On the plus, she never knows what time I get home.

Two quick beeps sound outside my bedroom window. I slide the curtain to the side. Josh air drums on the steering wheel. He's probably cranking up a Led Zeppelin album and pretending he's living the dream. I hop down the steps like a caffeinated rabbit and bounce out the door.

The damp air sends shivers along every inch of my skin. Winter's on its way and seems to last forever. I follow the white vapor of my breath and slide into the passenger seat. Josh spots me and turns down the radio.

"I was enjoying the concert." I lean in and give him a quick peck.

His cheeks burn crimson red. "You got a front row seat, wanna be my groupie?"

"I'm already there." I chuckle. It's pretty much the truth. I'm in the front of the field, cheering for him every game. I guess I'm a super groupie.

Josh fires up the engine and takes off. Shana's parents flew to New York for the weekend, something to do with her Dad's job, so we've got a place to party and stay tonight. She even saved a room for Josh and I. Why is this ride taking so long?

The car skids across the curvy road. It swerves across both lanes, fish-tailing through the pavement. Josh grabs the steering wheel, trying to take control. I grip onto the seat for dear life. He turns the wheel to the right and pulls over to the side of the road. *Thank God, we're alive.*

"You okay?" Josh leans over the center console so he's almost sitting in the passenger seat.

I nod. "Yeah, what the hell happened? Is there black ice?"

"We slid on some wet leaves." He sits back in the driver's seat and holds my hand. "Two more blocks and we're there."

"Good, I could use a drink." I tighten my seat belt and hold onto Josh's hand like it's my lifeline.

"Don't worry Al, you know I'd never hurt you." He brings my hand to his lips and kisses my fingers.

I melt into a puddle. How did I get lucky enough to win Josh's love? Fate stepped in and brought the most amazing man in the universe to the smallest town on earth and paired him with me. Most people don't find a connection like this their whole life, and I've got it at eighteen years old. Our life together is going to be amazing.

Music blasts through the air, barely muffled by the closed windows of Josh's car. It looks like the party is in full swing. He finds a parking spot at the end of the road, and we head inside. The moonlight glistens off Josh's still damp hair on the short walk to Shana's house. He's the epitome of a sex symbol on the field but when he wears those perfectly fitted jeans and his football jersey I can barely stop myself from tackling him right here.

We walk inside, hand in hand. A group of players rush toward us like we're in the middle of a play.

"Great game, buddy." A voice yells out.

"We're going to state, man," Another guy says and hands Josh a beer.

Josh holds it up in the air. "To the Seamist Tigers, the new state champions."

A roar of cheers drowns out the music. Josh takes a sip of his beer and puts his arm around me, guiding me to the living room. How can he be so humble? I mean, I love the fact that he never brags or takes the credit for himself, but he deserves some of it. If he wasn't the star quarterback, the Seamist Tigers would still be on a losing streak. No matter what happens, good or bad, he always calls it a team effort. There's no one else in the world quite like him.

"Hey, you guys made it." Shana pulls me into a quick side hug. "If you're looking for privacy I saved the last room on the left for you." She winks.

Josh nibbles his lip. "Your call."

Is he serious? I've been dying to get my hands on him for the past two hours. At least I have all night to revel in the wonder that stands before me. "Grab me a beer and let's head up." The words echo in my brain. Way to be romantic, Ali. It's like a line from a ridiculously under budget B-movie.

He finishes his beer in one massive gulp and takes two bottles from the ice-filled bucket near the corner of the room. I nuzzle his neck, nudging him toward the steps. Other than prom and a few impromptu parties, finding alone time to spend with Josh is no easy task. It's like I have to share him with the team, with the school, even with the town. Well, tonight he's completely mine, and I'm not wasting a second.

I turn the door handle and duck inside, almost dragging Josh behind me. Maybe he'll take it as uncontrollable desire, but I really don't want anyone else pulling his attention in a different direction. I lock the door behind us and switch on the light.

Ah, must be the guest bedroom. Light green walls adorn the decent size room. Josh sets the beer on one of the nightstands next to a figurine of a lighthouse. A large painting of the ocean, complete with seagulls and a wave breaking onto the shore takes up the far wall. Memories of our first time hit me like a freight train. I can almost smell the salty air.

I hop onto the bed. "I love the beach."

Josh joins me, turning toward me propped up on his elbow. "Duke's not that close to the beach."

"Always a downfall." I gaze into his dark blue eyes. "Good excuse for some weekend road trips."

He tucks a stray hair behind my ear. "Are you kidding me? When I finally get you all to myself all the time, I might never leave the apartment." He grazes my cheek with the back of his hand. "Probably fail out of school."

I chuckle. "You'll probably get sick of me… and definitely my cooking."

He scoots closer. "Not a chance." He slides his lips along mine, sucking hard as he pulls away. "I want to be with you forever, Ali... even if that means I'll eat nothing but burnt grilled cheese for the rest of my life."

"Trust me, forever isn't long enough to spend with you." I slide my hand under the hem of his jersey, slowing pulling it up.

He sits up on the bed and finishes the job, exposing his chiseled chest. I follow every curve of his muscle, memorizing him. He's perfect, a flawless specimen. For the life of me, I can't figure out why he chose me over everyone else. I mean, other girls are prettier, have better bodies, can bring a man to his knees with their seductive power, but he never even gives anyone else a second look. Every time I ask him, he tells me I'm crazy and that he's got the best girl in the world. Hearing those words spark more adrenaline in my body than if I was on the podium accepting an Olympic gold medal. It's like I've won the lottery and I'm living the dream.

He tugs at my sweater, easing it over my head. "You're so beautiful."

In reality, my hair is probably sticking up in a million directions from static cling, but right now I feel like Miss America. "Josh, you are amazing, and I love you."

His face lights up like a Christmas tree. "You're the love of my life, Ali Whitman and I can't wait to run off to college with you." He slams his lips against mine. "And someday, you'll be Mrs. Hanson."

Hot lava flows across my cheeks. "I can't wait for someday."

He grabs my face with both his hands. His lips glide across mine, slowly at first but increasing in passion with every breath. Josh's kisses could wake a sleeping maiden in any fairytale. Okay, so I'm not that experienced but when his lips touch mine, lightning strikes. A whole new world awakens. He reaches around behind me and fumbles with my bra, tugging at the clasp. Even Superman succumbs to Kryptonite, and my bras have that effect on him. He rips it off and tosses it onto the floor.

I lean back onto the bed, pulling Josh on top of me. He slides off his jeans and boxers, and hovers above me. The moonlight shining through the window glistens off his skin like he's glowing. A beacon in the dark night.

I wiggle out of my skirt and panties. The bra is one thing, but I can't walk in the house without those items intact. We stare into each other's eyes, naked and vulnerable. I don't even like getting changed in front of other girls in the locker room, but with Josh, I'm not embarrassed about any part of me. I'm completely comfortable baring it all in front of my football God.

He leans forward and grazes my ear with his lips. "You ready?"

"Yeah," I whisper.

He slowly eases himself inside. I gasp as he completely fills me. Making the trek to Planned Parenthood to go on birth control pills was the best decision. No more worrying about accidents from the condom breaking, which happens more than I deemed imaginable. Josh and I are as close as humanly possible at this moment.

We mimic each other's movements, creating a unique rhythm. The whole world suddenly disappears, and no one else exists but the two of us. Passion builds and within minutes Josh comes inside me at the same instant I release my desire. He rolls over next to me, hearts thumping so hard they could probably burst from our chests and fly around the room.

Loud knocks resonate through the air. What idiot is banging on the door? I mean, everyone knows party etiquette. I wrap the comforter around myself and Josh pulls on his jeans.

He opens the door a crack. "What's up?"

"Someone called the cops, party's busted."

Once I hear the words, I spring from the bed and get dressed in warp speed. Josh fishes for his keys in his pocket and takes my hand. Looks like there's no time to revel in the afterglow. We leap down the steps and funnel through the crowd until we're out on the sidewalk. Duke would be history if we have an underage drinking citation even though we barely drank. Nowadays, just being at a party with alcohol gets you in trouble.

The cold air douses my fiery skin. I leap into the passenger side and close the door in one smooth movement. He fires up the engine, and we take off.

"Damn, you're pretty quick. Maybe you should try out for the team." He slides a hand on my thigh.

"Nah, wouldn't want to break any of your records." I flash a quick smile.

"If we win state I'm having the party. No cops allowed." He moves his hand to mine, interlocking our fingers.

"If someone calls the cops after we win state, they may be banished from the town."

"Sorry we got cut short tonight." He slows the car to a stop outside my house.

"My mom's on the graveyard shift. We can have a four-hour sleep-over." I hate staying here by myself. I swear the house makes all kinds of creepy noises when it knows I'm there alone. If anyone in the world can protect me, it's Josh.

He shuts down the engine. "Okay, but no painting my nails."

I give him a love tap, and we head inside. Even though no boys are allowed in my room, Josh has slept here at least ten times. Mom's never home, and she'd never understand we're not just two high school kids hooking up. What Josh and I have is much more than that.

He follows me to my room, and we slip under my purple comforter. I set the cell phone alarm to 6 a.m. so he can make his escape before Mom comes home. He wraps his arms around me and we drift away together.

Hours seem like seconds. My cell phone chimes, sending me

into panic mode while my brain processes what's happening. I nudge Josh.

"I'm not ready to let you go yet," he says and pulls me close.

"Pretty soon you won't have to." I smack my lips against his.

He rises from the bed and I walk him out. In a few short months, we'll be together twenty-four seven. A lot of people would be scared to death of such a concept but I'm on cloud nine.

He opens the door, letting in a cool gust of wind. "See you soon." He kisses me and walks down the few steps to his car. He turns and gives me "our" wave.

I smile and wave back, watching him drive away. Once he's out of my visual field, I close the door, making sure it's locked and head up to bed. Within minutes, I'm back in dream land.

"Ali," Mom calls.

I blink, trying to will my heavy eyelids open. She never wakes me up, not even when I ask her to.

"Yeah."

She walks into my room and sits on the bed. "We need to talk."

16
INVITATIONS

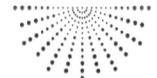

COLD SWEAT COVERS EVERY INCH OF MY BODY. I GASP AND PROP UP
to a sitting position, sucking in a few shallow breaths. My heart
drums, skyrocketing through my veins. I take a deep breath and
blink repeatedly, trying to get my bearings. The sun peeks
through my curtain casting a golden glow on Tyler's skin. Thank
God, just a nightmare. At least I didn't wake him. The way this
day went he might run for the hills if he has to deal with another
one of my freakouts. It's been forever since I had a dream about
my last night with Josh, more like a nightmare of a memory. At
first, I relived the tragic tale every night, then only a few times a
month, until it stopped completely. I always woke up the same
way, cold sweat, hysterical tears, and the urge to rip out my heart
so I could finally have peace.

Not today. It's weird. Kind of like my brain mustered up those
memories again to test me. Believe me, re-living that night is
nothing short of pure hell, but everything that happened before
was amazing. Like the complete euphoria was worth the total
devastation. Lightning rarely strikes twice in the same place, so
maybe I paid my dues in the love category. Everything could be
different this time.

Of course, I'm never going to be okay with Tyler street racing or taking other stupid risks, but I'll try and keep my freakouts to a minimum. I mean, Josh's car skidded on wet leaves, according to the officer it was most likely to avoid hitting an animal. His car flipped and slammed into a tree. Crushed like a tin can. Maybe destiny plans your every move and no matter how careful you are, you can't fight what's meant to be.

I turn toward Tyler, watching a few strands of hair dance when he breathes. Not sure what the great beyond is planning for Tyler and I, but I'm ready to find out. No running, no turning back, and no holding out. Time to turn up the heat. I know, I bet he hasn't done this in bed… at least not in a very long time.

I quietly slip out of the sheets and toss on my old KISS t-shirt from one of their million farewell tours. I head to the kitchen and grab a big mixing bowl. I've come a hell of a long way from burnt grilled cheese. I grab some vanilla, eggs, milk, bananas and cinnamon along with a loaf of bread. Chloe would kill me if she knew I made my famous Bananas Foster French Toast and didn't invite her. It's the only thing she's willing to splurge on without checking the calorie count.

I heat up the griddle and get to work. The kitchen smells like I just walked into Seamist Buns, home of the world's best sticky buns. Okay, so it's a self-proclaimed title, but I've never found any better… anywhere. Tyler loves diners and hidden hole-in-the-wall places, but I think I'll class things up a bit. I slice a strawberry and fill the plate with slices of French toast in a circle so it resembles a flower, or at least looks like the presentation of a breakfast dish at a swanky restaurant. I top it with sliced bananas and drizzle some syrup over everything. I brew some coffee and pour us each a cup. Tyler's about to have his world rocked.

I fit everything onto a TV tray that I use way too often, and walk to the bedroom at the speed of a sloth. Dousing Tyler with hot coffee and sticky syrup might make this more memorable than I hoped. Just as my toes hit the bedroom carpet Tyler opens his eyes.

"What's all this, babe? Is it Best Kick-Ass Rocker, Wave-curling Surfer Boyfriend in the World Day?" He sits up, shirtless, and leans his back against the headboard with the white sheet draped over his lap.

I shift my gaze from his chiseled torso, down to his six pack abs. It's like he's been photo-shopped. Dear God, he could grace the cover of any magazine and increase the company's shares tenfold. *Please let this image imprint itself on my brain.*

"Yeah, I think I saw that in a Hallmark card." I slide my feet forward, steadying my trembling arms. "I thought you might want some home cooking for a change."

The coffee sloshes to the top of the cup as I set the tray down on the bed. Okay, so breakfast in the bed might be a little on the corny side. It's in just about every Mother's Day commercial I've seen, except it's always the guy bringing the girl breakfast. Rock stars eat on the road 24/7. Who knows, they might appreciate breakfast in bed just as much as a tired mom. Ah ha, I might've just brainstormed a whole new advertising campaign.

Tyler stabs a piece of French toast with his fork and shoves it in his mouth. "This is the best thing I've ever put in my mouth… well, almost." He crams in another forkful.

Heat flashes across my cheeks. I slide over next to him and take my plate. "Glad you like it… Is your whole world changed?"

He takes a big gulp of coffee. "Yep, you're full of surprises, babe." He finishes the last bite. "You're more talented than anyone I know." He winks.

Clearly a lie, especially since he hangs out with people oozing with talent, but it's nice to hear. Tingles sweep across my skin. "I doubt that, but thanks." I finish up my two pieces of French toast and slug down some coffee.

"Today is a very special day, and not just because of the

awesome grub." Tyler sets the tray down on the floor and turns toward me.

Special scares me. On one hand, it can mean Tyler found another amazing adventure for us and on the other it might mean Tyler earned an awesome opportunity without me.

"Other than Best Kick-Ass Rocker, Wave-curling Surfer Boyfriend in the World Day?" I flash a smile.

"A close second… For the first time in months, I have absolutely nothing planned for the whole day." He wraps his arm around my waist and pulls me toward him.

The sheets ripple, following my movements. "What did you have in mind?"

"Anything you can imagine, babe." He nibbles my ear.

When he says it like that, my creative juices flow endlessly. He's all mine for the next twenty-four hours. Moments like these may be far and few between. I need to strike while the iron's hot, and it's spewing steam right now. Let's start at step one. "How about we stay right here, in bed all day." I nuzzle his cheek.

"Best idea I've ever heard." He brushes his lips against mine.

The doorbell sounds, pulling me out of the moment. Chloe probably smelled the French toast from across town. Then again, the whole building could be on fire, and I'd never have a clue. At this point, molten lava could spew from the earth's core sending us shooting into oblivion and I wouldn't care. A raging inferno's got nothing on the sparks Tyler creates.

"Hold that thought." I jump up from the bed and sprint toward the door, trying to waste the least amount of time possible.

I pull open the door. Huh, no one's there. I take a deep breath. Okay, no smoke so we're not on fire. A decorative white box wrapped with a gold bow sits on my doormat, gleaming in the rays of sun. Did Tyler have something delivered to surprise me? The Rock God oozes romance. He shocks me on a daily basis, in a million different ways. Plus, he's always got something up his sleeve. I snag the box and take it inside, closing the door behind me and locking it. Nothing is going to pull me away from Tyler for the rest of the day. I head back to the bedroom, still carrying the box.

"Let me guess, a subpoena from the wedding store you and Jenna visited?" He props himself up on his elbow.

"We only argued for like a minute. It's not like we were wrestling around and throwing dresses. Plus, Lexie found her dress. If anything, they'd be sending me a thank you card." Smart ass. Maybe I'll have a little of my own fun. "Probably a gift from one of the guys who always hit on me at work."

He scrunches his eyebrows and sits up. "Maybe I should drive you to work." He grabs me by the waist and tackles me onto the bed.

I burst into a mess of giggles. "Okay, the suspense is killing me." I sit up and slowly unwrap the ribbon. *Dear Miss Whitman,* Entertainment Rocks! *cordially invites you and a guest to their annual Black Tie event Saturday at the Savannah Ballroom of the Oak Lake Country Club. Cocktail hour begins at 7 o'clock.* I run my fingers over the raised letter.

My first professional event, I bet everyone who's anyone in the entertainment and reporting world will be there. And I've made the guest list. If Tyler weren't here, I'd probably jump up and down and squeal like I'm twelve years old but since he is here maybe I'll celebrate a whole different way.

"Sounds like a blast. Congrats." He runs his fingertips along my thigh.

Did he notice the *and guest* portion of the invitation? "I bet you look hotter in a suit than you do on stage." Wow, now I sound like one of the girls backstage. I swear, less and less blood makes its way to my brain when Tyler is anywhere near me.

"You've never seen me in either. We've got to change that."

"You up for it? Might be fun." What's wrong with me? If a guy asked me to a formal event like that… well, I'd probably still go.

Tyler deserves a proper invite. "I mean, do you want to be my date?"

He rubs his chin. "Hmm. I'd get to show those dudes that hit on you that you're taken." He nods. "Plus there's probably good booze."

I playfully slap his arm.

"Yeah, I'm in." He tosses the invitation to the side and rolls on top of me, hovering just above my lips.

So I embellished the part about the guys asking me out. No harm done. Tyler gets asked to do God knows what after every show when he's on the road. My stomach knots. How the hell am I going to handle that whole ordeal? I banish the negative thoughts from my brain. I'll cross that bridge when I come to it.

I'm showing up at my first black tie event with a rock star. Never in my wildest dreams could I conjure up this scenario. Last time I wore a formal dress was at prom. Sadly, my fashion sense hasn't changed since then. Chloe has her work cut out for her this time.

Dress shopping bonds females, or at least it did last time. I'll invite Jenna and Lexie too. The fearsome foursome takes Rodeo Drive. Assuming we don't kill each other in the process.

"Earth to Ali, are you planning your speech to thank the academy?" He brushes his lips against mine.

"Nah, more like deciding what activities we should partake in today." I feather my fingers along the muscles in his back up to his neck, weaving my fingers into his hair. "Let's start here." I press my lips against his pulling him close. Time for round two.

"DEFINE NICE." CHLOE SLIDES ON HER SUNGLASSES AND STRUTS down the sidewalk.

"Um, not bitchy or condescending. And that includes facial

expressions." I practically have to jog to keep up with her. When she's on a mission nothing stops her.

"And is she expected to play by the same rules?"

"Please do me this favor. God knows how she's going to act. It's like trying to predict when a volcano's going to erupt... I need to keep her on my good side." Chloe has no clue the influence Jenna possesses over the band. It's like she's the matriarch of a mafia family.

Chloe stops dead. "Why the hell do we have to kiss her ass? No one should have this kind of power over you. Who does she think she is?"

The master of the universe. Chloe's right, she's always right, but staying in Jenna's good graces is in my best interest right now. Tyler and I have enough going against us, no need to add more fuel to the fire. If getting along with Jenna is my biggest obstacle, then Tyler and I might actually have a chance.

I put my hand on her shoulder. "She's one of those girls who can be your best friend or your worst enemy... you know, like us."

She turns toward me and flips her hair over a shoulder. "Oh darling, even though I really want to clock her for all those things she said to you, I will be a lady. What are best friends for?" She blows me a kiss.

"Thank you, I owe you." I pull her into a side hug. *Thank God.*

"I'll take a new pair of Manolo's." She entwines her arm around mine, and we walk down the sidewalk.

"How about I buy the drinks we'll definitely need after this shopping excursion?"

She nods. "Deal."

If I had the chance to help humanity I wouldn't wish for world peace, nope, I'd pray that everyone has a Chloe. A best friend who stands by your side whether you're right or wrong, celebrates the good times, lends a shoulder to cry on when you're at your wit's end, and curses with you like a sailor with Tourette's when someone screws you over.

We turn the corner and spot Jenna and Lexie waiting for us outside of stop number one, Frederick's. Chloe dashes forward, to the point where I almost need to stop to catch my breath. I swear she blows off steam by smacking her high-heeled Louboutins against the concrete sidewalks. Hey, whatever works. She finally stops a few feet from the door.

I suck in a few breaths until my pulse is back at a normal level. "Jenna and Lexie, this is Chloe, my partner in crime and bestie since college."

"Nice to meet you." Lexie shakes her hand.

"It's a pleasure." Chloe flashes the fakest smile I've ever seen.

Jenna looks us both up and down. She holds open the door. "Ready to shop till we drop, girls?"

I can feel Chloe giving me the you've-got-to-be-kidding-me look underneath her dark glasses. "Let's do this." I head into the store. Everyone else follows suit.

Mannequins dressed in everything from elaborate ball gowns to cocktail dresses fill the large storefront window. Long wall to wall racks of dresses line both sides of the store, and a round center display shows off the newest fashions. I do a quick once-over trying to take in a glimpse of the inventory. Thank God I have help. I think I'm more confused about what to wear than I was before I walked in here.

"You okay?" Chloe slides her sunglasses on top of her head.

I nod. "Just a little overwhelmed." Not only am I attending my first professional event, but it's also the first time Tyler will meet my colleagues. Okay, so I've never taken a guy to any social gathering in the last five years. My stomach drops. For once I want everything to be perfect, starting with the dress.

Everyone scatters through the store, rummaging through the racks.

Chloe holds up a long black satin dress. "Black is classic. Especially for a formal event."

Jenna pulls a crystal-embellished silver gown from the rack. "It's your time to shine, might as well sparkle a little."

Chloe's face distorts into that you-can't-be-serious look. "She's not accepting an Oscar. It's a business event, so she needs to look elegant but not flashy."

Jenna shrugs. "I always like to stand out." She lifts her chin and continues to inspect the dresses, like she's a fashion designer.

I step on Chloe's foot before she opens her mouth. Luckily, she gets the point. The last thing I need is a brawl, especially in an upscale dress store.

"What about something like this?" Lexie holds up a black chiffon dress with a crystal brooch near the waistline.

"Great find." Chloe runs her fingers along the fabric.

"I love it." I close my eyes for a second and picture myself arm in arm with Tyler. I'm dying to see him in a suit.

"Hello ladies, welcome to Frederick's. I'm Mary Ann. Can I get a fitting room started for you?"

"Yes, please." I hand her the dress.

Jenna pulls a few dresses from the rack. "If you're going to get undressed, make it worth your while." She winks and hands the dresses to Mary Ann.

"Great advice." Chloe peruses the rack near the far end of the store.

I stop next to her, pretending I'm examining another dress option. "Really," I whisper.

"What... that's the most intelligent thing that's come out of her mouth so far." She gives me two dresses and nudges me toward the dressing room.

Okay, so this trip is more like a John Hughes movie from the 80's where two totally opposite groups of people are trying to impress each other. Of course, in the end, it always works out, usually to an awesome song and iconic image, but I'm pretty sure this will end with someone slamming shots at lunch. Most likely me.

I step into the dressing room and put on the black chiffon dress Lexie found. Goosebumps spread across my skin as I pull up the zipper. Huh, fits like a glove. I glance into the mirror. The brooch on the side of the dress gives just enough bling without being overly dramatic, classic with a hint of glitz.

I've imagined myself in this position a million times. Walking into a black-tie affair, turning heads as my leg peeks out from the high slit with every step, schmoozing with the bigwigs and drinking champagne. Never in my wildest dreams did I see a hot rock star standing next to me, especially one I'm completely in love with. I turn from side to side, watching the chiffon flow with my body. It's absolutely perfect. A perfect dress for my perfect night with Tyler.

I walk out of the dressing room like I'm about to step onto the red carpet. Lexie, Jenna, and Chloe all stand in a semi-circle around the fitting room door.

"Ali, it's fabulous. No need to try anything else on, you've got a winner." Chloe turns toward Lexie. "You've got a great eye."

Lexie twirls her hair around a finger. "I'm not much of a fashionista, but I've attended a few of *Global, Inc.*'s black tie events."

"I can use a few tips." I fidget with my fingers. Lexie has more experience in this area than anyone I know. I mean, she's an advertising exec. Maybe Tyler will take a few tips from her, too. What am I thinking? He lives for the moment, makes up the rules as he goes. He's a what-you-see-is-what-you-get kind of guy. One of the things I love about him.

"Sure thing." She nods.

Jenna stands tall, glancing around the room like she's interested in buying everything in it. It's her defense mechanism. All of us have some sort of experience in the corporate world, well, everyone except her. I get it, she left her dreams behind so

Marcus can live out his. But this situation right now is her kryptonite.

"Looks like we can head to lunch early." I do a once-over in the mirror. I've got to be crazy to rescue Jenna from herself, especially after all the shit she's put me through. I can't watch her search for an escape and do nothing. It's like when people asked me if I was okay after Josh's accident. *Oh yeah, never better.* I always nodded or said I was taking it day by day but my insides twisted into oblivion making me wish I could escape from the world.

Jenna glances at her watch. "How about Pierre's? Crepes and Cosmos."

Chloe turns toward Jenna. "I've been dying to try Pierre's. But you'd have to make a reservation like... three months ago."

Jenna takes out her cell phone and holds up her pointer finger. She dials and presses the phone against her ear. "Jess. Hey, it's Jenna. Yeah, you too... listen we just finished dress shopping. Tyler's girlfriend has a corporate event, and we were hoping to grab a bite. Any chance you can hook us up with a table for four?" She pauses for a moment. "Yeah, me neither but it's true. He's a taken man. Okay, we'll see you in a half hour. Thanks."

"Are we in?" Chloe bounces on her toes.

"Yep. Let's get Cinderella all set for the ball and we'll head." Jenna slides her cell phone into her purse, a knowing grin on her face.

"So what's it like to be married to a rock star?" Chloe sips her Cosmo.

Jenna raises an eyebrow. "It's got its perks."

I glance around the quaint dining room, taking in the essence of France. This is about as close to Paris as you can get here in L.A. A mammoth crystal chandelier hangs in the center of the room. Bistro tables line the perimeter near the picturesque windows, bringing the ambiance of an outdoor café to the room, while the center tables boast fancy linens and crystal water goblets.

Jenna's connection hooked us up with a round table right in the center of the room so we can take in the atmosphere. I don't get how she knows so many people in L.A. It's like she's lived here her whole life, even though she only visits a few times a year. If it weren't for Chloe, I wouldn't know a thing about big city life.

Chloe probably thinks I'm crazy. It's like Jenna's been reprogrammed and is on her best behavior. I doubt Tyler had anything to do with this sudden change in attitude. I mean, she never listened to him before so what's up her sleeve this time?

"Ali, did you mention to Tyler he needs a tux for Saturday?" Jenna nibbles on a baguette. "His idea of a party is a keg and some tunes."

Ah, there's the Jenna I'm used to. "I gave him the names of a few places he can try." Okay, so that's a total lie, but I'm not dealing with her insults today toward myself or Tyler. He's not a moron, I'm sure he knows what black tie means, right?

"Maybe you should give him a quick etiquette refresher." She smirks.

"Jenna, he's been to weddings before. It's not like he's clueless on how to act at a formal event... come on, give him a little credit. It's not like she's taking Chaz." Lexie sips her wine.

Jenna chuckles. "True. Listen, I'm not trying to be a bitch. I'm telling you he's out of his element. He might need a little help, that's all."

Now she may have a point. So Tyler's used to wild parties and back stage antics, which consists of God knows what, but he can function in society. I mean, Josh never even wore a suit until we went to prom. Just because Tyler's somewhere different doesn't mean he can't adapt.

"I'll give him a few pointers." Lexie winks.

"You guys are making me nervous. Is there something I should know?" Maybe Tyler doesn't want to go with me, and he conned them into trying to talk me out of taking him. I did serve him breakfast in bed before asking him to be my date. There's no way he'd turn me down even if he wanted to.

"Yeah, guys are idiots." Jenna closes her menu and sets it on her plate.

"Newsflash." Chloe chuckles.

"Does Tyler turn into a werewolf or something? Saturday is a full moon." I nibble my lip.

"Something like that." Jenna turns toward the waiter who just walked up to the table.

"Mademoiselles. I'm Jacque, and I'll be your server. Do you know what you'd like?"

Yeah, I'd like to find out why Jenna's trying to insinuate that taking Tyler to the event is the worst idea in the history of the world. She's acting like he's bipolar or something. I spent more than enough time with Tyler to form an opinion, and he's pretty close to perfect. I'd never lay my heart on the line again if he wasn't worth it.

"I'll take the Risotto aux champignons." Jenna speaks like she's lived in Paris for the last ten years.

I haven't even looked at the menu. "I'll have the same." God knows what the hell I'm eating, probably brains. Jenna's the kind of evil human being who'd revel in the flesh of another.

Chloe and Lexie order, but I have no clue what they're having either. It's like I suddenly forgot the little bit of French I still remembered. At this point I don't even recall the curse words. Doesn't matter, I can't stop hearing Jenna's words over and over again in my brain. Why the hell do I care what she says? She's been trying to keep Tyler and I apart since we met.

"Ali, you guys are going to have a great time. Don't worry. Jenna's trying to tell you he's a little rough around the edges when it comes to the corporate world." Lexie twists her hair around a finger. "He'll be fine."

"Yeah, doesn't play well with suits." Jenna chuckles. "Remember when he called Regina a whore."

Lexie almost spits out her martini. "Well, she was hanging all over the lawyer handling our contract."

"Um, that's her husband." Jenna shakes her head. "Tyler has strange views about shit like that. He thinks anyone who wears a suit is a sellout."

"Who's Regina?" Do I even want to know? I get it, Tyler is all about the freedom. I swear, if he wasn't in Devil's Garden he'd probably join the nearest chapter of Hell's Angels.

"Devil's Garden's manager," Lexie says.

"If he acts like an animal, he'll have to answer to me. Ali worked way too hard to have anyone ruin this for her. I'm scrappier than I look." Chloe flashes a smile.

We all laugh. Chloe might kill someone if they chipped her nail or scuffed one of her designer shoes but she's no brawler. Tyler's been nothing but a gentleman every time we've been together. Even when he stormed the elevator to rip me a new one, he still helped me out rather than kick me when I was down. They've all lost their minds. Tyler would never do anything to hurt me or my career.

"We'll have to see how she handles groupies." Jenna nods toward Lexie.

"Cheers to that." Lexie downs the rest of her martini.

"Wow, you guys are Debbie Downers today." I shake my head.

"Just wait, you didn't see what's it's like backstage yet... You will and you'll feel the same way." Jenna taps her fingernails on her glass. "Closest you can get to hell on earth."

I'm sure it's a million times worse when I'm stuck here, thinking about all the things Tyler is doing backstage when he's on another continent. And just like that, my appetite fades away. If I knew today was going to be like this, I would've pulled something out of my closet and avoided this disaster of a day. I stare down at the table trying to hide the frown creeping over my face.

Lexie puts her hand over mine. "Don't worry. The meet and greets only last around an hour, and we're out of there. Trust me, if I can handle it, you can. Are you thinking of coming to Europe?"

No. Well, Tyler never actually asked me but even if he did I couldn't go. I mean, I'm building a career for myself here in L.A. and I can't just pick up and leave to hook up with a rocker I've been dating for all of two months. I mean, I love Tyler, it's not that, but I love myself too, and I can't lose everything I've worked for. "No. I'm focusing on my career here in L.A."

"If it still exists after Saturday." Jenna leans back as Jacque puts her lunch in front of her.

"Of course it will. Tyler and I are going to have a great night. All my colleagues will love him. It's not every day they get to meet a rock star." Or maybe it is. I'm still not sure who's going to be attending, but I think Jenna got my point.

"Hope you're right." She shovels a forkful of mushroom risotto into her mouth.

"Trust me. I know what I'm doing." Heat flushes across my cheeks.

"Famous last words." She smirks.

Clearly, shopping does not bond women. She's still trying to sabotage my relationship with Tyler. I just can't figure out why. I mean, there's nothing in it for her. And I really didn't expect Lexie to agree with her. Wait, was this lunch an intervention to warn me about Tyler's demons? Maybe there's more to all of this than meets the eye.

17
SOIREE

SINCE WHEN DID HALLOWEEN ARRIVE MORE THAN ONCE A YEAR? I glance at the mirror on the back of my bedroom door. Damn, I actually look like I could be on the arm of a rock star. I sway side to side, letting the long black chiffon dress drape down. It sticks to my curves like a Mustang heading up Mulholland Drive. The brooch sparkles, adding some glamorous bling. I push a tendril back from along my forehead and fluff the curls in my half up-do. Here I am, dressed the part with no clue on how to actually pull this off. I guess I should've worried more about what to do and what to say rather than what to wear.

Memories of Josh's cousin's wedding flow through my brain. Mariah always wanted the swanky lifestyle and when she hooked a Wall Street broker her dreams came true. I'd never been to a wedding before, but I was psyched to spend a weekend with Josh at Martha's Vineyard. At the reception, we snuck way too much champagne. I grabbed the microphone from the string quartet and burst into my best rendition of Billy Idol's *White Wedding*. Clearly not my finest moment, but Josh stood there clapping like I had the voice of an angel. Mariah freaked and smacked me with her bouquet screaming about how I ruined her wedding. Note to self, stay away from all microphones or other voice amplifying devices.

Knocking resonates through the walls of my apartment. Okay, he's here and ten minutes early. I put on my dangling crystal earrings and trek toward the door.

"Who is it?" Nothing wrong with adding a little humor to the night, maybe it will relax my frazzled nerves.

"Your friendly neighborhood earthquake-stopping, shark hunting, rock God." His voice emits a frequency that sends my body into overdrive.

All the nervous energy suddenly leaves my body. "Ah, and modest, too." I pull open the door.

Tyler stands tall in a perfectly fitted three-piece classic black tuxedo. I follow the fabric from his chiseled biceps to the black vest buttoned along his abs, continuing to the silver and black tie that hangs just above the promised land. My body temperature skyrockets, like volcanic lava flows through my veins. *Dear God, how am I supposed to keep my hands off him all night?* Whoever made that suit should market it as male lingerie. I continue to stare like I'm in some sort of walking coma.

"You can stop drooling now." Tyler winks and walks inside.

I shake my head, jolting back into reality. Caught red-handed, nothing like embarrassing myself right from the get go. My face is probably a hundred shades of crimson.

"My turn to stare." He takes a step back and sweeps my body from head to toe. "You look gorgeous."

He pulls a dozen red roses from behind his back. I guess I was caught up in the moment I didn't even notice he had them. His hopeless romantic aura shines through, even though he'd never admit it. "You didn't have to do that." I sniff the beautiful red buds, taking in the sweet aroma. "I love them."

"Keeping it classy." He flashes a sexy half smile. "Looks like I've got some hot eye candy on my arm tonight," he says as I turn to put the flowers in a vase.

"Right back atcha." I may have to spend half the night, keeping the ladies away, like some kind of formally dressed ninja.

"You ready or are you going for that getting there late thing?" Tyler slides his hands in his pants pockets.

Well, I doubt I'll ever be ready, but I hate being late. I mean, I know people think it's fashionable, but I don't want to rush. One of my goals for tonight is to avoid falling on my face.

"Let's head to this shindig." I lock my arm with Tyler's and guide him toward the door.

He looks at me, sporting a devious smile. What's he up to tonight? Quiet and smirking spells scheming. My stomach quivers. Come on Ali, get it together. What's the worst that can happen? Ugh, note to self, don't ever ask that, especially when butterflies swarm in my stomach and I'm ready to spew out the panini I ate at lunch. We head down the three flights of stairs at the speed of a sloth. Walking in heels is not my strong suit, especially not in these black pumps. I wish I had my Louboutins back, but alas, they are now in shoe heaven.

We continue to the sidewalk. I scan both sides of the road but Tyler's flashy car is nowhere in sight. He's going to love this.

"Okay, this time I really can't see the car."

He lifts a finger, and a limo pulls up to us. "We're going in style tonight, babe."

I melt into a puddle right there. He did all of this for me? I close my eyes and take a deep breath holding back a few tears. No need to turn on the water works even though I feel like I'm in the middle of a really good chick flick.

Even if Lexie and Jenna gave him a few pointers, he really hit this one out of the park. A man dressed in a suit, complete with a chauffeur hat pulls open the door and Tyler and I slide inside.

I scoot as close to him as possible without sitting on his lap. "In case I forget to tell you later... I had an awesome time tonight."

"You ain't seen nothing yet, babe." He brushes his lips against mine as the car takes off.

～

ELABORATE CRYSTAL CHANDELIERS CAST A MOONLIT GLOW through the ballroom, sending flecks of silver starlight all around. I hold on to Tyler, tighter than necessary, as we make our way inside. Dozens of people form small groups, sipping champagne, and talking with their whole bodies like they might win an academy award for hand gestures. I guess impressing a colleague takes dedication.

Who am I kidding? I'm not cut out for the whole schmoozing thing. I get it, you need to get in with the right person, and there's a ton of them here tonight. Everyone in this room has one thing in common, we all want to write a killer article, get exposure, and make a name for ourselves. So how am I supposed to stand out? Other than having Tyler on my arm, I'm just like everyone else.

I grip my place card and scan the room for table number five. Maybe coming here was a mistake. I'm still a newbie, not even close to ready for this kind of event. I mean, I don't even know anyone here other than Jake, and I have nothing good to say to him. My stomach knots. Well, if all else fails at least I get to spend an amazing night with Tyler.

I shift my gaze toward him. He stands tall like he's the movie star everyone came to see. I guess he's used to all eyes upon him, walking out onto the stage to a massive crowd of people who came to see him play. What's it like to be so... confident?

He locks eyes with mine. "Wanna grab a drink, babe? Or should we walk around so I can show off my arm candy?"

Wildfire spreads across my face. I think he's got that backwards. "I definitely need a drink."

We make our way to the bar on the far end of the room. Eyes stare through me like they're not sure if I belong here either. I take a deep breath and stand tall, no harm in following Tyler's lead. Of course, I'm not the rock star, in this scenario, I'm one of the many fans vying for some attention.

He scans the room. "Don't forget to point out those guys who always hit on you." He lowers an eyebrow. "You okay?" He leans against the bar, turning the heads of at least ten women.

Of course, he'd remember that little white lie. I hate to break it to him, but I'm lacking groupies at work. I force a smile. "Yeah, just a little intimidated." I take a glass of champagne from a serving tray as the waiter glides past us.

"What? Are you kidding me? Look around." He grabs my hips and pivots me until I'm facing the crowd of people, mingling around the room. "Really take a good look. These people got nothing on you, babe. They're all clones of each other." He drops his hands and turns to take a slug of beer.

"I'm just like them." I down the rest of my champagne and set the glass on the bar.

"Are you crazy? You are nothing like any of them." He tips his chin toward a woman, probably in her mid-thirties wearing a painted on black dress. "Watch, she touches that suit she's flirting with every ten seconds."

Her hand caresses the man's bicep as she speaks. Okay, I get it. Some people are willing to do anything to get cozy with the entertainment execs. At least Tyler knows I don't go that route.

"And how about him?" He gestures toward a guy, probably fresh out of school, trying to hold back a grimace every time he sips his drink. "Bet he wishes he was playing beer pong instead of downing scotch."

"At least they're trying." I fidget with my fingers. Yep, and I'm here gawking like a wallflower dying for the popular kids to accept me into their group. People watching isn't going to help my career.

"That's the thing. You don't have to try... you've got it." He finishes his beer and sets the glass on the bar for a refill. "You know that first article that ripped us apart."

I lower my head. "Yeah." Worst thing I've ever done, even though it gave my career the jump start it needed.

"Everything about it was awesome... you know, except that it was about us." He moves closer and slides his arm around my back. "These people need you... not the other way around."

Tingles sweep along my skin. "That's the best compliment of my life." I lean into Tyler, giving him a peck on the cheek. What the hell were Jenna and Lexie talking about? Tyler's more in his element than me. Without him, I'd be lost.

"True story." He winks.

"Only one problem, none of them know it." I snag a stuffed mushroom from the server. Great, here I go eating and drinking everything in sight. Why wasn't I blessed with losing my appetite when I'm nervous?

"Then show them what they're missing."

"It's not that simple. I can't just pick up a bass guitar and shred it like no one's business. And I can't bring a portfolio to these shindigs. It's all based on word of mouth and who I can impress on my own." I nibble my lip and scan the room, looking for any familiar face.

"That's what's wrong with corporate America. It's not what you know it's who you know." He sighs and shakes his head.

"I've got to play the game if I want to make it." I take a cocktail napkin and gently dab my mouth. With my luck, I'd talk to the owner of J&C records with a big piece of spinach between my teeth. I rub my lips together, trying to even out any last bits of lipstick. What a day to forget my purse at home. "Do I look okay?"

Tyler tucks a stray hair behind my ear and leans in close. "You are the most beautiful woman here. Anyone who can't see that is blind." His eyes widen like they're about to devour me.

The heat of a thousand suns radiates through every inch of

me. The words melt my soul. For the first time in forever, I feel beautiful, and it has nothing to do with the elaborate dress or fancy up-do. Tyler softens his gaze, his clear blue eyes gleam. Right now, I'm the only person that exists in his world. I shift my weight, trapping him against the bar.

"I see you're having a good time." Jake smirks and points to the bartender. "Gin and tonic".

The voice rips through me like nails on a chalkboard. My chest tightens. I take a step back from Tyler, still breathless. I guess I lost myself in the moment, now I look like the girl in the painted on dress. When Tyler stands before me saying perfect things and looking hot as hell in that suit, keeping it G-rated is near impossible, I'm only human.

I take a deep breath. Okay, Ali, let's step up the professionalism a notch. "Tyler, this is Jake. We work together."

Tyler reaches his hand to shake Jake's just as Jane marches up to the bar. Her black fitted dress with a small sleeve and lace at the top screams professionalism with an elegant flair. The large diamond studs in her ears cast a rainbow of color with every step.

"I take it everyone's having a good time." Jane gives us a quick once-over. A pleased grin graces her face.

"Ali certainly is." Jake sips his drink. "Nice to meet you, Tyler. Jane, have you met Ali's date... you know, he's one of the band members from her first article." He flashes his anchorman smile.

My heart pounds in my ears. What the hell is he doing? Making me look unprofessional in front of our boss won't benefit him at all here. No, he just likes to get a rise out of me. Or maybe he's one of those assholes that like to bring others down to build himself back up. Either way, it's not happening tonight. My hands clench into fists.

She lifts a brow. "No, don't think I had the pleasure. Jane Reiser." She holds out her hand.

Tyler takes it and gives a soft handshake. "Pleasure's all mine."

He sips his beer. "You know Ali's article was hardcore, gave us great exposure."

"I can see you're very appreciative." Jake leans back against the bar like he's God's gift to the world. "Not many rock stars accompany the reporters."

Tyler's skin flushes. He stares at Jake with cold eyes. "Yeah, well Ali and I have known each other a while. We had a blast at her last party, to celebrate her promotion."

Jane wrinkles her forehead. "Oh, so you didn't just meet at the interview." She gives Jake a dirty look. "I'll see you two later. Nice to meet you, Tyler." She walks away.

Tyler darts forward, stopping inches before Jake. "What the fuck is your problem, man?" He mutters through clenched teeth.

Jake takes a step back. "Call off your attack dog before you embarrass yourself any more." He shifts his eyes to mine.

I wedge myself between them. Just what I need, a fight breaking out over me. Definitely not the way I want to stand out. Tyler's a tiger ready to strike and Jake's the annoying fly swarming around until he's finally swatted. I've got to get them away from each other if I plan on surviving tonight.

I press my hands against Tyler's chest, trying to back him up. He barely budges. A bead of sweat forms along my hairline. I've got to stop this before it goes any further. No doubt, Jake will torment him until he snaps. Stupid game plan but for some reason it works for the jerk. I slide my hands up and wrap my arms around Tyler's neck, resting my head on his shoulder. He takes a deep breath and relaxes his tense muscles. I let out the breath I'd been holding. *Thank God.*

I press my lips against his earlobe. "Please, just ignore him. This night is important to me and I know he's the biggest asshole on the planet but please, let it go for tonight," I whisper.

Tyler sighs and lifts my chin. "Wait. You want me to stand here and do nothing while he tries to burn you to the ground?"

I nod.

"You can't be serious, babe." He steps back and gestures for the bartender to refill his beer.

"He's making himself look like an unprofessional moron… he can bury himself." How can I make him understand I don't need a gallant white knight to fight for my honor? Not tonight. Sometimes saying nothing speaks louder than any words.

He blows air out of puffed cheeks and leans against the bar. "Whatever." He slams his beer and sets the empty glass down for a refill.

The night's hardly begun and disaster fills the air. Maybe Jenna and Lexie were right, Tyler's not equipped to deal with the dirty politics of the entertainment world. Rock stars can get away with temper tantrums and fights. Hell, most of their fans even think it's cool, but it doesn't work like that when you're on the other side of the fence.

I hold back a tear about to fall. "Please, I need you tonight." I lift my eyes and stare into his baby blues.

He hooks an arm around my waist and pulls me against him. "I've always got your back, babe. Just keep him away from me."

Easier said than done. "I'll try. Promise me… no more fights." I nibble my lip.

"Yeah." He kisses my cheek.

Okay, not completely convincing, but I'll take it. Half of me loves that Tyler throws down to protect my honor like I'm in the middle of an old time romance. The other half hides under the covers, scared to death that he's about to go all psycho. A pressure cooker can only take so much before it bursts open, steam spewing.

"Let's find our seats." I take a step back and glance at the place card still in my hand, crumbled to oblivion. Okay, table five. *For the love of God, please don't let Jake be at our table.*

Tyler gestures to the bartender for another beer. "Need a refill?"

I nod. Last time I drank this much alcohol, I woke up next to Tyler so maybe tonight will take the same route. At this point, I'm better off observing and planning my mingling strategy for the next event.

I grip my glass of champagne with one hand and take Tyler's with the other. He stands tall and follows my lead. We weave through the small groups, still mingling, some laughing like they've just heard the funniest joke in the world. Half the guests sit at their tables. The rest swarm the bar. I scan the crowd. Jake sits at a half-full table, sipping his gin and preaching to a group of people who stare at him like he's reciting the secret to immortality.

My heart pounds as my eyes peruse the table number. I take a deep breath as the black number comes into focus, table number six. The weight of a thousand tons floats from my body. I see table five and pick up the pace like I'm in the last leg of a marathon.

"This is us." I set down my glass of champagne and plop into a seat, so my back is to Jake's table.

Tyler's beer sloshes to the rim of the glass as he sets it down. He sits beside me. His lips form a hard line, like a chiseled sculpture unable to move.

Silence kills me. When Josh and I would have one of our five-minute fights, he'd refuse to speak. It drove me insane. Of course, if I nibbled his ear a smile burst through his stone cold face, and we'd be kissing the next minute. That tactic won't work in this scenario.

I set my hand on Tyler's thigh. "Thanks for coming here tonight, I know it's not your thing."

He lets out a muffled laugh and shakes his head. "Yeah, watching some douche insult my girl and not being able to do shit about it." He sips his beer and puts the glass down on the table, harder than necessary. "Definitely not my thing."

A wave of energy flutters through my heart. The words "my girl" repeat in my brain like a broken record. I close my eyes for a second, erasing the rest of the world. How does he make me feel like the luckiest girl in the world, even when he's just about ready to go on a killing spree, Jake his first victim?

I get it, Jake's way out of hand and thinks he's the master of the universe but causing a scene at a black-tie event isn't the way to deal with it. You've got to hit him where it hurts, his pride. I slide my hand over his. "He already made himself look like an ass in front of Jane. He's his own worst enemy."

Tyler turns my chin toward him. "No one treats you like that and gets away with it."

My lip trembles. I open my mouth to speak, but nothing comes out.

"Ali," Jane interrupts.

I lean back and shift my eyes toward Jane.

"I'd like you and Tyler to meet Roger Turner, CEO of *Entertainment Rocks!* and his wife Lynne."

I stand up and tug on Tyler's arm, giving him the signal. "Great to meet you." I shake both their hands. Tyler stands and follows suit.

"Ali, I loved your article on the Elle Crowley. It showed a whole different side of the issue." Lynne takes the seat next to me. "Are you a reporter too, Tyler?"

"No, I only write songs." He flashes a smile.

"That's fabulous. Music speaks what words can't express." She tips her glass toward Tyler and sips her champagne.

"Thank you." He lifts his glass and takes a swig of beer, finishing the glass.

Amazing, even though he wants to rip Jake apart limb from limb, he turned on the perfect gentlemen switch. Kind of like how a sociopath goes through all the motions but never actually feels anything. Great, I've turned him into a psycho, way to go, Ali.

"Want another drink?" He turns toward me.

"Yeah, I'll come with you." I stand and sip the small amount of champagne left in my glass. "Nice talking to you, Lynne."

"Likewise." She smiles.

I came, I saw, well I didn't quite conquer, but at least I know what happens at these events. Tyler struggled through something he obviously hates just to make me happy. He paid his dues. Maybe it's time we head out before things get any more intense.

I weave my arm through his and march toward the bar, trying to keep up with his fast pace. "Want to head out after this drink? I had enough of the corporate world for today."

He stops and faces me. "Ali…"

Jake rolls in like a tornado, unwelcome and ready to spin everything out of control. He smirks, staring at the two of us with glossy eyes. A low groan forms in Tyler's throat. Great, a showdown. I've got two choices, get Jake to leave or get Tyler out of here. Is either option possible?

Jake stumbles toward us, pointing his finger in our direction. "Looks like you're tight with Mr. Turner's wife. Maybe you can cover her cat's wedding," he slurs. "It would be a great accompaniment to your dog spa piece." He laughs, swaying from side to side.

"I'm going a different route, broadening my horizons. I can feature you in my article on sloppy drunks who can't even zip their pants."

A few people near us burst into laughter. Jake looks down and quickly pulls up the zipper, getting the material stuck as he struggles. The laughter turns into a small roar.

Jake's face turns crimson. "Whatever… hard to get a decent suit these days." He takes a step backward, knocking into a woman.

The woman lets out a loud sigh. She holds out her glass, champagne dripping down the stem. She flashes a death glare in Jake's direction and stomps away.

Tyler slides his hands in his pockets, a knowing smirk on his face.

Jake shoots fire from his eyes. He stands in front of us, like a linebacker. Doesn't he realize he's making things worse? Next, he'll slam his drink down and scream "you shall not pass".

I shattered his goal of making me look bad tonight, or maybe he did it himself. Whatever. The desperation in his eyes sends a chill from my spine to my feet. Why is my spidey sense suddenly kicking in?

I take Tyler's hand. "Ready?"

He intertwines his fingers though mine and navigates around Jake like he's the drunk uncle ruining a classy wedding. We head toward the door.

"Hey, Ali…" His voice makes my skin crawl.

Tyler stops. My heart rate triples. Every sense in my body screams run… get out, but my feet plant themselves to the floor. Tyler turns around. I spin toward the nemesis saying my name.

Jake smirks. "I've got a great idea. Beneficial for both of us," he yells through the room.

Jane shakes her head, she rushes toward him like she's about to duct tape his mouth shut.

He sips the last of his drink and tosses the glass on the table next to him. "How about I throw one of my decent assignments your way." He points toward Tyler. "And in exchange, you can bang me just like you did him. I bet you're a good fuck."

Tyler rips his hand away. Hellfire sweeps through his face, burning crimson. He charges forward, like a freight train out of control. Jake's sarcastic smile melts from his face, his eyes widen. Maybe his brain function kicked in enough to alert him of the severity of the situation. I stand still, paralyzed.

Jake holds up his hand. "Listen..."

Tyler doesn't even slow. He storms forward and punches Jake in the face. Gasps fill the room. Everyone stops, all eyes upon the two of them. Jake flails for a second and then falls backward, knocking over the table behind him. Tyler kneels above him, grabbing him by the vest of his three-piece suit.

"Dude, you think you know it all. Well, let me educate you, man. She's mine... got it?"

Jake stares up at Tyler through half-opened eyelids, blood dripping from his lip. He tries to nod.

"No one EVER talks to her like that... and if some scumbag like you even tries it, you deal with me." Tyler loosens his grip and moves to his feet.

"Sorry, your girl's a whore." Jake smirks through bloody teeth.

Tyler goes into attack mode. He pounces on Jake like a lion taking down an antelope. He holds Jake down with one hand and punches him with the other. Blood splatters along the white linen tablecloth, turning the elegant venue into a war zone.

"You don't know when to shut your friggin mouth," Tyler yells in between punches.

Jake's eyes roll back, and he lies limp on the floor. Mr. Turner yells for security. Four men, who look like they could be body slamming each other in a wrestling ring, rush to the fight. They yank Tyler off Jake and escort him out of the building.

Everyone turns their attention from Jake and stares up at me, squinting their eyes like they're trying to read my mind. A flush creeps across my cheeks. I fidget with my fingers, cringing. It's like I'm in the middle of a nightmare. How could Tyler do this to me? He promised, no fights.

Jane struts up to me and grabs my arm. She pulls me out into the hallway like a child being scolded. "What the hell is going on?"

My stomach drops to the floor. I swallow hard. "I'm sorry... Tyler shouldn't have handled it that way." It's all I could say.

She saw everything go down, heard the things Jake was saying. Just because he's lying unconscious doesn't mean I have to take the hit for his actions. He's an asshole and got what he deserved, even though it wasn't the time or the place. What am I thinking? Tyler knows better. I'm sure he deals with drunk fans who have a few too many and say things to piss him off. Isn't he beyond the solving problems with violence phase? Plus, he promised me he wouldn't fight with Jake tonight, and he broke it.

"You're damn right." She lets out a loud breath and paces in a small circle. "How am I supposed to explain this?" She wipes her hands across her face. "Jake has been shooting digs at you all night. Is there something going on I should know about?"

I shrug. "Not that I know of. I have no idea what his problem is with me."

"I've got to smooth things over in there. Go home now. I think your presence will make things worse at this point. I want both of you in my office first thing Monday morning." She pats down her dress, plasters a fake smile on her face, and marches back into the room.

Tears stream down my face. I should probably get used to the bottom of the barrel assignments if I can even get them at this point. Jesus, I may not even have a job. My arms tremble. I wipe my clammy hands against my dress. What the hell happened? Tonight was supposed to be amazing, instead it turned into a testosterone-induced World War III. Looks like Tyler's not the only one who's not welcome here. Nope, apparently I'm taking the hit too. I slowly make my way down the hallway to the main entrance. What am I going to say to him?

A cool wind greets me as I step outside. I wrap my arms around myself and navigate down the steps. The dark night gives way to a few bursts of starlight. I head down to the sidewalk, conjuring a speech for when I see Tyler. Where the hell is he?

I walk to the end of the block. "Tyler?"

Nothing, not even the chirp of a cricket. My chest tightens. I trot on my toes to the rear parking lot, "Tyler."

An aching resonates through my soul. I close my eyes, hoping for a voice in the distance. Nothing. I head back to the front of the building and sit on the steps. Third time's the charm. "Tyler," I yell a little louder. Still nothing. I cover my face, unable to stop the river of tears flowing through. How can he do this to me... again?

1 8

MOVING BACKWARD

THE LETTERS *TYLER* FLASH ACROSS MY CELL PHONE SCREEN YET again.

Chloe grabs it before I can send the call to voicemail. "Stop calling, don't text, forget Ali exists. You've destroyed everything." She presses her finger onto the screen so hard it's a miracle it didn't come through the other side.

I wipe away the millionth tear rolling down my cheek. "Thanks for rescuing me yet again."

Amazing he didn't take the hint after the twenty unanswered texts and ten phone calls gone straight to voice mail. I guess he just doesn't know when to stop. What can he possibly say to change things?

Tyler ruined Chloe's night too. She ran out on her date, clutching her purse like she just stole the silverware from the swanky restaurant where they were dining. Then she rushed to come pick me up. I owe her so much it's no use keeping track anymore.

"Like I was going to let him do any more damage." She puts her hand on my shoulder. "Don't waste another second crying over him." She lowers her chin and slides her hand away. "He's so not worth it. And the bastard flew right underneath my radar." Her lips move into the best pouty face made from anyone over six years old.

"Yep, just like a stealth bomber. Flies in surreptitiously to save the day but ends up leaving everything in flames." My life turned into a pile of ashes, charred from the flames of love.

I sigh. The worst part, I did this to myself. I broke my number one rule, stay out of relationships and focus on work. I mean, the whole reason I came to L.A. is to build my career. A one night stand with a rocker and everything's gone to shit. Did aliens remove my brain for examination and forget to put it back?

Maybe they should've taken my heart instead. It takes forever to put it back on the line but only a second to shatter it into pieces. Was everything he said to me a lie? I don't get it. He didn't pull out the charm for sex, he could get that anywhere. I screwed him, big time with the story. Was this all a ploy to get back at me, hurt me in the worse way possible? Bravo, he hit the goal.

A few stray tears fall down my chin. Hollowness fills my aching chest like a piece was ripped out leaving a void of emptiness. Why did I give him my heart and leave the rest of me exposed, vulnerable? God, I'm an idiot. Why would I put myself through this again when the first time nearly destroyed me? This time might finish me off.

I slump over, leaning against the arm of the couch. "Why did I do this to myself?"

"Are you serious? You did nothing wrong." Chloe pulls me into a side hug.

"Not true. I should've stayed single." I shake my head.

"Oh yeah, because you oozed happiness before you met him."

I slide from her grip and crinkle my forehead. "What the hell is that supposed to mean?"

She shrugs. "In the last four years, I haven't seen you as happy as you were these last few months… you know, except for today."

Is she insane? I throw my hands in the air. "I might as well shoot up drugs, take in the euphoria of the high and live for the moment, then wish for death when I crash." I regret the words as soon as they leave my mouth. Especially since Chloe's brother almost died from a heroin overdose a few years back. Thank God he cleaned up. What I'm going through now is nothing compared to the hell she and her family endured.

She shakes her head. "Would never work. You hate needles."

I let out a slight chuckle. Leave it to Chloe to make me laugh when I want take off and join a monastery. "Sorry, Chlo. I didn't mean it."

She nods. "I think the female praying mantis has the right idea... you know, ripping off the male's head after mating. Saves a lot of trouble."

We both erupt into a mess of giggles.

My laughter quickly turns to tears. The levee breaks again. Tears roll down my face like a raging river. I close my eyes, trying to shut off the water works but my tired body slumps. I cover my face with my hands.

Chloe hugs me, her arms trembling.

I take a deep breath and pull away, wiping away as many tears as I can. "The worst part is that I still wish he was holding me. Telling me he screwed up and he'll fix everything." I sink into the couch. "Nothing can repair this damage." I'm right back where I was six years ago, shattered into pieces. How can I pick them up this time?

Chloe reaches over to the end table and hands me some tissues. "He called you like, a million times. I bet he feels the same way."

I shake my head. "He ruined everything. I can't talk to him again... ever." I wipe my eyes with the tissue. "It sounds like you're sticking up for him. He singlehandedly ended my career by acting like an immature ass. Besides starting a fist fight at a black-tie event, he just left me there to fend for myself. How could he just leave me?"

"Sorry, momentary lapse of judgement. He's scum. Worst human being that exists on the planet." She hands me another tissue. "I just want you to be happy."

Yeah, me too. Right now, happy isn't on the cards. "Thanks."

She stands up and yanks my arm. "Come on, you're not moping around all day over a guy. That's not our style."

I slump back into the couch. "I don't want to go out. Not today."

"Fine, then I'll order pizza, and we're watching chick flicks and making cocktails." She grabs the remote and surfs through the guide. "Ah ha. Hot vampires turning a town upside down."

I peek through my stinging eyes. *The Lost Boys?* I've already lived through the mayhem and pretty much had the life sucked out of me. Watching vampires do it to someone else is like reliving it again. "Stop. Let's watch *American Psycho.*"

She presses the remote. "Christian Bale for the next two hours. Nice."

I grab Chloe's cell phone from the table and hand it to her. "Extra cheese and mushrooms."

"Your wish is my desire." She blows me a kiss and heads to the kitchen to grab the take out menu.

Ugh, why can't I rewind my life? My stomach drops. Jane's going to rip me a new one in about twelve hours. After that, I'm back to square one. I'll miss my cubicle. Of course, I sure as hell won't miss my neighbor. Maybe Tyler threw the first punch, but Jake started the fight.

My cell phone screen lights up, glowing through the dim lit room. I glance down, scanning over the bright white letters.

I'm sorry. Please forgive me, babe.

I flip it over and slide it across the table. A few more tears escape. Shutting him out is damn near impossible. I mean, with Josh he was gone. No choice in the matter. No wondering "what if" and "should I." This time it's my call. I keep second guessing myself. Am I making the right decision? Come on Ali, be strong.

Tyler and I were doomed from the start and what happened last night solidifies the fact we shouldn't be together.

I grab a pillow, pressing it close to my body like it might help hold me together. How am I supposed to forget the way his arms wrap around me, blocking out the rest of the world? Or the way his musky cologne jolts my body into a frenzy. The stray hairs that dance along my face when I'm nuzzled against him. An ache forms in my chest. Is it possible to feel your heart break?

I quickly wipe away a tear. He woke my body, making it come alive in a million ways. He knew exactly what to do and how to do it, bringing me to the brink of irresistible insanity that only exists between the two of us. That kind of chemistry only happens in chick flicks and romance novels but I had it. And now it's disappeared into oblivion.

How am I supposed to forget all of it? His voice echoes in my head like an iPod on repeat, calling me babe. The most derogatory, sexist term that I love to hear roll off his tongue. God, I just want him back. I take a deep breath. Come on Ali, this is for the best.

Chloe sets two pink drinks down on the table. "Pizza's on the way, what did I miss?" She plops on the couch next to me.

My world fell apart. I'm contemplating how I'm going to make it through another day living in hell on earth. "Not much. Christian Bale and his colleagues are showing off their business cards."

She scans me from head to toe. "You okay?" She grimaces.

Not even close. I'm the absolute furthest thing from okay possible. "Yeah, fine." What's the point in telling her the truth? Pity won't help me through this, and there's nothing else she can do for me. She's here and that's more than enough. I grab a drink from the table.

"Chloe's famous hurricanes" She flashes a smile and sips her drink.

Ah, how fitting. I gulp down almost half the glass. The cool liquid burns my throat. Whoa, she made these super strong. Maybe she knows exactly what I need. A concoction to shut my mind down for a little while. At this point, I'll try anything.

I slug down the rest and slide my glass on the table in front of her. "Hit me up again."

"You sure?" She taps her fingernails against the glass.

I raise my eyebrows and shoot her the you-can't-be-serious look. "Oh yeah." It's about the only thing I'm sure of at the moment.

"Coming right up." She mixes up another one and hands it to me. "To a fresh start." She raises her glass and clinks it with mine.

We both take a sip. I force a smile. Aren't new starts supposed to be filled with hope and infinite possibilities? I know exactly what's in store for me. I slug down half the glass. The concoction is mostly juice with a swig of alcohol. Maybe I'll be the bartender next time. I get it, she's trying to help, and I love her for it, but I don't want a new life. I want the life I had three days ago.

Tomorrow everything changes. A whole new world awaits me. A fresh new start filled with broken dreams and heartbreak.

THE FIRST DAY OF THE REST OF MY LIFE. THE WORDS ECHO THROUGH my brain like a war cry. I repeated them to myself over and over again the first time I walked into this building. Of course, today they have a whole new meaning. I take a deep breath.

My heels click on the tile of the long stretch through the foyer to the elevator. I close my eyes for a second and take in the sound; muffled voices, the tap of my shoes against the tile, the beeping of the elevator signaling it's time to jump in to enter a world of possibilities. My stomach drops to the floor. Why did I always think knowing this is the last time would make things easier? I mean, I wished on every fallen star for another minute with Josh so I could make the most of it. I've never been so wrong. Knowing this is it makes you focus on the inevitable instead of taking in the moment.

I step into the elevator and press the button with my trembling finger. Maybe I should've taken the stairs. The last time I stepped into the elevator and walked into work internally disheveled I summoned an earthquake. Just as the doors move to close, a hand slides in between them.

My heart rate triples. I focus on the smooth fingers and perfect cuticles, probably freshly manicured. I let out the breath I'd been holding. Did I seriously expect lightning to strike twice? Why would I even think Tyler was going to rush here to insist on talking to me? Last time, he demanded answers. No need to clear up what happened this time.

The doors slowly open back up. I raise my eyes and stare at the devil. Jake struts in, his head pointed to the ceiling like the air is better suited for him up above. I stand tall, refusing to move an inch. As far as I'm concerned, he could plummet down the shaft. He brushes past me and leans against the back wall, tapping at his cell phone screen.

I swallow hard, trying to force the wave of nausea to the depths of my stomach. I grip my purse strap, gazing at him from the corner of my eye. Dark glasses cover most of the purple mark on his left cheek. A line of dried blood holds together his bottom lip, swelled a quarter larger than its normal size. Despite the fact he looks like he just crawled out of an MMA octagon, a smug grin still graces his brutalized face.

My lips upturn into a small smile. Good for the bastard. He deserved everything he got and probably more. Maybe Jake learned you can only push people so far. And you won't always come out unscathed. You mess with the wrong person you get what you have coming. I mean, he bullied me for weeks. I guess he figured I'm just a feeble woman who can't do a thing about it. Too bad I didn't get to smack that smile off his face, at least for a little while. What the hell am

I thinking? Now I sound like we're meeting after school at the playground. Did Tyler have that much of an effect on me?

Jake walks out of the elevator like he's about to accept a Pulitzer. I fight the urge to stick my foot out and trip him. Doesn't matter, right now I'm about to face the inevitable. I swallow hard trying to alleviate the ache in the back of my throat like a thousand bees just stung me at the same time. The elevator doors move, closing me in. I step out a split second before they shut. Fresh new start, here I come.

I fidget with my fingers. Déjà vu floods through me. Was I this nervous the first time I stepped into her office? Probably, no chance of impressing her this time. No, it's pretty much a meeting to follow protocol.

Claire lifts her eyes from her desk. "You can both go right in." Her cold stare sends chills from my head to my feet.

Jake pulls open the door and walks inside, dropping the door right on my shoulder. I huff. Why not be an asshole until the last possible second? No sense in redeeming himself now. I push the door back open and slip inside. It slams shut behind me. I scan the room, taking in the panoramic view of L.A. one last time. Jake already made his way to the leather chair.

Jane sits tall in her chair. Her hair slicked back into a tight bun. My pulse skyrockets. She intimidates merely with her presence. You can literally feel her when she's in a room. It's almost like a superpower. I move my trembling legs forward, gripping onto my purse for dear life.

Her eyes burn through me, watching my every move. I pick up the pace. Procrastinating won't change things. Like I always say, best to get it over with just like ripping off a Band-Aid. Only this time, the Band-Aid is directly attached to all my hopes and dreams.

I slip out of my heel, buckling my knee. By some miracle from the heavens I catch myself before I plummet to the floor, but my purse spins off into oblivion. Why not add one last embarrassing moment to the list.

Jake bursts into laughter. He covers his mouth with his hand like he's trying to be discreet. The fakeness oozes through.

Jane stands up. "Shut it… now." She points at Jake and then turns toward me. "You okay, Ali?"

Heat spreads across my face, no doubt it's pure crimson. I nod. Might as well leave my last impression the same as my first, clumsy and unprepared. I scurry to the far end of the office and throw the mascara, keys, and loose change that escaped from my purse back inside. I head back and plop down into the hard leather seat next to Jake.

Jane sits back down. "Take of your sunglasses. This isn't happy hour at the Cabana."

I muffle a laugh.

Jake slides off his glasses. The white part of his eye blotches with red, as if he'd been drinking straight gin for a week. His entire eyelid gleams dark purple, getting lighter as it reaches the brow. Last time I saw that type of disaster was when I tried a smoky eye technique to match my vampire Halloween costume.

"What were you both thinking?" Jane rises from her chair and paces the length of her desk.

Neither one of us say a word. I'd like to tell her this is all Jake's fault. He pushed me, bullied me, and insinuated I sleep with the interviewees to get a good a story. I mean, he did all of that. She's seen it, he said it in front of her many times. Truth be told, I let him get away with it. I never once stood up for myself or told Jane I met Tyler before the interview. Tyler told her that himself. Maybe if I grew a set and put him in his place long ago I wouldn't be sitting here right now. Never again.

"You both represent me when you are at these events. You know how this looks?" She rubs her forehead. "You look immature and unprofessional… and you made this office look like recess at preschool." She shakes her head, still pacing. "What's going on between you two?" She puts her hands on her desk and leans forward. "Well?"

"Sorry Jane. I can't deal with Ali's unprofessionalism." Jake looks at me, and then back at Jane. "It's disgusting if you ask me."

Jane huffs and sits back in her chair.

I let out a low growl and spin around toward him. "And what exactly do you have a problem with? Is it that I brought Tyler to the event? For your information, we've been dating for months. I did nothing unprofessional. You concocted these scenarios in your brain. Maybe you should use some of that creativity on your stories. Or get a life so you don't have to worry so much about mine."

Oh my God, did I say that out loud? The words flow like hot lava. I sit back in my chair and press my lips closed, obviously not my most professional moment. Jane might throw me right out the window at this point.

Why stop now, at this point there's nothing to lose. I sit up tall. "Jane, I think Jake will do whatever it takes to make me look bad so he can get the best assignments. I stay away from the dirty politics of this world. I want my writing to speak for itself." I fold my hands across my lap.

"And it does. You are an amazing writer, Ali. But you can't have your boyfriend starting brawls at black tie events. Don't ever let a guy hold you back. You've got a great future ahead of you if you can stay on track." She turns toward Jake. "And you, were you at a corporate event or a frat party?"

Jake flashes a smug grin. "You know how it is, Jane. The guys were handing me drinks and the finest cigars. I wanted to fit in with the gentlemen. You know, make connections."

She raises an eyebrow. "Really. Well, look around. This isn't the boys club and we're not living in the 60's." She taps her fingers on the desk. "Your stories need depth, the writing is mediocre at best, work on that rather than impressing the gentlemen." She makes quotation marks in the air with her fingers. "And one more sexist comment like that I'll make sure you never work for any magazine in L.A.... Got it?"

He nods. I resist the urge to jump out of my chair and cheer. Did he seriously think that mentality was going to fly with Jane? I mean, hello, she's a woman. God, he's even stupider than I give him credit for.

She looks at me, then turns toward Jake. "Whatever this is between you two ends now."

We both nod.

She sits back in her chair. "You only get one second chance. Don't make me regret it." She flips through her folder. "You're both on probation for a month. During that time, you'll be checking quotes and research."

Jake huffs. "You can't be serious. It's prime time for fall television... hell, it's an election year."

"And you won't be covering either. Claire will set you up downstairs. Please close the door on your way out." She leafs through papers like we're not even in the room.

The dark cloud lifts, spreading its silver lining. I survived the wrath of Jane. A month of research and quote checks is nothing compared to unemployment. Of course, Jake made it through this too but not completely unscathed. I bet his skin crawled when Jane praised my writing and ripped his apart. Good, he deserves a little dose of reality. Plus, now he knows there's no boys club here. Nope, girl power.

Jake storms out of the room. Jane looks up for a second, shakes her head and goes right back to the paperwork. I navigate my way through the office, paying careful attention to my footing and slowly closing the door behind me.

Jake stands at Claire's desk, quickly sliding on his sunglasses to hide his dirty little secret. He got his ass kicked from running his mouth. I lag behind, waiting until he steps into the elevator before heading to Claire's desk. I could care less what he has to say and I sure as hell am not afraid of him. I just would rather stay away. No need to let his negative black soul infiltrate me.

I step up to Claire's desk. "Any chance you can set me up as far away from him as possible?"

She holds back a smile. "I'd have the same request if I had to work with him," she whispers. "Oops, did I say that out loud."

I smile. It looks like Jake made quite an impression on all the staff here.

She hands me a mountain of paperwork. "You can head down the basement, pick any table you want. It's like a huge library down there."

"My kind of place." I hold the papers close to my chest. "Thank you."

Just as I'm about to head to the elevator my phone rings, vibrating through my purse. I set the paperwork down on a chair and pull it out. My eyes peruse the white numbers flashing across the screen. Oh my God, it's happening.

19

DREAM JOB

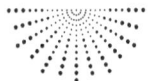

MY BODY FREEZES, PARALYZED. I STARE AT THE SCREEN, IT'S ALL I can do. My hand trembles, slowly willing my body to move. Everything happens in slow motion, like one of those dreams where you struggle to run but you move at a turtle's speed. Suddenly the vibrating stops.

I suck in a breath, my eyes still glued to the screen. *Dammit*, I missed it. What the hell is wrong with me? It's like I'm afraid to grasp an opportunity, or maybe I'm scared of the words coming from the other end.

My phone chimes and the voicemail icon flashes across the screen. I exhale slowly, releasing the breath bottled up in my chest. All hope isn't lost, not yet anyway. I shove my phone back in my purse and hit the elevator button. I've got to hear the message, but not here, not like this.

I stop on the main floor and rush through the foyer like a raging river chases me. I'll have the next month to fact check in the basement, no need to hurry down there now. I keep going, paying careful attention to my footing. With my luck, I'll crash into a pillar and smash my phone. I escape into the mammoth parking lot, trekking forward until I see the silver hue of my car. At last, a safe haven.

I click the key fob and plop into the driver's seat, slamming the door behind me. I lean back and take a deep breath, staring out of the windshield. The cloudy sky turns dark, like an evil took over in a few seconds flat. *Please don't let this be an omen of things to come.*

I dig in my purse and take out my cell phone. The voicemail icon still graces the homepage. A few drops of rain smack against the windshield growing in intensity. A split second later, the heavens unleash their fury. The pounding rain drums against my car, blocking out any other noise. Why is there always an obstacle? I don't get it. Some people float their way through life with no setbacks, taking everything that comes their way. How the hell do they get off so lucky? Every time I try, divine intervention makes it take a turn for the worse. I can't even hear my goddamn voicemail.

I fling the phone onto the passenger seat and rest my head on the steering wheel. A few tears roll down my cheeks. Yeah, I know life isn't fair, but I've paid my dues, where the hell is my break? I take a deep cleansing breath and wipe away my tears. Come on Ali, suck it up. Sulking or feeling sorry for myself won't make a difference. Time to put my big girl panties on and see what's in store for me.

I sit up and grab my phone. It's now or never. I press the voicemail and hold the phone to my ear. Light flashes into the corner of my eye. I turn to the left and gaze out the window. The rain stopped, leaving behind a brilliant rainbow, boasting its colors throughout the sky.

"Allison, it's Kate Winters from *Newswatch Weekly*. I wanted to let you know your article comes out tomorrow. I've had a shipment sent to your home. I've got to tell you, it's a big hit here. Everyone cringes when they read about your ordeal. Being trapped in an elevator during an earthquake brings out the worst fears for some of us. I was hoping we could chat. Tyler was right about your talent. I'd like to discuss working together on a more permanent basis. I hope to hear from you soon."

I press play again as soon as the message stops. Okay, so it's quirky, but I need to make sure I didn't imagine all of this. Trauma clouds memories and today was a cyclone. Kate's voice fills the car. The words sing to my soul. I pinch my arm. Ouch, yep it's real. Kate Winters wants to discuss working with me and it's all thanks to Tyler. My dream job sits before me on a silver platter held in part by the man I love. Only one problem, his world collides with mine, causing a supernova of destruction. Can I crawl from the ashes of the aftermath again or will we both go down in flames?

"TELL ME YOU CALLED HER BACK," CHLOE YELLS AS SHE FLIPS through the pages of *Newswatch Weekly*.

"I will." I hold the magazine up trying to control my trembling fingers. *Shake, Rattle, and Roll: By Ali Whitman* sits smack dab in the middle of the periodical. A smile spreads across my face like wildfire. It happened, my first byline in a nationally acclaimed magazine. No smut reporting, no digging for juicy gossip from the past, just professional honest writing.

Did Tyler see this yet? A brick drops in my stomach. Devil's Garden has a hero, and everyone now knows it. Maybe it'll have some impact on their new record, bring in a whole new genre of fans. He deserves success. He brought mine directly to me. I nibble my nails.

"Ali, this article is amazing. You didn't tell me the half of it. And Tyler... every woman in America is gonna want some of that now. I might want to date him."

I swing my head around and give her a death stare.

"Ah, good, I got your attention." She closes the magazine and turns toward me. "What's up? You're acting like you broke a heel off your Manolos."

I scrunch my eyebrows. "Uh, I don't have Manolos... but yeah, I know." I drop the magazine on the table and sink into the couch. "What do I say when I call her... I mean, I want to work for *Newswatch Weekly* but do I lie and say Tyler and I are still... on speaking terms?"

She puts her hand on my shoulder. "Listen, you wrote the article. You earned this. Tyler may have gotten you into the club, but you danced on the tables all on your own." She winks.

I laugh. "Yeah, great comparison. Maybe you should write."

She smacks my arm, playfully. "Call her."

I nod and grab my cell phone. A kaleidoscope of butterflies swarms my stomach, sending my heartbeat into overdrive. My hand trembles as I press the call back number. Chloe was right, like always. A fresh new start awaits me. Am I ready for it?

"Kate Winters."

I clear my throat. "Hi Kate, it's Ali Whitman." I break out into a frenzy of shivers like I'm trekking across the Himalayas in the middle of a blizzard. Thank God we aren't on a Skype call.

"Ali, your article is burning through the pages of *Newswatch Weekly*. The CEO personally called me to ask where I found you hiding." She muffles the phone for a second. "Would you like to be part of the team? There's an opening for a news reporter in our L.A. office."

I bounce on my toes. Oh my God, a news reporter. I close my eyes and picture my name on a feature article... *Supreme Court's Landmark Ruling by Ali Whitman*. Warmth radiates through my body like the heavens shine down upon me. This is it, my big break. I slowly open my eyes and pace around the room.

Chloe mouths "What?" All I can do is flash her a full-teeth smile.

"Hello... are you still there?"

I jolt back to reality. "Yes... Kate, I'm very interested in the position."

"Wonderful. Let's set up a meeting to discuss the details. How about Monday morning at ten?"

"I'll be there. I look forward to seeing you." I press end on my cell phone and set it down on the coffee table. "I got the job." I sprint toward Chloe. She meets me in the middle of the room. We both lock arms and jump up and down like we just won the lottery.

"Congratulations, Al." She pulls me into a hug.

I take a deep breath, letting my brain fully comprehend what just happened. I'm a news reporter for *Newswatch Weekly* magazine. Everything I've worked for has paid off. I'm finally exactly where I want to be. It's completely perfect... well almost.

Chloe pulls away. "We've got to celebrate... where to this time?"

I take a step back. "Oh no... no celebrating. We can order in. No clubbing, no dancing, no drinking... no going out to celebrate, period. You know where that got me last time."

She raises her eyebrows and smiles. "Yeah, it ended up getting you your dream job. Maybe you should be thanking me, dear."

I grab a pillow from the couch and throw it at her. "You know what I mean."

She catches it and nods, a smirk still gracing her face. "Okay, how about a fancy dinner. We'll celebrate elegantly."

"Deal."

Knocking radiates through the apartment. Did Chloe order something while I was on the phone with Kate? No way, no delivery is that quick. Maybe she's got something else up her sleeve.

"You expecting someone?" I nod toward Chloe.

She cocks her head. "My guests usually come to my apartment."

I shrug. My heart beats in double time. Did Tyler see the

article? Déjà vu floods through me. Doubt he'd have the same reaction twice, but then again he never fails to surprise me. I take a few steps toward the door. Jolts of electricity flow through my core. Why is my body ignoring my brain? It's not him... we're over. Amazing, hope exists even though all rational thought proves otherwise. I grip the handle and pull open the door.

Jenna and Lexie stand in the doorway, each holding up a copy of the magazine.

"Congratulations." Lexie smiles.

I let out a deep breath. The smile gracing my face melts into a frown. See, not him. Why would he show up? There's nothing here for him. Not anymore. Just burning passion and an endless river of love that I can't give to him, we're better apart. Now, if my heart would just listen to reason.

"Don't be so excited to see us." Jenna lowers the magazine, exposing a black strapless sundress that looks runway worthy.

I blink repeatedly, pulling myself back into reality. "Sorry, my brain's on overdrive today. Come on in guys."

"Uh huh." Jenna flings her blond locks over a shoulder and struts inside.

Lexie follows. "Great article, Ali. Superb quality writing."

"Thank you. I'm glad you guys like it." A compliment from Lexie means a lot. Not just because I've fixed the tension with the band from the last article. Jenna probably cares more about that than anyone. Lexie truly understands what I'm trying to achieve. I mean, she's done it. Plus, she knows if an article's well written or just a bunch of words on paper.

They make their way inside and head to the living room. Chloe stares at the pair like the devil's summoned them to steal my soul. She slides over, making room for them on the couch.

"I see you girls read the article. Let me guess, now you're in Ali's fan club?" She points to herself with both pointer fingers. "You're looking at the president."

"I'm in." Lexie hi-fives Chloe and sits next to her on the couch.

Jenna takes a seat on the last cushion. She sets her purse on the table. "Everyone loves your article. Even Chaz… guess he can read." She sweeps her gaze from my feet to my head, locking eyes with me. She stares through my soul. "Yeah, *everyone*."

My heart drums against my chest, skyrocketing through me. *Dammit.* She knows exactly what I'm thinking. How the hell does she do that? At least I know Tyler's read it. One question erased from my frazzled mind. I sit in the living room chair adjacent to the couch. "That's great. I was hoping they all were happier with this article."

Chloe looks at me, then back at Lexie and Jenna. "How'd you guys find Ali's apartment?"

Lexie twirls her hair around a finger. "Tyler had it written on a piece of paper. I guess from the first time you guys met. He left it in the practice room. We figured we'd surprise you and congratulate you on the article. I hope that's okay."

"Of course. It's great to see you two." Okay, there's more to this than an impromptu visit. No way they kept a paper with my address on it from months ago. Lying isn't one of Lexie's strong points and Jenna's never beats around the bush. "Can you guys stay a while? I'll order in." What are they up to?

"Sounds good to me. I won't have to listen to Tyler mope and whine all damn day." She slips off her stilettos and leans against the arm rest.

Ah ha, here we go. I look down at the floor trying to suppress the tears threatening to fall. What is she talking about? Tyler doesn't whine or mope. He lives for the moment, like an outlaw cowboy. No risk too great to take and no regrets. He's made it more than clear he never wants to be stuck in one place or tied down. Why would he send his cronies here? He knows we would never work out.

Lexie slaps Jenna's leg.

"What... are we not saying his name?" Jenna shakes her head and huffs. "You're both acting completely ridiculous. I mean, he's a mess. And look at you." She points in my direction.

I get it, Jenna's back into her mama-bear mode trying to fix everything, if it was only that easy. I slowly lift my head, trying not to look her directly in the eyes. She turns me to stone.

"You just had an article published in a national magazine, and you're acting like you lost your best friend." She throws her hands in the air. "I get it, he fucked up. I warned you he's not cut out to be the GQ model at these events. Honestly, I'm surprised you weren't the one to clock that guy."

Chloe scrunches her eyebrows and turns toward Jenna, almost crushing Lexie in between them. "What the hell are you talking about? He fought with Ali's co-worker, and then left her there. Why would Ali fist fight... especially at a black-tie event? She's like the most professional person."

"I think your BFF skipped a few parts of the story." She shifts her eyes between me and Chloe. "That Jake idiot threw digs at Ali all night, then got sloppy drunk and called her a whore in front of everyone." She folds her arms across her chest. "If Tyler let that asshole get away with talking to you like that, I'd kick *his* ass."

Chloe holds up her hands. "Whoa. So Tyler basically fought for your honor in front of everyone." She jumps up from the couch and heads to the kitchen. "Yeah, that information kinda changes things... don't you think?"

"I almost lost my job, was made a spectacle of at my first ever event, and the ballroom was pretty much destroyed. It's not as romantic as it sounds." We're not in the middle of a chick flick. In the real world, it causes havoc and destruction. I mean, everything changed in a matter of minutes. Something I know all too well.

"I can't believe you omitted all of this. You should've jumped into his arms and ridden off into the sunset." Chloe grabs some glasses and a bottle of white wine. "Looks like he's your hero yet again." She points to the magazine article.

"I couldn't... he left me there remember?" God, why is everyone turning on me and joining team Tyler? No matter how you look at it, he was wrong. End of story.

"He got scared and ran. Driver took him halfway home, then he regained some brain function and went back. You were already gone." Jenna grabs a cup and pours some wine.

Okay, I get it. Facing a life you never expected terrifies anyone. I've run too. It never changes anything but he didn't just run, he left me. And what the hell was he scared of anyway? "How can I trust someone who literally leaves me when I need him most?"

"You don't get it, Ali. He came back. He realized he can't leave you." Lexie takes a glass of wine.

I grab a glass of wine and slug in down in one gulp. The cool liquid perks up my senses. Maybe even enough to get this room of hopeless romantics to understand reason. "Doesn't matter. It's over and it was destined to fail from the start."

"Why? If you want it to work it will. Trust me, I've been there." Lexie sips her wine.

What is she talking about? Not even close to the same situation. "You can travel with your work. You have it all. Plus, Van didn't tell you... like a million times that his biggest fear is to settle down." I take a deep breath. "Long distance relationships are torture... and I need to focus on my career."

"Did you talk about it with him, or are you remembering things he said forever ago?" Lexie twirls her hair around her finger. "Everything can change in an instant."

A stray tear rolls down my face. I quickly wipe it away. No one on earth knows that better than me. "That's exactly what happened."

Jenna jumps up from the couch. "That's it, I can't take it anymore. You're both torturing yourselves like two morons." She grabs her cell phone and presses a few buttons, turning it on speaker. "You can decide yourself how he feels." The ringing sounds throughout the room.

"Hello." Tyler's voice pierces my ear drums. It's a voice I'd know anywhere but never thought I'd hear again. Tears stream down my face. I want to run to the phone, tell Tyler I love him and we can make it work. My feet plant themselves firmly to the floor.

"Hey, it's me. We're heading back soon. Want anything?"

"Nah, I'm reading Ali's article again. It rocks," his shaky voice cracks.

Oh my God, he's read it more than once? I pick at my lip. Maybe he just thinks it's good reading material. Yeah, that's probably why. He is the hero of the tale.

"Did you call her?" Jenna sets her cup on the table.

"About a hundred times. She won't talk to me." He sighs.

Not won't, can't. He doesn't understand I'm making things better for both of us. Why prolong the inevitable? It just makes things worse.

Jenna rolls her eyes. "What's your problem? Where's that love 'em and leave 'em attitude you and Chaz live by? We'll be in Europe soon. You'll forget all about her."

"Not this time. I fucked things up big time."

"What the hell is so different about Ali? I don't get it." Jenna flashes a smile and points at the phone.

"Everything."

"That's a lame answer." She steps back and points to the phone.

"She's different, Jenna. Not like the chicks on the road." He exhales loudly into the phone. "She'll try anything, and if she's scared she sure as hell won't tell ya. She's tough, calls me on my bullshit. She doesn't give a shit about the whole rock star deal. And being with her makes me think your life doesn't suck so bad."

"What the hell is that supposed to mean?" She gives a death glare to the phone.

"I don't know. I guess I get it now. Why you and Marcus got hitched once we got signed. When I'm with her, it's like the lights on the stage just blazed down, the energy from the crowd blasts me, like catching a gnarly wave. She's the perfect high," his voice cracks. "I'm really fucked. I can't stand being without her."

A live wire of tingles sweep through me. Do I make anyone else in the world feel like that? Tyler awakened me, turned me human again. He saved me way too many times and now I'm the only one who can save him. I can't. I won't be that broken girl... not again. An earthquake ripped through our souls, leaving a path of destruction. I can't let it happen to us again.

A split second later, the levee breaks. I cover my face with my hands trying to stop the river of tears. My heart sinks to the ground. *Dammit Tyler.* Why? Why did I let myself fall in love with you? I run toward my bedroom.

"Jesus, Tyler. I think you just wrote a ballad. Newsflash, maybe you should tell her all of this." Jenna pivots, watching me flee to my safe haven.

"Yeah, I would if she'd talk to me."

"I got this. I gotta go."

I close the door behind me and launch onto the bed, hiding my face in the pillow.

Chloe comes rushing in. "Are you okay?"

I lift my head. "Not even close."

Jenna and Lexie follow. Lexie sits on the bed next to me. She sweeps a few strands of hair away from my tear soaked face. "I hope those are happy tears."

Is she insane? I sit up and wipe my face. "Why would I be happy?"

Chloe plops next to me. "Oh darling, are you for real? I mean, hello. He just professed his love for you to Jenna. And I think I just melted into a puddle in there."

I shake my head. "It doesn't change anything."

"What?" Jenna folds her arms across her chest. "It changes everything. Are you deaf?"

"Ali, he pretty much said he wants you no matter what. I mean, what else do you want from him?" Chloe smirks. "Does he need to bring you the Hope Diamond or something?"

The trio stares at me like I'm some evil demon set on selling Tyler's soul. They don't know a Goddamn thing about what I went through and I sure as hell am not putting myself through it again. Maybe they need a dose of reality.

"What gives?" Jenna taps her foot.

Heat creeps across my face from my cheeks to my ears. "I'm not doing this to myself, not again." I take a deep breath. "I had love before. Real, true love. I know what it is and I never thought I'd find it again… but I did." I swallow hard. "When Josh died I didn't want to live. I prayed a million times I wouldn't wake up. But every morning my eyes opened and a few seconds later the pain gripped my heart like a vice." A few more tears escape. "I can't go through that every time Tyler leaves. I won't see him for months or maybe longer." I clear my throat. "I know it's not the same but it sure as hell feels that way. Why should I let myself live in pain?"

Lexie covers her mouth with her hand, slowly letting it drop down her chin. "I'm so sorry, Ali."

"Isn't that exactly what you're doing to him?" Jenna's cold eyes burn through me. I swear, she lacks the sympathy gene.

"This may be the absolute worst celebration ever," Chloe says. Leave it up to her to break the tension. At least someone still has my back.

"Yeah, let's have a do-over. Jenna and I are planning a celebration for you Saturday and we won't take no for an answer." Lexie puts her arm around me.

"I'll make sure she's there." Chloe pulls me into a hug.

Jenna joins the crowd turning the heart to heart into a four-way hug. God, another celebration with them might kill me. I'm pretty much dead inside anyway.

I bow my head toward the floor. She's right. There's no easy way out. We either both stay away from each other and try to pick up the pieces of our shattered hearts or stay together and completely destroy each other. No one wins.

20

CELEBRATION

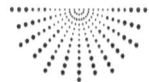

LIVEWIRE SPELLED OUT IN HUGE LETTERS BRIGHTENS THE DARK sky, sending flickers of neon red sparks through the crowded street. I stare up at the flashing sign gracing the entrance to one of L.A.'s hot new night clubs. My stomach quivers sending waves to the pit. Why do I feel like I'm about to enter hell? Ah, maybe because one of Lucifer's children planned tonight's events.

Okay, so Jenna isn't so bad, but she definitely has her moments. We walk up to the club, our heels clicking, creating a unique rhythm like we're about to break into a choreographed dance. A line of people waiting to get in wraps around the corner. I step to the side and file in behind them. Looks like we'll be heading back to my apartment and celebrating with take out and wine. We have a better chance of getting into the Oval Office than we do this club.

Jenna adjusts her painted on black mini dress and struts forward. "You guys coming?"

Lexie walks by Jenna's side, her brown hair falling in perfect curls along her red tank dress. She gestures for Chloe and me to follow.

"I'm so out of my league right now." I pat down my plain black skirt.

"You're gorgeous. Less is more." Chloe winks and grabs my hand. "Come on." She pulls me forward, invoking her inner Mighty Mouse.

Easy for her to say, she could make a plastic bag look stylish. I almost run to keep up with her. Maybe those three have a shot at getting in using their, ahem, assets but I'm not playing the seductress card.

Jenna walks up to a man that looks like he just walked off the defensive line of a pro football team and whispers in his ear. Great, God knows what she's promising. Probably things I'll have to look up in the Urban Dictionary.

She tips her head toward the door. "Let's go, we're in." She flashes a sexy smile at the man.

"The fabulous foursome rides again." Chloe blows the man a kiss.

He muffles a smile and stands aside, waving the four of us in. I can just imagine the perks of his job. I fold my arms over my chest and march forward. Why did I agree to this?

Striking black and white décor greets me, giving the brand new club a cool retro vibe. Red laser-esque lines of lights hang along the walls. Black leather semi-circle booths surround a dance floor. A huge stage takes up the back wall. Sophistication meets Rock and Roll evoking a classic rock 70's vibe. Okay, so the club is cool. Not really a dance club, more of a stand and sway style.

"This place is freaking awesome," Chloe says as she swings in a circle.

"The band playing tonight rocks." Jenna sports a sinister grin.

"Not Devil's Garden, right?" My lips form a hard line. I mean, I'd love to see them live someday. Once this wound forms a scar and I have full function of my brain again, if that ever happens.

"Sorry, not that lucky. They're called Riptide." Jenna heads toward the bar.

Okay, never heard of them. Maybe tonight isn't the disaster I anticipated. Hearing a new band and hanging out with the girls may be just what I need. Might as well live it up.

I push through the crowd, getting elbowed in a variety of places and make my way to the bar. Chloe dashes forward and wiggles her way to the front. She'd make a hell of a jewel thief with her stealthy ways. She leans forward, trying to get the bartender's attention.

Jenna slides in between two guys. They move to the side like Moses parting the Red Sea. She struts forward, flicking a blonde lock over a shoulder. If a gust of wind blew her hair back, I'd think I was in the middle of a beer commercial. She takes a place at the bar next to Chloe. The bartender spots her and immediately comes to her aid. Lexie and I squeeze in next to her. What's it like to live a day in Jenna's shoes?

"Pick your poison, girls." Jenna leans forward, exposing cleavage from the top of her strapless dress. "How about some Cosmo's?"

The bartender smiles. "Coming right up." His eyes suck into Jenna's cleavage.

"Make mine a virgin," I scream, louder than necessary.

The bartender nods.

"Seriously? Not even one drink?" Chloe tips her head and raises her eyebrows.

"Nope. Not after the last celebration." I tap my foot on the tile floor. "Not happening." No need to repeat history. Waking up with a guy I hardly know is not on my to-do list.

The bartender returns with our drinks. "The one with the cherry is the virgin." He smirks. "Oh, drinks are on that guy." He points to a guy on the other side of the bar.

"I got dibs." Chloe waves to him. "You're all taken anyway."

I jerk my head back.

"Yeah, you too. Whether you know it or not." She turns away, not giving me a second to respond.

Why is everyone in fantasy land except for me? I get it, they're all Team Tyler but this is real-life, not some twisted fairytale. Love doesn't conquer all. When too many obstacles exist, you can't blindly follow your heart, it's a recipe for disaster. I take a deep breath trying to release the negative energy from my body.

The guy from across the bar walks over. I give the quick once-over, brown hair, athletic build, cute dimples when he smiles. Hey, maybe they'll hit it off. Things seem to happen when you least expect it. One of us deserves a happy ending.

"Come on, the band's about to start." Jenna grabs her drink and makes her way to the stage.

We all follow, along with Chloe's new friend. It's been years since I've seen a live show. The lights dim, casting a red hue over the crowd. A lull takes over, like someone just pressed the mute button. My heart beats, pounding through my chest. Electric energy fills the room. Shadowy figures take the stage. The bone-rattling drum beat pulsates through my chest. A frenzy of loud cheers emerges, piercing through the calmness as the crowd jammed to the rafters erupts. I take a deep breath and stare at the silhouettes slowly being illuminated.

My mouth falls open. Tyler's head hangs down. His blond locks a perfect mess. His fingers dance along the guitar strings, effortlessly. My eyes lock onto him, like a missile finding its target. Slowly he lifts his head to the crowd. An atomic bomb of energy bursts through. I freeze. My heart goes rogue, frantically beating. The singer belts out lyrics from the center of the stage, but I keep my focus on the bass player, commanding the left side of the stage.

His muscles flex with every pluck of the string, sending the tiger on his left forearm into attack mode. Electric sparks bolt through every cell in my body. His head sways, keeping in time with the melody. He transports to another dimension, owning the stage.

I follow his every movement, unable to break my stare. I'm in a trance, captivated by the rock God standing before me. He swipes the strings one last time, letting the bass hang from the guitar strap. He runs a hand through his hair and sweeps the crowd. His radar detects me in a split second.

"Hope you all liked that one," the singer yells into the microphone. "We are Riptide and we're here to rock you tonight!"

The crowd cheers, almost blocking out his voice. I keep my attention focused on Tyler, barely listening to the singer. The bright lights reflect off his baby blues. No one else exists at the moment but the two of us.

"Thanks to our friend Tyler from Devil's Garden for filling in for our bass player who just got here." The singer points to Tyler and the crowd goes crazy.

Tyler jolts back into reality and waves to the crowd. He pulls the strap over his head and hands the bass to a guy who emerged from backstage. Tyler heads to the back, my eyes sticking with him until he disappears.

The band huddles in the middle of the stage, and then moves to their positions. They break out into another song. Doesn't matter, my heart thumps in my ears blocking out all other sound. I shift my gaze toward Jenna. She shrugs her shoulders. Yeah, like she had no idea he'd be here. Heaviness fills my chest. God, I can't ignore him, but how am I supposed to face him? There's nothing left to say except goodbye. Tears well in my eyes. Time to do what I do best, run.

I turn toward the wall of people, trying to sneak in between the droves of bodies. It's like trying to scale a brick wall. Fans sway from side to side, creating an obstacle course. I'm trapped.

Someone grabs my arm, holding me back. I try to wiggle away but no luck. I swing around to face them.

Lexie loosens her grip. "Stop. You can't leave like this. Trust me, you'll regret it."

A tear escapes. I quickly wipe it away. "I need some air."

"I've got this." She pushes through the crowd, turning sideways and weaving in between the horde of people.

I follow her, sandwiching myself between a plethora of sweaty bodies. I suck in shallow breaths. *Please just let me go home.* I can't be here right now.

The crowd dissipates as we get closer to the door. She pulls me to the only vacant corner of the club. I take a deep breath and compose myself.

"You okay?" She steps back and twirls her hair around a finger.

I shake my head. What's the use in the lying anymore? "No. Not even close. Look at me, I'm a mess and you guys just made it worse. How could you set me up?"

Lexie holds up her hands. "Not a set up, I swear. Well, not really." She lets out a breath. "Listen, this band is a bunch of Tyler's surfing friends. We told him you were coming, that's it."

"So that's how we got in tonight?" Typical, Jenna would sell my soul to Satan himself if it would benefit her in any way.

She puts her hand on my shoulder. "I know how you feel and I know you'll regret it if you don't try."

I bow my head. Am I on mute? I told everyone a million times why it's not going work out yet they seem to ignore me. Lexie of all people should understand. Staying away from Tyler kills me. Did they think getting us together in the same room would help either one of us? I'm not the selfish one here. I'm trying to prevent more anguish for the both of us. I love Tyler. I mean, I love him so much I know it's best for both of us to let him go, no matter how bad it hurts. I blow out a breath from puffed cheeks.

"I get it, I really do. It's hard, seems impossible sometimes, but so worth it. And you make your own choice but at least talk. Nothing worse than wondering what if or did I make a mistake." She drops her hand.

She's right. If we're going to end things we need a clean break. After everything that's happened between us, I owe him that. "Okay. I'll talk to him."

Jenna and Chloe, dragging her new friend by the arm, emerge from the crowd. I stare as they walk toward us. Tyler appears behind them, standing about ten feet away. Fire sweeps through my soul. He runs a hand through his hair and takes a few steps toward me.

I swallow hard, mustering enough courage to speak. They spot us and trek forward. Every muscle in my body quivers.

"What'd ya think about the band?" Jenna smiles.

Couldn't tell you a note they played. "They were good."

I look down at the floor. Black boots invade my field of vision. I nibble my lip, slowly raising my gaze. My eyes find Tyler's like a moth to a flame.

"The article was killer." He flashes that sexy half smile that can bring me to my knees.

"Thanks," I say so quiet it's almost a whisper.

Tyler points to his ear. "Can we go outside for a sec?"

I nod. It's all I can do.

I turn toward the door and will my feet to take a few steps. Tyler rests his hand in the small of my back, guiding me forward. His touch sends a million volts of electricity through me. How can I live without feeling that spark again?

"I'll introduce you to Mason when you get back," Chloe yells.

"She's not coming back," Lexie's voice rings in the distance.

Nothing they say matters right now. I walk slowly, trying to control my wobbling legs. If he touches me again I might burst into flames. We head out the door and continue around the back to the parking lot. Tyler's red Camaro sits in the last spot of the lot. A cool breeze blows through, dousing my fiery cheeks. My heart races, faster the closer we get. It realizes what's about to happen.

We stop at the flashy muscle car. I take a deep breath, trying to hold back the tears about to well up in my eyes. Tyler turns toward me. His feverish eyes lock with mine.

He rubs the back of his neck, slowly letting his arm drop. "I flipped. Screwed up big time." He exhales slowly, still locked on my face. "I won't let anyone hurt you. Ever. When that idiot ran his mouth, I couldn't stop myself. No one talks to you like that." He runs a hand through his hair and paces back and forth. He stops, taking a step forward to face me. "You drive me insane. You can destroy me with one look. Bring me to my knees begging for more without even trying."

He brought my lifeless soul back from the dead. No one else has done that before and probably never will again. Chloe's right, I've been happier these last three months than I've been in years. No matter how much I tell myself being with Tyler is a disaster, it's perfect bliss. I breathe in the aroma of his musky cologne. It creates a frenzy inside me.

"Tyler—"

He lifts my chin, moving so close to my face our lips almost touch. "You don't get it. I love you, babe." He closes his eyes and presses his forehead against mine. "Didn't get how much until I punched that asshole. Scared the hell out of me. I took off, shouldn't have left you, babe." He presses his hand to my cheek, taking a step back and staring directly in my eyes. "I know we've got a lot going against us, and it'll be hard and probably suck sometimes, but I want you. Everything I never wanted I want with you, babe."

My eyes well with tears. All lines of self-defense retreat. All rational thought shuts down leaving burning passion behind. Tyler had me the second those baby blues locked with mine.

"I love you, too... babe." I can't hold back my smile.

He lets out the breath he'd been holding and presses his lips against mine, planting the ultimate knock-your-socks-off kiss onto my quivering lips.

Maybe I am a glutton for punishment? Or maybe my brain realizes what my heart already knows, I need him. New territory awaits in this imperfect scenario. We both have no clue how to handle it, but there's no one else in the world I want. I pull away, trying to catch my breath. "It's gonna be tough, but you're worth it… you're completely worth it." I smack my lips into his.

"Your new boss is a fan," he says breaking contact with my lips for a second. "That's a plus."

I pull away. "So you heard about my new job."

"That reminds me." He takes a step back and digs in his pocket for his keys. "I got you something."

Looks like tonight's full of surprises. I follow Tyler's every move, almost bouncing on my toes. He leans over the driver's side to the passenger seat and pulls out a gift bag.

"Trying to buy me off?" I flash a half grin.

"Whatever works, babe." He hands me the black bag spewing with red tissue paper. "You need these."

I crinkle my forehead. Lingerie? I rip through the paper like a kid on Christmas morning and open the box. I gasp and then melt into a puddle.

I pull out a pair of black Louboutin heels, like the ones that got ruined in our elevator disaster. "How did you…?"

"I told Jenna and Lexie I needed shoes that are red on the bottom. They knew exactly what I wanted. Jenna even smacked me for ruining yours." He shakes his head. "Girls and their shoes."

I put the shoes back in the wrapping. "They're perfect." Just like Tyler. I jump into his arms, pushing him against the car. I slam my lips into his, putting every ounce of passion built up into this one kiss. He wraps his arms around me holding me close.

I take a step back, sucking his lip as I pull away. "What happens now?"

He tucks a stray hair behind my ear. "I know this great place for breakfast."

We hop into the Camaro and ride off into the night. Who knows what the future holds for us? For once, I'm going to enjoy the ride. Sometimes what starts out as a complete disaster turns into perfect bliss.

PLEASE REVIEW

We hope you enjoyed *Blissful Disaster* by Amy L. Gale. If you did, we would ask that you please rate and review this title. Every review helps our authors.

Rate and Review: Blissful Disaster

MEET THE AUTHOR

USA Today Bestselling author Amy L Gale is a romance author by night, pharmacist by day, who loves rock music and the feel of sand between her toes. She's the author of USA Today Bestsellers *Resisting Darkness* and *Resisting Moonlight;* Amazon New Adult Bestsellers, *Blissful Tragedy and Blissful Valentine,* along with *Christmas Blitz, Blissful Disaster, Bear Creek Cowboys: Bear Creek Rodeo series, Mine Before Midnight, Pull Me Under, and Fight For It.* When she's not writing, she enjoys baking, scary movies, rock concerts, and reading books at the beach. She lives in the lush forest of northeastern Pennsylvania with her husband, daughter, five cats, and golden retriever, Sadie. You can find her at

Read More from Amy L. Gale www.authoramygale.com

OTHER TITLES FROM

5 PRINCE PUBLISHING